THE DIVIDED REALMS
BOOK 2

THE DARKENING

MAGGIE L. WOOD

Divided Realms, Book 2: The Darkening

Text © 2011 Maggie L. Wood

Published by Lobster Press™
1620 Sherbrooke Street West, Suites C & D
Montréal, Québec   H3H 1C9
Tel. (514) 904-1100 • Fax (514) 904-1101 • www.lobsterpress.com

Publisher: Alison Fripp
Editor: Mahak Jain
Editorial Assistants: Simon Lewsen & Ryan Healey
Graphic Design & Production: Tammy Desnoyers
Production Assistants: Vo Ngoc Yen Vy & Janet Hardcastle

 Canadian Patrimoine
Heritage canadien
We acknowledge the financial support of the Government of Canada through the Canada Book Fund for our publishing activities.

Library and Archives Canada Cataloguing in Publication

Wood, Maggie L.
       The darkening / Maggie L. Wood.

(The divided realms ; 2)
Previous title: The Princess Mage.
ISBN 978-1-77080-072-4

       I. Wood, Maggie L. Princess Mage II. Title. III. Series: Wood, Maggie L. Divided realms ; 2.

PS8595.O6364D37 2011   jC813'.6   C2010-906524-7

Alvin and the Chipmunks is a trademark of Bagdasarian Productions; Dark Crystal is a trademark of Jim Henson Company, Inc.; Elmer Fudd is a trademark of Warner Bros. Entertainment Inc.; Indy is a trademark of the Indianapolis Motor Speedway Corporation; Muppet is a trademark of Muppet's Studio; Saran Wrap is a trademark of Johnson Home Storage, Inc.

Printed and bound in Canada.

To Chelsea, the kissing scenes are for you.

– Maggie L. Wood

THE DIVIDED REALMS
BOOK 2

THE DARKENING

⤜❦⤛ **MAGGIE L. WOOD** ⤜❦⤛

Lobster Press™

CAST OF CHARACTERS

THE GALLANDRIANS:

King Ulor Farrandale: Grandfather to Princess Willow

Queen Aleria Farrandale: Grandmother to Princess Willow

Prince Alaric Farrandale: Father to Princess Willow

Princess Diantha Farrandale: Mother to Princess Willow

Princess Willow Farrandale: Previously known as Willow Kingswell of Earth

Nezeral (Nezzie) Thornheart: Adopted brother of Princess Willow; formerly a Faerie Prince of Clarion

Lady Gemma Fletcher: Best friend to Princess Willow

Sir Brand Lackwulf: Sworn knight and boyfriend to Princess Willow

Malvin Weddellwynd: Mage apprentice

Queen Cyrraena Silvenfrost: Faerie Queen and guardian of Mistolear

Headmaster Ewert: School Headmaster to apprentice mages

Sir Baldemar of Tamarvyn: Mage Knight to King Ulor

THE CLARIONITES:

King Jarlath Thornheart: Head of the House of Jarlath; father to Nezeral

Princess Dacia Thornheart: Daughter to King Jarlath

Prince Theon Thornheart: Second son of King Jarlath

THE GAUNTLET DWELLERS:

King Gobb: Goblin king

Prince Pitt: Prince of the goblins; son of King Gobb

PROLOGUE

Dacia's breath caught, excitement strumming over her like urgent fingers on lute strings. Father sat at his desk, eyes blank, face inscrutable. But Dacia knew. She *knew* he meant to make her his crowned heir. With Nezeral defeated, he had no choice. *She* was next-born. Had proven herself in countless Games, even besting the crowned heirs of two different faerie houses. She would be Father's pick – the next crowned heir to the House of Jarlath Thornheart.

"The girl will come."

The girl? A flat note soured Dacia's jubilance. What did Father mean by that?

"It's all set now. The Game is in motion."

Dacia stared, careful to hide her confusion.

"Council has agreed to the Game. The rules are ratified. All that's required is to select the players." Jarlath's brilliant eyes penetrated Dacia. "You, my dear, will be the main player in a Game to win back your brother."

No! No! No! On the inside, Dacia felt her world collapsing. On the outside, she didn't stir a muscle. "Nezeral has been defeated," she said dispassionately. "And by a human. Why bring him back, when he has brought such shame to our house?"

"Bringing him back is not the immediate purpose." Jarlath toyed with a feathered quill. "The first purpose will be to win the heart of the human girl. She must agree to bring you back to Mistolear."

Mistolear? Humans? Despite her tight control, fascination crept over Dacia, her mind swarming with lurid pictures of the primitive creatures, of their clumsy magic and small crafty brains. Father would send her to be with *them*? The thought made her shiver in anticipation.

"No Game," Jarlath continued, "can change the outcome of another. We can't take Nezeral back. He must stay with the humans until he reaches their age of sixteen years. We *can*, though, *win* him back – in a fashion." A smile stole over his face. "You will go to Mistolear, Dacia, and stay there till Nezeral is grown again. You will keep him unsullied by human customs, instructing him all the while in the ways of Dark. Then when he is returned to us, he will be untainted."

Awareness hit Dacia like a cold air blast. Father had no intention – now or in the next millennium – of naming her the crowned heir. He would bring Nezeral back and pretend that nothing had changed. Her mouth twitched. Only her clenched toes indicated her fury.

"Of course, you'll be as free as your brother was to make new Games with the humans. Games to sway the Balance to Dark." Jarlath's glance pinned her like a moth. "What say you, my daughter? Shall you be the Game Master in my new Game?

Or shall I ask Theon?"

The mention of her twin brother decided it for Dacia. "*I* will be Game Master, Father." Only crowned heirs or *potential* crowned heirs could lead a Game as a Game Master. No way would she give Theon a chance to usurp her. She rose from her chair, bowed to Jarlath, and left the study, rage propelling her down black marble corridors and out the castle doors.

At the foot of the great entrance steps loomed the lion gargoyle statues. Dacia fumed in their shadow. So Father thought he could pass her over as heir, yet still dangle the opportunity like a prize? Well, she would show him! She would find a way to turn the Game to *her* advantage.

On a whim, she magicked herself atop the stone base of one of the gargoyles and slid down into its hollowed-out middle. As a child, she'd made all her Game plans here. It was a tighter fit than she remembered. But Dacia liked the comfort of squeezed-in places. They helped her think better.

After a minute, though, her neck began to cramp. It had been eons since she'd last hidden under the lion gargoyle. Its belly used to barely brush the top of her head. She touched the cold black stone with her hand. Marble groaned and grated, the belly above her magically rising a few inches. Dacia straightened her neck. Around the tiny cavity, rune graffiti shimmered like silvery snail tracks. She chuckled at her childish script, at the overly elaborate schemes she used to hatch.

Someone snorted. Dacia ducked as footsteps pattered down the stairs. She peeked over the lion paws at a pair of shiny black boots.

"Dace, if you're going to hide under there, I suggest you raise *both* gargoyles. I could see that one is higher than the other from a mile away."

Anger, twinged with spite, ripped through Dacia. Theon was the real reason Father hadn't named her the crowned heir. Twins embodied the Balance – one Light, one Dark. But which was which? No one knew. Dacia glared past Theon and his insufferable grin, instantly raising the other gargoyle to match her own. "Satisfied?" she spat at him.

He shrugged and continued grinning at her. "If anyone asks for you, shall I say you're a bit – *under* the weather?"

This was too much for Dacia. She materialized two steps above Theon, so that she could stare down at him haughtily. "Little Brother," she said, reminding him of his place – he was a full two minutes younger than her – "be careful whom you mock. I will not always be merciful in my wins against you."

Theon's face reddened. It was Dacia's turn to grin. They had been pitted against each other in Games since childhood and she had trounced him memorably more than once. If there was to be a competition between them, she would most likely be the victor, and he knew it.

Bowing his defeat, Theon turned away from her, evaporating from sight. Dacia eyed the spot where he had stood, her anger fading. She remembered a time when they had hidden under the gargoyles together, he on one side, she the other. It seemed so long ago now. When had Father forced them to become enemies?

Her thoughts turned back to her father's new Game. Jarlath had her completely cornered. No matter what she did, Nezeral would still be crowned heir. She slumped against a gargoyle leg. *How could she beat them? How ...*

Suddenly, it became clear. She remembered her human studies. The lessons on low intelligence and simple instincts. Humans wouldn't care for an infant faerie. *They would want revenge.* Dacia smiled. Father had lied to her. His worry wasn't that Nezeral would learn to be like a human – but that he would learn to fear them.

She ran the tip of her tongue along her teeth, the inkling of a plan beginning to take form. She knew what to do now. She would best the human girl, go to Mistolear, and teach her elder brother to fear. Only he would not fear humans. He would fear *her*.

Oh yes, she would bring Nezeral back *and* be the crowned heir. She would win it all.

CHAPTER 1

"If I may be so bold, Your Highness, might I suggest that you move to the shade? Your skin, I fear, is becoming as brown as a sheepherder's."

Willow glanced at her lady-in-waiting, Tavia Huxley, who sat sheltered under a golden canopy in an elaborate pink silk dress that covered her body from neck to ankles. "Thanks, Tavia, but I'm fine here. I *want* my skin to brown. It's called a tan."

Tavia sniffed. "As you wish, Your Highness," she said, and went back to needlepointing.

From atop the east tower, where she was stretched out on a lounge chair, Willow could see past the inner and outer castle walls to the lush green forest on the horizon. Pine-scented breezes fanned her warm face. She inhaled deeply. *This* is what summer vacation was all about!

A musky fragrance filled the air as she rubbed rose oil on her arms. *And I'm not brown*, she thought. *I'm golden*. Her tawny skin gleamed in the sunlight. No freckles either. Willow looked down at her legs. Nice even color. She rolled up her tank top, exposing her tanned stomach. Tavia gasped. *"Your Highness ... it's not seemly ... I mean ..."*

Oh for pete's sake. Willow rolled her eyes. Tavia gasped at every little thing. Bare legs. Bare arms. Now bare stomach. Ladies-in-waiting were about as risqué as Victorian grandmothers.

"Tavia, relax. There's no one here but us. I just want to get a little sun on my stomach." She'd been about to hitch her shorts down as well, but decided against it. Tomorrow, she would come alone and wear the bikini she'd bribed the seamstress mage into making.

Another gasp escaped from Tavia. "Er ... um ... Y-Your Highness ..."

"No, *really*, Tavia. It's okay." Willow turned to the other girl and realized she wasn't stammering about Willow's indecency but pointing at a scroll that had appeared in midair and was now unrolling itself. Elegant curlicued words appeared on the parchment:

My dear Netherchild,

I bear glad tidings. The Faerie Council of Clarion has at last settled on a date for you to enter Clarion. You shall be the first human to visit our fey realm and the first to sit amongst our Council. It is indeed a great, great honor, one that I hope you are as pleased with as I am.

There is, however, one stipulation of which I feel you should be made aware. I cannot accompany you to Clarion, nor can anyone else. You will go without an entourage of any kind. I know this will appear unseemly to your family.

Please inform them that I shall arrive at week's end to allay their fears and to transport you to Clarion.

Headmaster Ewert has a special book for you entitled The Complete History of Fey Magic Lore. *I suggest you read it before my arrival. It will help in your understanding of faerie culture and custom. I look forward to our meeting.*

Queen Cyrraena Silvenfrost
House of Cyrraena Silvenfrost
Realm of Timorell

The sun suddenly felt hotter. Over the past ten months that Willow had been in Mistolear, she and Queen Cyrraena had had many meetings with each other. But the faerie queen hadn't mentioned the offer to sit on the Council since the breaking of the Game spell. Truthfully, Willow had hoped Cyrraena had forgotten all about it, as going to Clarion, the dangerous world of the fey, was not on Willow's top ten list of fun things to do. And now the faerie queen was saying Willow had to go *completely alone? By the end of the week?* Willow's heart fluttered. Cyrraena certainly hadn't given her much time to prepare. Or to object. She started to sweat. Just the thought of being the only human in a realm full of faeries terrified her.

"This is outrageous!" Tavia stood over Willow's shoulder, her eyes bulging with indignity. "You cannot go alone to a foreign realm. How dare she even make such an improper request?"

Willow grabbed Cyrraena's scroll out of the air and quickly folded it.

Tavia stood up. "I shall go to King Ulor and Queen Aleria."

"No." Willow grasped her hand. "Please don't. Not yet, anyway. I'll tell them myself, okay? I – I just want to think about it first."

"Think about it? But Your Highness, this is a matter of great importance. Their Majesties will wish to know at once. As will your parents."

"I know." Her family *always* wanted to know everything at once. Willow let go of Tavia. "But I will tell them myself. Give me your word you won't say anything."

The lady-in-waiting frowned, looking ready to argue further. Finally, though, she nodded and returned to her shaded tent seat. Willow lay back on the lounge chair, but found her peaceful enjoyment of the morning sun spoiled. Nearly a year had passed since she had come to Mistolear as a pawn in a terrible, magical chess Game. The faerie prince Nezeral had trapped both sides of her family in a spell, forcing them to play against each other as live chess pieces. After she'd defeated him, he had told her that in Clarion all the great faerie houses competed in Game after Game.

We play for one reason and one reason only, he'd said. *Power*.

Willow shivered despite the heat. Queen Cyrraena would send her alone to Clarion? Send her to Nezeral's powerful, pissed off family – *all alone*?

"Your Highness?" The tower door burst open. Another

lady-in-waiting, Petrina Hottspear, came huffing through it. "Prince Nezzie," she panted, "he's on the loose again!"

Chubby legs tottered out from behind the low hedge, followed by a gleeful squeal. Willow scrambled to her feet. *"Come back here!"* she shouted, giving chase to the small, naked boy romping across the garden. He plowed into a patch of bushy ferns and squatted, his impish blond head sprouting through the greenery like a flower top. She slowed, pretending not to see him.

"Where are you?" she called out. Little muffled giggles answered her. She craned her neck deliberately. "Oh dear. I wonder where Nezzie could be?" More giggles. She lunged at a rosebush and then at the birdbath, each time looking crest-fallen when she came up empty-handed. The giggles became belly laughs.

"I here, Will! I here!"

She spun around, scooping the waiting toddler up into her arms. "Aha! Gotcha!"

He squealed and tried to escape, but Willow clung to him tightly. "Oh, no you don't," she growled. "You're mine now and I'm gonna feed you to the crocodiles!" She held him high, nuzzling his round tummy until a wheezy, aggravated voice interrupted their fun.

"Oh, Your Highness," the voice gasped, "thank heavens you

caught the little mite. Here, put this back on him. *Quick.* Before he changes us both into the gods know what."

Nurse Minna, her ginger hair frizzing and her plump cheeks puffing, held out a tiny blue undershirt, its collar festooned with a delicate chain of magic-warding iron bumblebees. Nezzie tried to squirm away from Minna, but she deftly dressed him and lifted him into her arms. "You're a fine one," she cooed, shaking her head ruefully, "turning your own head nurse into a hammer and then whacking her against the wall. No doubt the old girl's fit to be tied. With a good thumping headache to boot."

Willow burst into laughter. Nurse Minna frowned at her. "Really, Your Highness, it's not a bit funny. He changed Mertice the chambermaid into a top yesterday. Spun her all around the nursery, he did. Poor chit was dizzy the rest of the day. And then there was Filmore and Ned, the two kitchen boys. His Nibs, here ..." she mussed Nezzie's short, silky curls, "turned them both into frogs and tried to *feed* them to the cat."

Willow nodded sheepishly, pursing her lips together to keep from laughing again. She knew where this was leading. Ever since Nezzie had learned to walk, he had decided that *au naturel* was the way to go. Only problem with that, though, was that every time the little guy peeled down to his birthday suit, he wreaked magic-havoc wherever he toddled. The servants had had enough and Nurse Minna had been elected their spokesperson.

"Did you happen to notice," Minna said softly, "how close he came to the pond this time?"

The humor faded from Willow's face. She glanced back at Nezzie's hiding spot, realizing the tall ferns masked the edge of the murky goldfish pond.

"You know how he loves them F-I-S-H," added Minna. "My guess is, if you hadn't come along when you did, the little mite would've headed right for them." She gave Willow a shrewd look, letting her draw her own dire conclusions. Faerie immortality, Willow knew, had exceptions. Exceptions that, under rare circumstances, meant Nezzie could actually die.

"Mama ... *Mama!*" Nezzie wriggled and pointed across the gardens. Willow and Minna turned to see Princess Diantha, Queen Aleria, Nurse Tibelda, and about half a dozen ladies-in-waiting bustling across the grass, their skirts and veils streaming behind them like an armada of storm-blown ships.

"Oh, my sweet Nezzie!" cried Princess Diantha, snatching the baby from Nurse Minna. "Are you well? He's not hurt, is he?" Despite Minna's assurances, Diantha twisted Nezzie this way and that, checking for injuries. Finally, she sighed and squeezed him tightly. Nezzie snuggled against her gold veil, closed his eyes, and promptly fell asleep. Diantha glared at Nurse Minna. "This ... this *negligence*," she whispered hotly, "cannot continue. If you are not able to keep proper watch over the prince, then I will find someone who *is*."

"Aye, Ma'am." Minna cast hangdog eyes to the ground. Her hand, though, reached behind and pinched Willow.

"Um ... Mom ... Mother," Willow faltered. Nine months had gone by since she'd first met her mother, the princess Diantha, and still she hesitated when calling her Mother. "You can't blame Minna, okay. Nezzie's not like a regular one-year-old. Nobody can watch him every single second." Willow paused, forcing herself to ignore her mother's sharp look. "He needs warding bands."

Minna's eyes shot up. This, Willow knew, was what all the servants wanted. Iron bands around Nezzie's wrists that he couldn't take off.

"The bumblebee shirts aren't working, Mother," said Willow gently. "He was this close to the pond when I caught him." She held up her hands with a two-foot spread. "If I hadn't come along ..." The thought hung in the air, the same way Minna had let it.

Diantha's eyes widened then narrowed back to a stubborn glare. "No. I will *not* have Nezzie wearing shackles."

"Really, Diantha, this has gone quite far enough." Queen Aleria, imposing in her sapphire-studded tiara and full crimson court regalia, frowned impatiently at her daughter-in-law. "The child is a danger to himself and to others. Just look at Nurse Tibelda." She drew the older lady forward and lifted the edge of her brown wimple, exposing a bruised and bloodied forehead. "This," ordered Queen Aleria, "simply has to stop. You *must* let us make the warding bands."

Diantha's chin and bottom lip quivered as she stared at Nurse Tibelda's forehead. Willow instantly felt guilty. Since taking over the care of Nezzie, her mother had developed an overprotective streak that had grown into a neurosis. *And I made her do it,* thought Willow bitterly. *I made her take responsibility for Nezeral.*

That day, months ago, still weighed heavily on her conscience. Turning an evil faerie prince into a baby and then adopting him had seemed a good way to end the Game spell. Everyone had been smiling and kissing and looking so happy. The idea had just blurted out of her mouth. *Why don't we raise him? We could bring him up right.* She hadn't thought about what her mother had been through. The year of stress while she'd been pregnant. Her abduction and emotional torture. The shock of seeing her fifteen-year-old "infant" daughter. No, all Willow had thought about was herself. How *she* had wanted to do what *she* thought was right.

She glanced at Nezzie. No one saw him as Nezeral anymore. The image of his sweet, silvery curls spread over Diantha's shoulder tugged at her heart. Willow loved him. Plain and simple. They all did. But her mother ... Willow's eyes rose to Diantha's beautiful, troubled face ... her mother was completely consumed by him.

"Diantha, dear," Queen Aleria embraced the young woman and softened her tone, "the bands don't have to be like shackles. My ironsmiths are quite clever. They can forge bands light as feathers and filigreed as fairy wings. Nezzie, I assure you, will love them."

Willow arched an eyebrow. *Light as feathers? Filigreed as fairy wings?* It wasn't like her pragmatic grandmother to wax so lyrical, but it did seem to be working. The trapped animal look had left Diantha's face, and she was nodding, allowing the ladies-in-waiting and nurses to lead her back to the castle. Minna threw Willow a grateful smile, then scurried ahead to shoo away the queen's scampering lapdogs.

Queen Aleria hung back for a moment, frowning at Willow. "My dear," she said, voice tight. "I fear we must discuss your apparel." Her eyes swept severely over Willow's cotton shorts and tank top. "Or lack of it. I will expect a visit from you after the noon meal." She lifted her heavy brocaded skirts, spun around, and marched rigidly after the others.

Willow's face flushed red. She'd forgotten about the shorts and tank top. She gazed after the retreating line of Queen Aleria's stiff back, her embarrassment suddenly turning to defiance. She was sixteen years old. She didn't need anyone's permission to wear Earth clothes.

Obstinately, she started along the path to the west tower. Overhead, birds chirped and sunlight wove bright arcs through the summer green trees, but Willow noticed none of it. She was going to Headmaster Ewert's to have a look at that faerie book Queen Cyrraena had mentioned.

A wave of heavy perfumed air hit Willow as she started up the stairs to Lord Ewert's classroom. She breathed it in. Mmm. Apple blossom today. The wind must be blowing east. Her mouth broke into a grin. The tower, located right next to the stable dung heap, could get a tad rank on a hot, breezy day. Magical air fresheners were the usual antidote.

She came to the door and peered around its corner. "Lord

Ewert?" No one answered. He was probably in the library. Headmaster Ewert never strayed far from his classroom, even during summer vacation. She stepped inside and wandered over to her empty desk. Since the great feast after they'd won the Game, when Queen Cyrraena had alerted Willow to the fact that she still had some of her powers, she'd been going to mage school with Malvin. Headmaster Ewert was their teacher.

She sat in her chair to wait. Lord Ewert, by the looks of his just-lit air freshening candle and Leaning-Tower-of-Pisa pile of paperwork, would be back soon. She tipped her chair against the wall, peering up at the narrow, wide-open windows. The headmaster had picked the west tower because of them. Five windows, each seven feet tall and two feet wide, filled the room with breezes and bright, warm sunlight. Only problem, though, was that they were way up near the ceiling, where no one could see out them. In Lord Ewert's class there was "no daydreaming or gawking at stablehands."

Which, Willow admitted grudgingly, was probably a good thing. Now that the Game was over and her powers reduced, she needed to concentrate to develop the little magic she did have. Her gaze fell on the headmaster's desk. Lord Ewert, as well as the Gallandrian mage knight Sir Baldemar and the Keldorian mage knight Sir Lachlan, had tested her over and over again, and found that all her extraordinary magical talents had left with the Game spell. Her only talent now was healing. She was just a beginning mage student – "undisciplined and inexperienced" as Lord Ewert put it.

Willow grimaced at the thought of her final exam in fire conjuring. She was supposed to make a row of candles light with fire, but instead had somehow burnt a hole in Lord Ewert's hat, which had then singed a large patch of his balding head. Not very impressive for someone who'd once turned a grown boy into a baby.

Malvin had tried to explain about magic aptitudes to her. How they were very similar to other abilities. *No one,* he'd said, *is talented at everything. Some people are math whizzes. Some are wordsmiths. And some excel at physical things, like sword fighting and archery. Magic is the same way. Some have talent for fire conjuring and some do not.*

Willow smiled. Malvin had shown her the C he'd received in healing. It still didn't make up for the D she'd gotten in fire conjuring and all her other Cs and Ds, but at least with her A+ in healing she'd beaten him. And since she had removed that terrible servant brand from Gemma's shoulder, Willow had decided that healing was the most useful magic talent to possess.

A man cleared his throat over by the doorway. "Ah, Your Highness." Lord Ewert bowed before entering the room. "I am pleased to see you."

Surprised out of her reverie, Willow let her front chair legs crash to the floor. Lord Ewert strode past, his thin lips pursed with disapproval. The headmaster did not approve of princesses tipping back their chairs like common schoolboys or dressing in an outlandish fashion.

Willow sat up straighter and smoothed out the creases in

her blue cotton shorts. Her grandmother and ladies-in-waiting weren't the only ones with old fogey ideas about clothing. No one approved of her summer wear. The Gallandrians – well, the rich ones anyway – used cooling spells under their long heavy robes and found her "short breeches" indecently revealing.

"I have just been to the library," Lord Ewert said, "and, as per the faerie queen's instructions, I have fetched you this book on fey history." He gripped a large, leather-bound book, all the while eyeing Willow dubiously.

She blinked. *Faerie queen's instructions?* Did *he* know about the trip too? Who else had received notes? "Um ... er ... did she say anything else in her ... instructions?"

Headmaster Ewert fished around in his robes and brought out a square of paper the size of a business card. "This just appeared on my desk a moment ago," he said. "It says that I am to bring you this fey history book and that you are to read it by Friday." He placed the note on his desk and frowned again at Willow. "I cannot impress upon you enough, Your Highness, how truly rare and valuable this book is. It's one of a kind. You *will* promise to take special care with it?"

She gave him a solemn nod, trying to look responsible, and peeked down at the note. It looked short and sweet. He wouldn't know about the trip.

Headmaster Ewert set the book on her desk. "Friday morning," he asserted, "I expect to see you and this intact, immaculate copy of *The Complete History of Fey Magic Lore* in my classroom." His worried eyes squinted from behind gold, wire-framed glasses. "And of course, Your Highness," he bowed deferentially, "please come to me if you have any questions."

Willow nodded, averting her eyes from his bowed head. After she'd healed his burnt bald patch, she'd covered it with hair for good measure. Lord Ewert had been so pleased that he'd given her the A+ in healing and had stopped wearing his mage cap. Gold curls popped from his scalp like coiled springs. Willow bit her cheeks to keep from smiling.

"Well, off with you then." Lord Ewert waved a dismissive hand. "You have a great deal of reading to do between now and Friday morning."

That was for sure. Willow eyed the history book dismally. The thing looked like it weighed as much as Nezzie. She picked it up and sighed. So much for summer vacation.

CHAPTER 2

Willow tugged irritably on her bodice ties. On the way back to her bedchamber, she'd met up with Brand and Malvin, both of whom had blushed like a pair of bashful ten-year-olds at the sight of her naked legs and bare midriff. She loosened the ties a less-constricting inch. The fun of wearing silk and velvet princess gowns had worn off a long time ago. Now, she just wanted to be comfortable. Put on low-riders and a T-shirt if she felt like it or – like today – a pair of shorts and a tank top. But every time she did, there was always someone around who either turned beet red in embarrassment or acted prissy and offended.

Frowning, Willow stared at her reflection in the mirror. White muslin sleeves covered her arms, while an amber-colored skirt and bodice covered the rest of her. Obviously, no one here cared about getting a tan. She twisted her hair into a messy ponytail. Wearing the dress was one thing. She drew the line at having long hair sweeping over her shoulders as if she were a heroine in some romance novel.

A soft knock sounded outside her door. "Your Highness?" Another lady-in-waiting, Desma, curtsied and barged in, her arms overflowing with gowns and hats. Like Queen Aleria and Princess

Diantha, Willow had her own pack of annoying, ever-present ladies-in-waiting. "There you are," Desma exhaled windily. "Your new riding dresses have arrived from the dress mage."

"But ..." Willow struggled with her temper. She'd asked Queen Aleria for riding *pants*, not riding dresses. Had even drawn a design for the dress mage.

"Are they not lovely colors," said Desma, holding up a russet jacket and pressing it to Willow's neck. "Like fall leaves. I warrant they will make a fiery sunset of your auburn hair." Desma dropped the jacket, her eyes widening as she noticed Willow's twisted bodice ties and feeble attempt at a hairdo. "Oh, Your Highness, do forgive me. I should have been here when you returned." She smiled as she began to retie Willow's bodice. "Your lacing skills, though, are beginning to improve."

Willow sighed and let Desma redo her bodice. Ladies-in-waiting, she'd discovered, were like pit bulls – once they had a hold of you, they never let go.

"Are you planning on staying here to rest?"

The question seemed harmless enough. "No," Willow answered.

Desma cocked her head. "Are you joining us in the queen's solarium?" She finished tying the laces and reached for a hairbrush. Willow glanced at her, realizing where this was heading.

"I'm not changing my clothes, Desma."

Willow was wearing the most casual outfit she could find that didn't raise eyebrows or blood pressure. The problem was that the muslin shift and cotton skirt resembled the dresses the servants wore.

"Good day to you, Your Highness. Lady Desma."

Relief swept through Willow when she heard the familiar voice. Gemma, her best friend and ally, regarded Desma from the doorway the way one of Queen Aleria's lapdogs eyed Grisard the cat. *She* would rescue Willow from the fashion police.

"Fancy duds you got there, Lady Desma. Is there some new shindig in the works?"

Desma's eyes skimmed over Gemma – and Gemma's even plainer dress – with distaste. "Nay, Lady Gemma. There is no *shindig* as you so quaintly put it."

Willow's irritation heated to anger. Though the king himself had given Gemma a castle and a title, the ladies-in-waiting still thought of her as a commoner. Her plump figure, her preference for plain clothing, and her colloquial way of speaking ignited snickers and snide comments whenever she was among them. Willow hated it but was powerless to do anything.

That was another aspect that sucked about being a princess – constantly having to endure people you couldn't stand. Every lady-in-waiting had a father, an uncle, a brother, or a cousin who was a powerful ally of Willow's grandfather. She had been read the riot act from day one – she had a duty to kingdom, duty to family, and *lastly* duty to herself. So actually *telling* Lady Desma she was a spiteful cow was out of the question. Willow had to be more subtle.

"Lady Gemma, what's this rumor I hear about you and

Squire Harley?" Desma's head tilted in Willow's direction. Squire Harley was the hottest squire in the castle. It drove all of Willow's ladies-in-waiting nuts that he liked Gemma. "I heard he's taken you out riding two evenings in a row now."

Gemma blushed. "Aye, he has."

Desma grimaced. She pulled out a gown from Willow's wardrobe. "This one," she said, holding out the pale green dress like a flag, "is quite fitting for the queen's solarium. And it is simple in style, as Your Highness prefers."

"Best to stay in the duds you're wearing." Gemma pointed to a window. "Prince Nezzie's on the loose again and Nurse Tibelda's looking for you."

Giving up, Desma gave an exaggerated sigh, and returned the green dress back to the wardrobe. "By your leave, Princess," she said stiffly, "I shall await you in the solarium." She bowed low and waited for Willow's permission.

Surprised, Willow dismissed her. Usually it took more than an argument over dresses and a Nezzie-chase to get rid of Desma. After the other girl left, Willow turned skeptically to Gemma. "Is he really loose again? I just caught him fifteen minutes ago."

"Nah," Gemma chortled. "I made it up. Figured Her Ladyship was giving you a hard time again over wearing a servant's muslin." Her blue eyes gleamed with humor. "Knew she'd leave right quick, though, if she thought we were going chasing after Nezzie. He changed her into a ball the other day and threw her about with the queen's wee dogs. I heard she hasn't come within ten feet of him since."

Willow snorted with laughter. "Oh no. Poor Desma. No wonder she left in such a rush."

"Aye," Gemma nodded. She wandered over to the bed and spied the pile of riding gowns. "So, was I right then?" she asked, picking one up. "Was she again badgering you over the servant's dress?"

"Well, you know Desma. She doesn't badger. It's more like ..."

"Wearing you down."

Willow grinned. The *ladies-in-wearing-you-down* was Gemma's nickname for the ladies-in-waiting. Not that Desma and the others were against everything that Willow did, but if Queen Aleria was against it then so were the ladies-in-waiting. And when Queen Aleria didn't like an outfit or an inappropriate behavior, the ladies-in-waiting acted like her henchmen, plying Willow with delicate hints as to what was proper and what was not. It drove Willow crazy. But even though technically Gemma was her lady-in-waiting too, she stood by Willow, siding against the others.

"It wasn't just Desma." Willow tossed Gemma her shorts. "My grandmother gave me a hard time over those too. I just can't seem to win with you Gallandrians."

Gemma held up the shorts and sniffed as if they were made of cat poo. "You'll get no sympathy from me. For once I agree with the queen. You may as well go naked as a mermaid as wear these short pants of yours. I still can't believe the dress mage actually made them for you. She must've thought they were for wee Nezzie."

Willow rolled her eyes. Mistolearians were so stuck in the 90s. The *1390s*. "So, what's up?" She pushed the riding dresses aside and flopped onto the edge of her bed. "Want to go meet Brand and Malvin down by the training grounds?"

Gemma frowned and scanned the room until she spotted *The Complete History of Fey Magic Lore* stuck between some pillows on a window seat. She retrieved the book and held it out to Willow. "Tavia's been wasting no time telling all who'll listen about the faerie queen's letter. And hanging around the training grounds is not what you need to be doing." The book thudded onto the bed beside a gold pheasant-feathered hat.

Irritation flared in Willow again. Tavia had given her word not to say anything. But obviously her word didn't mean much. Willow ignored the book. "Ah, c'mon Gem," she pleaded. "I'll read it tonight. It's such a nice day. I don't want to be stuck in here."

Gemma sat down on the bed. Her mouth flattened into a puckered, worried line. "Is it true? Are you really being asked to go to Clarion all on your own? Without even a single knight or mage for protection?"

Willow reached for the shorts still in Gemma's hand. She retrieved Queen Cyrraena's letter from the pocket and passed it to Gemma.

The other girl's eyes widened as she read the note. "Does the faerie queen think to serve you up to the fey like a lamb to slaughter? Surely, you'll not go, then, under them conditions?"

Wincing at Gemma's crude words, Willow shrugged and cupped her chin in her hand. There had been no mention of choice in the letter.

"Go to your grandmother," urged Gemma. "She'll know how to handle Queen Cyrraena."

Willow felt a wave of resentment over Queen Aleria's earlier imperiousness. That was the problem. Her grandmother knew how to *handle* everyone.

She gave Gemma a humorless smile. "My grandmother and I aren't exactly getting along today. Think I'll wait until she comes to me." As no doubt she soon would with Tavia blabbing about the letter to everyone.

Gemma nodded. "Aye. I see your point." She set down the letter and rose back to her feet. "I'd stay," she said, "and help you with your studying, but I'm already late for my lessons. And you know what head mage Gerda's like when she's riled." She gave a little curtsy. "With your leave, Highness, I'll be on my way. Maybe after the noon feast we can get together for your reading." A suspicious look came into her eyes. She pointed at the fey history book. "Now, I'm sure that's more important than hanging round them training grounds. You're going to stay put, aren't you, and study it?"

"Yeah, yeah," grumbled Willow. Gemma curtsied herself out of the room. Willow called out a parting shot. "You know you're starting to sound like my grandmother, don't you?" A loud snort echoed from the hallway. Willow grinned, sinking back against her pillows. Maybe she *should* go to the kitchens with Gemma. Watching the cake mages work was always fascinating.

Willow chuckled. She remembered when Gemma had first discovered her magic talent. The head cake mage had brought in a "flowered gardenry" cake for dessert one evening. As she paraded it by, the blue sugar flower buds opened slowly and sweet aromas wafted over the feast hall. Gemma had been so enthralled by the presentation that she'd gone over to the cake table for a closer look, dragging Willow with her. She'd then innocently made a comment about there being no such thing as blue roses and the next moment the entire cake had turned blood red.

After the initial shock, the head cake mage had hauled Gemma and the ruined cake back with her to the kitchens and discovered that Gemma had the talent of a cake mage running through her. Not a usual talent for a royal lady, apparently, but one that Gemma took to with gusto. She started apprentice lessons the next day and was fast becoming the head cake mage's prize student.

Willow's hand settled on the fey history book cover. Gemma was right, though. She really should get started on her reading. She leafed through the book halfheartedly. A curly, hard-to-read script lined the pages. She squinted at a sentence, barely able to make it out. *Nomenclature is difficult in the faerie realms ...* Nomenclature? What was nomenclature?

Sunlight cast warm bands of yellow across Willow's skirt. She stretched her arms into the rays, feeling the sun's late

August heat. A light breeze blew in from the open window. Willow left the book on her pillow as she rose from the bed. *I can't do this now,* she rationalized. *It's summer. I'm a teenager. And Brand's finally back from Rueggan.*

The last thought made her face go hot. After being knighted by the king last winter, Brand had been away all summer, visiting his family in their fiefdom of Rueggan. True, he'd never seen her in shorts and a tight tank top before, but she certainly hadn't expected him to blush. Jeez, he was a year older than her! Not that she was all that experienced or anything. Brand had been the first boy she'd kissed. But still, they'd sort of been going out for nearly a year now, and he treated her like ... well, a princess. Someone he had to keep at arm's length.

Willow caught her reflection in the wall mirror. She had grown another half inch over the summer and was a full five foot ten now. Her hips were still narrow like a boy's, but her chest had suddenly sprouted breasts the size of grapefruits. Willow squinted. Or maybe more like oranges. Whatever their size, though, they were definitely noticeable. She stretched the fabric down on her bodice to see if she could produce any cleavage. Not quite there yet, but soon. She wondered if Brand would blush while she was wearing the dress as well. She hoped not. In this one area, she wished he was more like Earth boys. She remembered that day long ago when Dean Jarrett had hooted at her from a car. He'd had no problem showing his interest.

The memory of Dean, though, also reminded Willow of what a jerk he'd been to Abby Addams in the high school cafeteria. And then she remembered what a jerk she herself had been. She frowned, the familiar guilt niggling at her. She'd asked Queen Aleria half a dozen times about visiting Abby, to let her friend know she was okay. But each time, the queen devised some story about why "an Earth visit was just not possible at this present moment." Willow wondered if maybe a trip to Clarion might knock loose her grandmother's restrictions on realm traveling to Earth.

Harp music echoed down the corridor from the queen's solarium. Willow stuck her head into the hallway. Desma would know by now that Gemma had lied about Nezzie. It was now or never. She'd better escape while she could.

The hallway was empty. Willow scurried down it, ducking into a narrow staircase and sneaking out through a rarely-used side door. The warm sun and fresh breeze tantalized her senses. Magic or no magic, a stone castle was still a cold, dark place to live, even in summer. She much preferred to be outdoors. She sucked in a fortifying breath, and shoving the faerie queen's missive and her grandmother's rules and regulations to the back of her mind, set out to find Brand and Malvin.

CHAPTER 3

Long grass grazed deliciously against Willow's bare feet. She meandered along the edge of the fishpond, tucking stockings and flat satin slippers into her skirt pocket. There had been a lady-in-waiting lurking on the stone pathway, and Willow, not sure whose she was – her grandmother's, her mother's, or her own – had ducked behind a hedgerow, taking the long way around to the training grounds. Glad now for the detour, she stopped to dip her feet into the still, green waters of the fishpond.

Beneath the surface, fat fishy outlines wriggled away into dark murk. She watched them, absorbed by their frantic escape from her toes. A frog hopped into the water, making a rippling splash. Willow's spine tingled. She saw a clear image of Nezzie as he might have been this morning, alone and unprotected, trying to catch a frog or a darting fish and falling into the pond. Her stomach clenched uneasily as she recalled a conversation she'd once had with Queen Cyrraena.

The faerie queen had told her that all fey beings, despite being immortal, could die. A sword thrust through their heart or any other type of physical trauma would kill them just as it would a human. But except for the one time Willow had magicked iron around Nezeral's wrists, no non-fey creature could ever get past a full-grown faerie's magic to cause the faerie harm. And no faerie would ever physically harm another faerie. It was anathema to their nature. So they just kept living forever, their cells rejuvenating to keep their bodies youthful.

Willow thought of Cyrraena's otherworldly beauty. The faerie queen had lived for thousands of years but looked, by human standards, to be in her late twenties. She had said that from infancy to the human age of sixteen, a faerie grows just as a human would, except for a somewhat quicker mental development, but after that their aging process stops almost altogether. Changes happen in the span of centuries instead of years and are imperceptible to the human eye. Because of this, Willow and her family would be allowed to keep Nezzie until his sixteenth year, but then he would be returned to Clarion.

Keeping him safe, though, was a challenge. At least until he was older and could understand his magic better. Right now his magic put him at risk, as he could so easily use it to escape his caregivers. And since he didn't comprehend danger, he might not use his powers quickly enough or in a manner that would save him from harm. He had to be watched even more diligently than a human baby.

Willow smiled. The little guy was a holy terror without his warding shirt. She banished the thoughts of Nezzie drowning in the fishpond. Once he had those warding bands, the nurses would put a stop to his bare-butt Houdini escapes. She walked along the pond bank, chuckling over some of her adopted brother's more memorable getaways. There was that one time he'd given Nurse Minna giant butterfly wings and flown her like a kite over the moat bridge. And the time he'd turned Malvin into a monkey. She laughed out loud thinking about that one. Poor Malvin had been squeezed into silky drawers and a doll's dress before being rescued by Nurse Tibelda. The weird thing, though, was that Nezzie had never once tried to change Willow into anything. As soon as he saw her coming, he'd hide, waiting for her to discover him. It was his new favorite game. Of course, that meant that whenever he went missing now, everyone expected *her* to find him.

Willow headed back toward the path and peered around a thick-trunked oak tree to see if the coast was clear. No ladies-in-waiting. But just then Brand came into view, storming along the path, intent on going somewhere fast. She watched him for a moment, noting his hard-eyed glare and the determined line of his jaw. Something had ticked him off. Big time. She almost let him pass but waved him over at the last second. "Brand," she called out. "What's the hurry? The king's hunting dogs digging up Cook's herb garden again?" She'd meant the last part as a joke. Brand, though, didn't seem to take it that way. He aimed his scowl at Willow and stomped toward her.

Oh crap! From the accusing look on his face, Willow figured he must've heard about the faerie queen's letter. She inhaled deeply, preparing for Brand's complete and total opposition to Queen Cyraena's plan. Truthfully, she didn't blame him. She'd feel the same way if the situation were reversed and he was the one going to Clarion alone. But she hadn't spent any time with Brand in almost six weeks. This was not how she envisioned their reunion.

"Is it true, then?" Brand stood cross-armed, eyes sparking defiance. "I am not accompanying you to Clarion?"

"That's what the letter said."

"Well, it's an outrage. You are a princess of Mistolear! A contingent of knights and at *least* two mage knights should accompany you."

"Brand, I haven't actually spoken to Queen Cyrraena yet. Maybe there's more to it than she says in the letter. She's coming on Friday. Why don't we just wait until then before jumping to any conclusions?"

"And what of Nezeral's family?" Brand thundered. "Does Queen Cyrraena mean to hand you to them like a plump chicken ripe for the plucking?"

Gemma's "lamb to the slaughter" remark came to mind. A frown crossed Willow's face. She didn't like being referred to as livestock. "Brand. Did you hear me? *I said* let's not jump to any conclusions. I –"

"Do you have the letter? I wish to read it."

Willow sighed and shook her head. Clearly, she was just going to have to let him get everything out of his system.

Suddenly, he squinted at her in puzzlement. "Why are you dressed that way? In servant garb? And before when you were ..." He colored, obviously remembering her tight tank top and short shorts. "Where are your shoes?" he finished lamely.

"Oh, not you too!" Willow rolled her eyes. "It's freaking eighty degrees out." She hiked her muslin skirt up to her knees. "This is light and cool. Who cares if it's a servant's dress?" The thin material fluttered against her bare legs. Brand stared, his face flaring red.

"It's not ... seemly," he began, averting his eyes, "for a princess to display herself so ... so *wantonly*."

Hurt mixed with anger. Wanton was not a nice word in Mistolear. It was like calling somebody a hooker. Willow dropped her skirt, turned away from Brand, and marched back along the pond bank. She'd had enough of people trying to make her feel bad.

"Willow, wait!" Brand caught up to her. "I didn't mean ... that is ... I ..."

A messenger dressed in the king's purple livery came running toward them. "Your Highness," the man puffed before bowing to Willow, "His Majesty requires your presence in his chambers. I am to escort you there at once."

Willow's eyes met Brand's, both of them guessing at the same time why the king wanted to see Willow.

"He must know of the letter," said Brand.

Willow nodded. And no doubt so did her grandmother, her father, and her mother, and they would all be there to question her. She slipped her satin shoes onto her bare, somewhat dirty feet. "May as well get this over with," she sighed. She straightened and gave Brand a cool, haughty look. "Coming?"

She hoped he would but couldn't bring herself to say so. The "wanton" remark still hurt.

Brand didn't answer. He offered her his arm and together they followed the king's messenger back to the castle. No one spoke. Willow felt embarrassed. She wished Brand had just taken her hand instead of doing the formal princess-arm thing. It always made her feel like she was on display, like a well-groomed dog at a dog show. Only today she wasn't so well-groomed and didn't want everyone staring. No luck there, though. Ironically, if she were wearing silks and velvets, no one would notice her. But dressed in servant garb, her hair in a ponytail, she was the object of much whispering and many curious stares.

"Your Highness." A glittering, chartreuse-gowned courtier bowed low. Willow nodded, ignoring the woman's surprised expression. The king's chambers were at the end of the hallway. Willow straightened and took a deep breath. Dealing with royal grandparents could be daunting. Kings and queens didn't discuss matters. They gave orders. She glanced at Brand. Firm chin. Square shoulders. He could be a strong ally when he wanted. But whether he would back her today, or whether she even wanted him to, was a good question. She didn't know yet if going to Clarion by herself would help Mistolear or not.

Guards opened the doors to the king's chambers. "Your Majesties," the messenger announced, "I have brought the princess." He bowed and left the room, closing the doors with a resounding thud.

Right away Willow noticed that her mother was missing

from the small group of inquisitors. She also noticed a long scroll of paper in King Ulor's hand that looked suspiciously like her letter from the faerie queen. Brand escorted her across the room to a table where King Ulor, Queen Aleria, Prince Alaric, and Sir Baldemar sat, their faces pinched and unsmiling.

Queen Aleria reacted first. Her stern eyes brushed over Willow's servant attire. She frowned but said nothing. At the moment, Queen Aleria had bigger fish to fry. She took the letter from King Ulor and held it out to her granddaughter. "Why did you not speak of this earlier? I was told it arrived *before* Prince Nezzie's escape this morning."

Willow let go of Brand's hand and reached for the letter. A part of her wanted to turn the question on her grandmother. *Oh yeah, and just how did you get the letter? And how did you know when it arrived? Are you spying on me?* Another part, though, a larger part, had grown tired of fighting Aleria. "I was going to tell you after lunch. Sorry. I should have told you sooner." She set the letter on the table and sat in the chair that Brand had pulled out for her. "Where's Mother?" But even as the words left her mouth, Willow figured out the answer. They hadn't told Princess Diantha yet.

"She's resting." Prince Alaric's eyes stayed pinned on the letter. "Under the, um, circumstances," he explained, "we felt it best she not know."

Willow's stomach lurched. Shadows marked her father's handsome face. She hadn't seen much of him lately. Since the breaking of the Game spell, he had thrown himself into his princely duties, making long treks across the kingdom to meet with his father's many liege men, helping them put their towns and villages back in order. He hadn't noticed, or had refused to see, the gradual worsening of Diantha's emotional and mental state.

He obviously saw it now.

Willow's heart reached out to her father. She had been away on Earth for the first fifteen years of her life, but due to the spell they had cast on her, only a few months had passed on Mistolear. Prince Alaric was twenty-three, more like an older brother than a father. His lopsided smiles and joking manner had easily captured her affections. It hurt now to see him so grim and low-spirited, his eyes clearly showing his fear over Willow's trip to Clarion and how it might affect his beloved wife and daughter.

King Ulor reached for Willow's hand. "My dear, we know it's a great honor the fey have bestowed upon you." Her grand-father's voice quavered. Willow's head jerked in his direction. Did he have no faith in Queen Cyrraena either? "We fear, though," he continued, "that this plan to have you go to Clarion alone is only a plot devised to harm you in some way. Thus, when the faerie queen arrives, we shall deny her request to transport you to Clarion." He squeezed Willow's fingers and smiled. "You shall remain *here* with your family, where you're safe from fey plotting." King Ulor let go of Willow's hand and rose from the table. "Come," he said. "We shall have a midday feast."

Prince Alaric and Sir Baldemar pushed back their chairs and stood, Sir Baldemar offering his hand to the queen. Willow stood too, but stayed by the table, watching as her royal family and Sir

Baldemar left the room, their long silken robes whispering behind them.

Brand didn't offer her his arm this time. He looked at her warily. "I know that expression," he said. "It doesn't bode well."

Willow snorted and shook her head. "I know they're right and everything, but why do they have to talk *at* me, instead of *to* me? I'm not five years old or mentally challenged. They didn't even ask me what I thought." She slumped in the chair. "You know, *you* didn't ask me what I thought either. Does *everyone* believe I'm incapable of thinking for myself?"

The question seemed to confuse Brand. "I'm not sure what you mean," he said. "Of course you think for yourself. But you're a princess. Your actions will always be ruled by others."

"What does *that* mean?" Willow frowned. She didn't like where this conversation was going.

"The king rules your parents and they rule you. When you wed, then your husband will rule you." He looked suddenly uncomfortable and added, "It's no different for me. I too am ruled by the king, and then by my father."

"But your *wife* won't rule you, will she?"

Brand gave her a crooked smile. "No. If I had a wife, I would beat her each day and make sure she obeyed my every whim." He leaned over and gave Willow a quick kiss. She clouted his shoulder in return.

"I'm serious, Brand." But she wasn't really. The kiss had made her want more of the same. She blushed. "I missed you," she said softly. "Next time you go away for six weeks, I shall *command* you to let me come visit." He chuckled, but Willow caught the flash of tension in his eyes. She had asked to accompany him to Rueggan, to see his birthplace and meet his family, but Brand had adamantly refused. The hurt of it still needled. Didn't he *want* her to get to know his family?

"I wouldn't subject you to such tedium," he joked. "My father had me patrolling mountain borders. It would hardly have been an enjoyable visit for you."

"Well, I still could have met your brothers and your stepmother." She'd met his father last year at Brand's knighting.

"Perhaps another time." He pulled her to her feet and kissed her again. Willow let the matter drop. They were alone so infrequently, she didn't want to waste this stolen time arguing.

"I missed you too," he whispered. His arms tightened around her, his next kiss making her dizzy.

Brand drew away first. "Princess, I ... we shouldn't ... We'd better go."

Ugh. Not again. Willow rolled her eyes. "Is this about your honor again? I thought we'd settled that before you left." She grimaced. "I told you, I don't want to be on some kind of princess pedestal. If you're going to be my boyfriend, then *be my boyfriend*. Stop being so damn formal all the time! I mean, I don't expect you to ravish me right here on the floor or anything, but we're only kissing. There's nothing wrong with that."

A turmoil of emotion crossed Brand's face. "I know it's different on Earthworld, but Willow – I am not from there. I am from here. And in my world, you are my king's granddaughter, my liege lord's daughter. Unless we are betrothed, just being alone with you dishonors me. Dishonors *you*."

"Argh!" Willow threw up her hands. "I already told you, I don't *care* about all that honor/dishonor stuff. It's stupid! And I'm not getting betrothed to you or anyone else. I'm only sixteen years old!"

"You may not have a choice."

"What?"

"Remember what I said before? We don't always rule our own actions. If my father betroths me to some lady, and her father agrees, then I would be bound to wed. As would *you*, even more so, if your father chose a match for you. As a princess your hand will be used to garner wealth and cement alliances." His dark eyes gripped hers. "I don't know if I would even be considered a match for you. Do you see now why I can't be as ... familiar with you as you wish?"

Shocked, Willow just stared. It had never even occurred to her to think that she and Brand would have no choice about their relationship. Or that her family could or *would* try to force her to get married. Some things, though, began to make sense. There had been many great feasts at the castle throughout the year, where neighboring kingdoms had brought their sons. *Princely* sons. Had they been courting her? Is that why Brand would fume for days if another boy so much as danced with her? Because he worried that he wasn't good enough?

"Brand, listen." Willow took a deep breath. "*I* didn't grow up here. *Nobody* is going to force me to marry someone I don't want to. Don't you understand? Those archaic royal values mean nothing to me."

Brand stiffened. "They mean something to *me*." He gave her a curt bow and offered his arm. "Shall we? I believe we're expected for lunch. "

Willow turned her back on him and waited until she heard his footsteps retreat. After he left, she sighed heavily. Knight-in-shining-armor boyfriends were not always as great as they were cracked up to be.

CHAPTER 4

Willow's shoulders slumped against her headboard. She stared at the faerie book on her lap, candlelight flickering over its gold-etched cover. All her anger at Brand and her family had disappeared. She knew something about this Clarion trip that they didn't.

It wasn't about sitting on a council. It wasn't about Nezeral's family. It wasn't even about magic or honor. It was about change. Life-altering, system-shattering change. Over the past year, she had spent a lot of time with Queen Cyrraena and one thing was clear – the faerie queen wanted to establish a new bond between faeries and humans. She wanted new rules, new beliefs – basically, a whole new world.

Willow opened the book and flipped aimlessly through its pages. *I'm the faerie queen's tool of change. There will probably be no choice.*

That's the part that nobody understood. She'd be going to Clarion whether anyone liked it or not. Queen Cyrraena's cosmic plans would not be thwarted by the possible sacrifice of one insignificant human.

Her eyes burned with unshed tears. She realized that she

would be taken away from her family – a second time – when she had only just begun to know them, especially her grandmother, who had started to feel like a true mother to her.

When she thought of her grandmother, the words "stiffnecked" and "controlling" usually came to mind. But that was Aleria the queen. Aleria the woman was another person entirely.

Willow sighed. Deep down, despite the bickering, she had begun to rely on Aleria. Rely, in fact, on them all – her grandfather, her parents, her friends. She knew they cared for her. She just hadn't grasped until now – when she might lose them – *how much* she cared for them.

A knock at the door interrupted her thoughts. Willow wiped at her eyes and tucked away her book. "Come in," she said gruffly.

Something little and fast streaked into her bedroom. "Will, yookit my new bwacelets! *Yookit!*" Nezzie, draped in a flowing white nightshirt, curls still damp from his bath, wriggled onto Willow's bed, offering her his small iron-banded wrists. Princess Diantha followed after him, a wan smile on her pale face. "He insisted there would be no bedtime until you saw his special bracelets." She sat on the edge of Willow's bed, a frail ghost in the dim candlelight.

Bracelets thrust beneath Willow's nose. "Yookit my dwagons."

Willow smiled, her sadness lifting a bit at Nezzie's Elmer Fudd imitation. "*Dragons!*" she exclaimed. She lowered his hands. Black, ruby-eyed dragons seemed practically tattooed onto his wrists. "Wow! These *are* nice!" Willow prodded one of the bands. "Can I have one?"

Nezzie snatched his hands out of her reach. "No, Will." He frowned reproachfully. "They're just for boys."

"Boys, eh." Willow couldn't resist his innocent charm. She grabbed his leg and pulled him off balance, knocking him backwards onto her bed. "Then *this* is just for boys too!" She crawled fingers up and down his sides, tickling him into squeals of laughter.

"Here now, Your Highness!" Nurse Tibelda, whom Willow hadn't noticed hovering outside the doorway, charged into the room, her eyes sparking with disapproval. "It's the prince's bedtime. This play, I fear, shall wind him too tight for sleep." She scooped Nezzie up into her arms and turned to Princess Diantha. "Shall I take the prince back to the nursery now, Your Highness?" Diantha nodded and Nurse Tibelda, holding on tight to a struggling Nezzie, bowed and left the room, closing the door behind her.

As Nezzie wailed down the hallway, Willow glanced curiously at her mother. Diantha had her head cocked toward the door, listening to Nezzie's fading cries, anxiety radiating from her and making her sweat. Willow wondered what was going on. Diantha rarely denied Nezzie the slightest thing, let alone anything that would cause a tantrum. Willow patted her mother's hand, hoping to keep her from bolting after Nezzie. "You did the right thing, Mom. He'll be a lot safer now with those bands on."

Diantha blinked and stared at Willow as though she'd never

seen her before.

"The bands," explained Willow. "You know, Nezzie's warding irons."

"What? Oh yes. Yes, the bands ..." Diantha's words died off. She wrung together nervous hands, darting antsy looks around the room. Willow had seen her act this way before. As if there were some kind of elastic between her and Nezzie that, if stretched too far, snapped her back to him.

Gently, Willow pulled Diantha's hands apart. She breathed deeply and closed her eyes, letting a calming spell flow through her and into her mother. Diantha's tense fingers relaxed. Willow opened her eyes. Diantha looked back at her, relief smoothing the strained lines of her face. Willow stared. She knew her mother didn't sleep at night. The bruised circles around her eyes confirmed that fact. But the rest of her appearance – the thinness, the pale sickly skin, the dull hair – hinted at something else troubling her. Something far more sinister than lack of sleep.

Healing mages from every part of Gallandra had been brought in to examine Diantha, but none could find anything wrong with her. They could not even get rid of the symptoms. Only Willow's magic had had any effect on her, though always short-lived.

"I wanted to talk about tomorrow." Diantha clung to Willow's hands, holding them like a lifeline. "Your father tells me that you won't accompany us to Keldoran. My parents, I'm sure, shall be greatly disappointed. Is there no way you can postpone the faerie queen's visit?"

Alaric was taking Diantha and Nezzie away tomorrow to visit Diantha's parents in Keldoran. Everyone had agreed that she should have no inkling of Queen Cyrraena's plans. Willow would remain in Carrus and politely refuse the faerie queen's request. Of course, Willow was pretty certain that Queen Cyrraena wouldn't accept a refusal. So, it'd been her idea to have her parents leave the city. She didn't want Diantha worrying about her on top of everything else.

Willow sighed and gave her mother's hands a comforting squeeze. "You know I can't do that. Queen Cyrraena doesn't postpone visits. But ... maybe after she's gone ..."

A smile lit Diantha's face, so that she almost looked like her old self. "Yes," she said. "It would be lovely to have us all together. As if it were a holiday."

Willow nodded, trying to keep her guilt from showing on her face. Maybe she was wrong about Cyrraena. Maybe the faerie queen would accept a refusal and Willow could stay in Mistolear and not make her mother's world come crashing down around her. She gave Diantha a hopeful smile. "Do you think Grandmother Morwenna will have her cooks serve those little unicorn desserts that melt into strawberry sorbets? Nezzie would get such a kick out of those." Too late Willow realized her mistake. Mentioning Nezzie broke the calming spell. Severed it, in fact, sharply enough to make Willow wince in pain. Her mother's face grew tense again. Reluctantly she withdrew her hands from Willow's.

"Yes ... I believe he would enjoy those." Diantha paused,

trying, Willow thought, to fight her compulsion to run back to Nezzie. The compulsion, though, won. She leaned over and kissed Willow's cheek. "It was lovely to chat with you, darling. But I – I must look in on Nezzie. Sleep well." She rose from the bed and without a backward glance hurried from the room.

Willow stared at the closed door for a few moments, fear gnawing at her gut. It was more than just the mention of Nezzie's name. Something else had broken that spell. Not just pushed it away or discharged it, but shattered it. And Willow was almost certain it hadn't been her mother.

In mage school, the healers had learned to distinguish between the magic of different mages. One of Willow's homework essays had described the two main attributes of Diantha's magic pattern as "flowing" and "gentle." Not harsh and aggressive. And while mental disorders could affect a mage's magical strength, they could not disrupt his or her pattern.

Willow's eyes widened. *Harsh and aggressive.* Suddenly she recognized the alien magic pattern. She'd felt something like it once before.

When Nezeral had tried to strangle her.

CHAPTER 5

Willow's heart drummed in her chest. A soft breeze from an open window spider-crawled over her skin, sending shivers prickling up her spine. Nezzie slept in his cradle, moonlight winking against the ruby eyes of his dragon bands. He had no power. The bands were still there. And Cyrraena had said that faerie babies could only cast extrinsic spells, spells that didn't become a part of their subjects. Willow's body went limp with relief. For the past hour she'd worked herself into a panic, imagining Nezzie as a psychic vampire, siphoning off her mother's strength, growing plump and healthy while she thinned and weakened. But ...

He had no power.

That strange shattering of her magic couldn't have come from him. It couldn't have.

A moan disturbed the quiet night. The bed beside the cradle creaked with movement. Willow padded toward it. Her mother lay tangled in blankets, her skin coated with a fine sheen of perspiration. She moaned again. Willow knelt beside her. This time she did all the preliminaries for an intrinsic calming spell that would last through the night. She focused on her mother's green-yellow aura, hovering her hands just over the bright-tipped edges. Then she passed the calming spell into the aura.

Diantha's breathing deepened. Her twisting face and body relaxed. Whatever demons pursued her, they were now subdued. Willow began to draw her hands away, to finish off the spell. But suddenly she felt a sharp tug as though someone had yanked her forward. Something was grabbing at her magic. Something incredibly strong. This time, though, it didn't just break the spell. It held her fast, pawing through her magic pattern like a hungry animal. Willow's mouth opened to scream but no sound came out. The attack suddenly stopped. Whatever had just mauled her savagely spit her out. She slumped to the floor, shaking from the violence of the assault.

Holy crap!

Willow gasped desperately for air and gawked in terror at the bed. Diantha thrashed to and fro, writhing uncontrollably. *Jeezus!* Her mother looked possessed! Willow heaved herself up, stumbled past Nezzie's cradle, and blindly careened through the adjoining room where the nurses slept, tripping over the prone guards she'd sleep-spelled on the way in. Her knee throbbed. She didn't care. She clambered back up and scrambled down the corridor.

Torches flickered brightly around the doors to Queen Aleria's suite. A guard awoke the queen and then escorted Willow inside.

"My dear, whatever is the matter?" Aleria had risen from bed and thrown a thin, gauzy robe over her nightgown.

Candlelight illuminated the trail of red hair that streamed down her back, softening her strong features.

Willow struggled to calm her breathing even as her mind raced. Now that she was here, what the heck was she going to say? *Your daughter-in-law's possessed by a demon. Bring on the exorcist.* She teetered, feeling suddenly faint.

Aleria grabbed her arm and half-carried her over to a chair. "Sit," she commanded.

Willow obeyed, sinking gratefully onto the plump cushion. Aleria sat across from her, concern tightening her lips. "Child, you look as if you have seen a ghost." She placed warm fingers over Willow's shaking hand. "And you're trembling like a leaf. What has happened? Are you well?"

"It ... it's Princess Diantha. I think ... I think there's a spell on her. Or in her, or ... or something."

Aleria looked alarmed. "On your mother? Her illness has worsened?"

"No," blurted Willow. "I'm telling you right now, it's not an illness. It's a spell. There's magic inside her. A malignant magic that's *not* a healer's pattern. She came to me tonight. I ... I held her hand. I passed a calming spell to her. And something ... something broke it. Something totally aggressive and *not* my mother."

Willow rubbed her forehead. "There's more. I went into Nezzie's room. She was asleep, but it looked like she was having a nightmare or something. I wanted to help her sleep better, so ... so I gave her a calming spell. An intrinsic one this time that would last all night." Willow took a deep breath. She had to get this part right.

"Just when I was finishing the spell, something grabbed my magic." She clutched Aleria's hands. "And it *attacked* me. It *groped* my pattern! Now is that something Diantha would do? Or *could* do?"

Aleria stared at Willow. "No," she said finally. "It's not." She rose from the chair. "Come, we shall awaken the healing mages and solve this mystery at once."

The three royal healing mages stood by a sleeping Diantha, their palms outstretched and hovering as if they were warming cold fingers over a fire. Willow had seen them work before, fascinated by how the mages interwove their powers to form a net of magic that they then trolled through their patient. No illness or spell could escape. Willow held her breath, waiting for the malignant magic to attack.

The head mage, an elderly woman with sparse gray hair and sharp, avian eyes, dropped her hands first. "Your Majesty, it's no use. I feel no magic pattern other than the princess's own." The other mages followed suit, dropping their hands and agreeing with the head mage.

"Aye. Perhaps the princess Willow was mistaken," said the one male mage condescendingly. "She is, after all, but a first year healer."

"Though nightmares *can* cause magical aberrations," the other mage was quick to point out. "The young princess could easily have confused one of these irregularities with an outside spell."

The head mage patted Willow's arm. "Your mother sleeps well, child. Better than I have seen in a long while." She frowned at the male mage who'd belittled Willow's skill. "Our calming spells have not taken hold since Her Highness's illness. But somehow she allows her daughter to soothe her. It is something, I believe, we can learn from."

Willow stared at Diantha. Her mother lay peacefully, her breathing deep and her features smooth. This wasn't right. Willow knew her spell hadn't worked. It had broken at the end. And broken spells don't miraculously pull themselves together and start functioning. She held her own palms hesitantly over Diantha, reaching for her aura. *Maybe the spell will only attack me. Because my magic can sometimes get through it.* But Willow felt nothing. No strange magic pattern. No illness. Nothing. Her mother felt completely normal.

Queen Aleria covered Willow's hands with her own, breaking the aura connection. "My dear, it's late. Let us retire back to our beds, and we can all discuss this further in the morn."

"You don't believe me." Willow looked indignantly from her grandmother to the three healing mages. They appeared sympathetic but unconvinced. Willow's face flushed with anger as she shrugged Aleria's hands away. "Look, I know what I felt. It wasn't some *irregularity*. I recognized the pattern. It was strong and aggressive, like ... like ... Nezeral's." There, she'd said it out loud. The four adults gaped at her.

"Faerie magic?" The head mage's black eyes pierced Willow.

Queen Aleria quickly stepped in. "It has been a long night," she said tightly. "My granddaughter has obviously made a mistake. Come. We are all weary. Let us go to our beds." She gave Willow a stern look and strode from the room, the mages following behind her. Willow stood dazed for a moment. Aleria didn't believe her. And, judging from the nasty look she'd just given her, thought her a liar as well.

But before Willow could feel truly hurt, Aleria suddenly reappeared. "What's the meaning of this?" she accused. "Do you intend to go to Clarion against our express wishes?"

"What?" Willow had no idea what Aleria was talking about.

Aleria took a deep breath, her face pinched with concern. She gently cupped Willow's face in her hands. "My dear, I know how you, Brand, and Malvin slipped away from Ulor to go after Nezeral on your own. No one questions your courage. But Willow, this is different. The fey cannot be trusted. Allowing you to go to Clarion alone would be akin to letting you walk into a trap. Don't you see that?"

"I don't understand." Willow blinked at her. "You think I'm lying?"

"Not so much lying as ..." Aleria sighed. "I've checked Diantha myself many times. I've never experienced what you described." One hand circled Willow's shoulder. "You're very brave, my dear. But truly, it's not necessary for you to go to

Clarion. You ..."

"Grandmother, I'm not lying." Willow stared directly at Aleria. It had finally hit her. Her grandmother thought she *wanted* to go to Clarion to protect them or something and was making up the faerie-magic story as a ploy to do it. "Please believe me. I don't want to go to Clarion. But I don't know what else to do. Don't you see? They could still be playing a Game with us. And if that's true, I may not have a choice. I may *have* to go."

Aleria seemed to struggle with Willow's words, as if she wanted to argue them away, but then her eyes filled with tears. Willow could see she believed her now. The queen pulled her into a hug. "I won't let them have you," she hissed. "Whatever we must do so that you can remain here, we shall do. You won't be Queen Cyrraena's or anyone else's pawn ever again!"

"But what about ... what about Diantha?"

"I don't know." Queen Aleria shook her head and smoothed back Willow's hair. "But *you* won't be the sacrifice."

CHAPTER 6

Willow shivered as she read the fey history book. Apparently, in the old world of humans, the fey had first acted as if they were gods. But after the Great Earth Exodus of Magic, the fey were cast in the lesser role of "Once Upon a Time." Magic left the world, and humans went on to develop their own philosophies and religions.

The Great Exodus occurred in the Earth time that came to be known as the Dark Ages. Humans with fey bloodlines up to the seventh generation were taken from Earth and given rights to a realm of the middle dimension, known as Mistolear. All fey, honoring the new rule against commingling with mortals, settled in the high dimension of Clarion.

Humans must not be fooled, though. The last guise of faerie, the fairy-tale world of "Once Upon a Time," is not the real world of faeries. Their real world is and always has been one of power, their values and ethics far removed from anything that humans might comprehend. They do not think or feel in the same way that humans do. They are alien creatures, incomprehensible to humans, and thus, harmful.

Willow sighed and bookmarked her page. The passage

she'd just read from the fey history book reminded her too much of Nezeral's horrible Game last year, and how he'd wanted Mistolear and its inhabitants to be used like some kind of vacation playground for him and his faerie buddies. Just like they'd once used Earth. Yawning, she rose from the window seat to stretch.

Sleep had eluded her last night, so she'd paced the floor of her room with feelings that kept fluctuating between hope and fear. Finally, she'd picked up *The Complete History of Fey Magic Lore* and begun to read it. The textbook writing style and stilted language had bored her at first, but once she read past the snoozer chapters like "Fey Nomenclature" and "Abbreviations and Authorities," she'd been enthralled with the strange fey views on mortal concepts like justice and government, or their thoughts on love, marriage, and child rearing.

Like, who knew faeries never married? They formed alliances. Ones that could last for centuries or days, depending on their mood. Love was just a fluid, ever-changing concept to them. And when it came to kids, faeries pretty much had the parental skills of cult leaders. Fey kids withstood years and years of what seemed to be mind-numbing indoctrination into the cults of Dark and Light.

What had really interested Willow, though, was the whole concept of "houses." Instead of being separated into kingdoms and nations, the faeries divided themselves into houses. Each house had a king or queen, who either would have been a fey from the beginning of time or a descendant of one of those first faeries. The first faeries ruled all the major houses. There were minor houses as well, ruled by crowned heirs that had advanced to ruling on their own. But since faeries didn't die, crowned heirs didn't actually inherit anything. Only direct descendants of a house ruler could qualify as a crowned heir. Once they qualified, however, they had to be incredibly astute Game players to defend their title from covetous siblings, who would stop at almost nothing to topple them. It took many centuries and many wins before crowned heirs finally graduated to ruling their own houses. But then the process would start all over again with their remaining siblings and then again among their own children in their own houses.

A whole society that revolved around Games. Nezeral had once told her this, but the intricacies of it all still boggled Willow's mind.

When dawn streaked the horizon, she dressed and went down to the courtyard to say goodbye to her parents and Nezzie. Diantha, for once, looked rested, her dark circles only smudges beneath eyes lit with anticipation. Willow hugged her parents and ignored the measured stares of the courtiers and servants. News of what she had said about faerie magic infecting her mother had spread through the castle like wildfire. Queen Aleria had decided to combat the rumors by saying it was all a mistake. Willow, however, didn't think people were buying it. She saw mistrust in their eyes – mistrust and fear.

Willow didn't blame them. She was scared too. Aleria said she had a plan but wouldn't give details. So, as soon as her parents and Nezzie left, Willow was back in her room, studying the fey book and keeping a low profile. When a loud knocking sounded at her door, she ignored it resolutely. Last thing she needed were ladies-in-waiting pestering her.

"Princess, may I come in?" It was Brand. He waited a moment and then knocked again, softly this time. "Malvin and Gemma are here too," he coaxed. "We wish ... we wish to be of service."

"Your Highness?" Malvin's muffled voice came through the door. "Don't lock us out. Please, we want to help you."

"Aye," added Gemma. "We've heard all the talk. But we want to hear from you what *really* happened."

Willow smiled. At least her friends couldn't be fooled by rumors. She opened the door, and Brand, Malvin, and Gemma filed into the room. Each had a face glum with worry.

Willow shut and relocked the door. "So, what's going on out there?" she said. "Does everyone think the place is crawling with faerie magic again?"

"Aye, you might say that." Gemma found a spot to sit on the edge of Willow's bed. "But I want to know, is it true? Did you feel faerie magic in your mother, or was it a mistake like the queen keeps saying?"

Willow sighed. "It's true."

Malvin, his mage's curiosity clearly piqued, looked Willow over hopefully. "Were you marked in any way? Sometimes a powerful spell can leave scorch marks."

Spreading her scorch-free fingers, Willow held them out to Malvin. "Sorry to disappoint you, but I'm not burned."

Malvin had the good grace to look embarrassed.

"What of the Imp, then?" asked Brand, using his nickname for Nezzie. "Is he the cause of it all?"

Willow shook her head, but didn't admit that she had suspected Nezzie first too. From day one, Brand had mistrusted the idea of changing Nezeral into a baby and adopting him. Willow didn't want him thinking he'd been right. She told him about the iron bands.

"Grandmother finally convinced my mother to use the warding irons on Nezzie. He was wearing them last night. There's no way he could've had anything to do with that weird magic pattern."

"This strange pattern, then," said Malvin, "can you describe what it felt like?"

What it felt like? Willow shuddered. She remembered something that had happened in fifth grade. Two boys had held her down, while a third had shoved snow in her face and into the open neck of her jacket. "Helpless," she said. "Weak. I – I couldn't move. If it'd wanted to hurt me, it could have."

"But what made you believe it was a faerie that made the spell? Couldn't a powerful mage have made it as well?"

"Maybe." Willow chewed a nail to hide her tension. "All I know is that when it attacked, it *felt* the same as the time when Nezeral tried to strangle me."

"So if it wasn't Nezzie, then," said Brand, "who or what could it have been?"

Malvin winced. "The speculation is that faeries are still

playing Games with us."

"Aye," said Gemma. "And the Queen's trying to diffuse it all by saying Her Highness made a mistake. For we all know if faerie magic's in the land again, every councilor and courtier will be calling for the princess to be on Queen Cyrraena's next portal call to Clarion."

"Well, no one needs to worry about that." All eyes blinked at Willow's cryptic comment.

Brand spoke first. "What do you mean ... no one needs to worry?"

"They don't have to worry because ... I don't have a choice." Willow let the statement sink in before she continued. "When Queen Cyrraena offered me the Council seat, I didn't say no. I didn't say yes, either, but with faeries that's beside the point. I didn't know it at the time, but by not saying no, my agreement was considered implicit, and once you agree to something with faeries, it's like a contract. So I have to go to Clarion on Friday. And nothing my grandmother or anyone else can do will change that."

"You know this for a certainty?" Brand gave her a dubious look.

Willow turned away, went over to the window seat, and picked up *The Complete History of Fey Magic Lore*. "Look, I've been up all night and most of the morning studying this. I *know* how faeries think. And trust me, it's nothing like we do. They're all about rules and contracts. They cook up bizarre deals with each other all the time. And it doesn't matter if only one side knows the rules. In fact, they kind of prefer it that way."

"What do you mean? Are you saying that your implied agreement to sit on a Council seat has locked you into some kind of faerie deal? The same as when the Keldorian mage called out to the Higher Powers and brought us Nezeral?"

Gemma had hit the nail on the head. Willow nodded. "That's exactly what I'm saying."

"But Your Highness," broke in Malvin, "it was the faerie queen herself that offered the Council seat. Do you mean to say that she has betrayed you? Betrayed us all?"

"Okay, that's the tricky part." Willow sat down on the cushioned window seat and thumbed through the book's ancient pages. "You see, she wouldn't see it that way – as a betrayal. To her ... Okay, here it is.

"There can be no Light without Dark, no Dark without Light. Faeries believe and adhere to this tenet. Some align themselves with the Light and some with the Dark, as their entire immortal lives are lived as an eternal struggle to balance these two elements.

"There's more," said Willow. "But the gist of it is this – faeries believe this Light and Dark thing is ... is some kind of mystical force. Like it's alive. Like ... God or something. It uses them to keep a balance. So they make up all these Games and rules and stuff, but to them it's really the Balance that manipulates everything. So if someone enters a Game and doesn't know all the rules, the faeries don't see this as being unfair. They believe the Balance keeps everything in check anyway, so not knowing the other side's rules actually adds more excitement to their Game."

Malvin looked incredulous. "Then this ... this Balance," he sputtered, "uses them to play Games the same way they used us?"

"Yeah, well kind of," agreed Willow. "But the faeries don't look at it as being 'used.' I mean, they like it. It's what they live for."

"Aye, but they're immortal," pointed out Gemma. "A Game can't end their life like it can ours. I say Malvin's right and the faerie queen has betrayed you."

Sighing, Willow closed the history book and set it on the window seat. "I don't know, Gemma. At first, I felt that way too. But after reading this I'm not so sure anymore. I don't think Queen Cyrraena means to hurt me specifically. I think she sees me as a tool for the Light. And ... well, as a faerie, she has to use the tools that the Light sends her."

"And if you refuse?" Brand's grim face struggled to hide his apprehension.

"I'm not sure I can."

"But you will try?"

Willow stared into Brand's worried eyes. She saw the way he felt about her. Knew he wouldn't hesitate to save her, just like he hadn't hesitated in the Game last year, when he'd stepped in front of a crossbow bolt meant for her. She didn't want to lose him. She looked from Brand to Malvin to Gemma. She didn't want to lose *any* of them.

"Do you know why Queen Cyrraena chose to leave Clarion

and come here to Mistolear to be its guardian?"

One by one, Willow's friends shook their heads. "Well, she told me," said Willow, standing up from the window seat. "She said that she, and the faeries that came with her, are tired of Game playing. They want to evolve and change like the rest of the universe. But that's not what the Council wants. The Council says that faeries are already the highest life-form, which in their minds means they don't need to evolve. So basically, Queen Cyrraena's here to prove them wrong. She's like an experiment that demonstrates to the Council that faeries don't have to separate the Dark and Light inside themselves. It can all be one. She also wants to show that she can interact with humans without using them as Game players and ... well, without being a Game player herself."

"It would seem then that she has failed," said Brand dryly.

"Yes," agreed Malvin. "She has both played the Game against the faerie prince Nezeral and used you as her champion."

"Well, yes and no." Willow stared at her friends. "Queen Cyrraena played the Game, yes, but she played it in a way that the faeries have never played before. She made it so that we ourselves won the Game. In the past when faeries played Games with humans, we were only their playing pieces, following orders and not making decisions for ourselves. Queen Cyrraena did things differently. She helped us, but she didn't tell us what to do. She made it so *we* won the Game and not her."

Gemma shook her head. "But don't you see, it's still a Game. You going to Clarion is like ... is like a win for her. She's using you as a playing piece in her own little Game of change. I say we call her on it and refuse to let you go."

"If we do that," sighed Willow, "I think we might be opening the door for more faeries to come here. Because if I break my side of the contract, then it opens clauses and loopholes for them to break their side. And maybe they would be allowed to come here again. Not something, I'm sure, anyone is too keen to have happen."

Brand, his color climbing to a red flush, spun around and stomped toward the door. In the hallway, he turned back to glare at Willow. "There is one thing certain in all this," he snarled. "*You*, Your Highness, shall not go to Clarion alone." The door slammed behind him.

CHAPTER 7

The next few days, while Queen Aleria prepared for the faerie queen's visit, Willow remained closeted in her room with Gemma and Malvin, studying the fey history book. Brand took a while to come around but eventually joined in to help as well. The whole time, Willow felt sorry for Queen Aleria, who was busily preparing for Cyrraena's visit. Aleria still thought she could stop the faerie queen from taking Willow to Clarion, but Willow knew better and prepared for the worst.

Queen Aleria paid Willow a visit the morning Cyrraena was supposed to arrive. It'd been days since they'd really talked. Aleria looked around the room, noting the empty breakfast dishes at Willow's feet and the mostly-finished fey history book open on the window seat beside her.

"I see, Granddaughter, that you have kept yourself busy these past few days. But it's all for naught." She smiled brightly, her face filled with confidence. "You won't have to leave Mistolear, not even for a moment. My mages and I have found the perfect way to protect you. Come." She held out her ringed fingers and took Willow's hand.

Curious, Willow followed her out the door and down the

71

hallway. "Grandmother, I don't know what you've got planned, but you do know Queen Cyrraena's not going to listen, don't you? She has no choice in this either."

Aleria lost none of her optimism. "That, my dear, remains to be seen. For now, though, your grandfather and I will meet with Queen Cyrraena on your behalf. And *you* will be kept safe from any fey influence."

"But how ... how can ..."

"You shall see soon enough. Be patient." Queen Aleria turned down another corridor, tugging her granddaughter along behind her. It was strange how empty the hallways were. Usually mornings meant high traffic. The corridor twisted into a gloomy staircase. Willow recognized her surroundings and stopped abruptly.

"Oh no," she said. "No *way* am I going down there!" Down there being the castle dungeon. Aleria appeared not to hear her. She sent a charge of magic into Willow that forced her feet to follow.

"*Grandmother!*" Aleria didn't answer. Willow's feet moved down the dingy stairs despite her best efforts to stop them. "What are you going to do? Keep me locked up like Varian and then forget about me?"

The nasty remark didn't make Aleria stop, but she did throw Willow a caustic glance. Prince Varian, Willow's great uncle, was still a bit of a touchy subject. Since his capture last year, the king and queen had been arguing over how to dispose of him. Queen Aleria, and most of the councilors, wanted to follow the traitor laws to the letter and execute Prince Varian. King Ulor, however, refused to do away with his own brother and wanted him banished instead. They'd settled on imprisonment – Varian was locked in the north tower – but it was still a source of contention between Ulor and Aleria.

Cool, dank air crawled along Willow's skin. Not having left her room yet this morning, she still wore only a thin nightshift and slippers. She began to shiver. From the top of the stairs, she watched Aleria descend into the darkness. "You know, this isn't funny," she growled. "I could catch pneumonia down here." The odor of urine and wormy earth engulfed her as she helplessly followed the queen into the dungeon's gloomy belly.

Willow's heart began to pound. There were no prisoners down here. Her family treated the dungeon like a big dirty storage basement, but Willow thought of it as a big dirty nightmare. She called out to her grandmother. "This isn't going to change anything. She'll still find me."

They rounded a corner. Torchlight flickered over an open cell door, illuminating the pasty face of the dungeon master. Willow, forced by Aleria's magic, stepped inside a cell decked out like a royal bedchamber, and then found herself frozen in place. Two other guards appeared, and with the help of the dungeon master, they started loosening a rope to lower something from the ceiling. Willow couldn't see what it was at first. Then iron bars came swinging into view. They were lowering a cage over her.

The queen peered through the bars, her face alight with

triumph. "The faerie queen doesn't rule here," she crowed. "She can't take you without our consent. And if she tries ..." Aleria tapped a bar, flinching when she touched the iron, "these will stop her."

Willow tried to speak, but the spell had frozen her mouth shut too. Aleria seemed not to notice and continued excitedly to explain her plan. "You will be secure here, as no one shall guess at your whereabouts and the iron will safeguard you from the fey. Trust me, my dear. The freezing spell will wear off in a moment or two. And I promise that all will be well." She patted Willow's shoulder through the bars, gave her a big encouraging smile, and left the prison cell, the two guards following after her. The dungeon master shuffled out too, closing the door behind him. Willow heard the dull click of a lock.

Slowly her limbs began to unfreeze until she could move them again. She looked around her prison, surprised at its opulence. Aleria had thought of everything. Rugs. Furs. Pillows. A brazier. Even a plush velvet couch piled with blankets and clothing, and a table laden with food, drinks, and books. Red silk hung in one corner from the top of the bars and fell to the floor like a curtain. She reached out and pulled the cloth aside. A white porcelain chamber pot came into view.

Oh great. Just how long did her grandmother plan on keeping her here anyway? She dropped the curtain and plunked down on the couch, wrapping herself in one of the blankets. The stone walls outside the cage blazed with the light of several torches. She could smell a hint of lemon and soap. Someone had scrubbed the floors and walls so that not even a cobweb or a speck of dust could be seen.

Willow sighed, leaning into one of the pillows. So this is what her grandmother had been doing for the last few days. Willow should have guessed Aleria was up to something questionable when she hadn't asked for Willow's help in planning for the faerie queen's visit. Another missed red flag popped into Willow's mind. She remembered when she'd first suggested sending Diantha to Keldoran. Aleria had jumped right on the bandwagon, insisting that Alaric and Nezzie should accompany her too. Willow shook her head. She'd been asleep at the switch. *Of course Aleria* knew *my parents would have no part in locking me up.* But where was King Ulor in all this? Could Queen Aleria have planned the whole thing behind his back?

A sinking feeling came over Willow. Where family was concerned, her grandfather didn't like to do the dirty work. He'd let Aleria arrange all the details for Prince Varian's tower cell and even now couldn't bring himself to visit his brother. No doubt he had agreed with Aleria's plans but had let her carry them out. Willow would get no help from him. So that left ... *who?* Who was going to help her escape? Because her grandmother's plan only worked on one level. It would keep Cyrraena from finding her. But it wouldn't stop a Game.

Brand, maybe? Malvin and Gemma?

But no. No one had seen her and Queen Aleria go to the dungeons. And even if any of the ladies-in-waiting had actually seen them, none of them would tell her friends. Willow snorted, ruefully acknowledging Queen Aleria's superior shrewdness. After all, who would suspect a loving grandmother of locking her only grandchild in the freaking dungeon!

A stab of anger spurred Willow to her feet. She wasn't just going to sit here and do nothing. Her fingers encircled the iron bars, numbed a bit, but her immunity kept the metal's power-leaching effects at bay. She tried to remember how it felt to magic iron. To make the molecules dance to her command. She could see the aura lights. She focused on them, visualizing the bars coming apart. Nothing happened. She kept trying, straining her mind, pushing herself to focus, but no matter how hard she concentrated she couldn't make the iron molecules obey her.

Sighing, Willow rested her forehead against the bars. Since the Game's end, the talent that had let her make slippers out of air, that had allowed her to pass a hand through a book, and that had cuffed Nezeral in irons, had left her. She felt like a singer who couldn't hit any high notes. The ability was there. Just not the range. Her magic only worked on living tissue now. Nothing inanimate would respond. Headmaster Ewert had assured her that with practice and study she would eventually relearn non-organic magic, but her true talent would always lie with the organic.

Willow returned to the couch. She reached for a book and a pear. Apparently, her only option was to wait things out.

A thudding sound awoke Willow. She lifted her head from the pillow, confused for a moment about where she was. The bars, though, quickly brought everything back. She was a prisoner. Albeit for a good cause.

She stretched and yawned, surprised that she had fallen asleep. How long had she been down here? A few hours? A day? There was no way to tell. Her windowless cell was deep in the ground. Even the door was solid, with no window for the guards to check on her. Not that she wanted that creepy dungeon master guy leering at her or anything, but ...

Willow cocked her head. She'd just heard another thud. Loud. As though someone had dumped a sack of potatoes by the door. The lock clicked. Willow's breath caught in her throat. She rose to her feet, clutching the bars as Malvin, Brand, and Gemma came stumbling into the cell.

"See, I told you!" proclaimed Malvin. "My spell *did* work like a tracking charm."

Brand brushed past Malvin, ignoring his triumphant crowing, and immediately set himself to lifting the cage. The heavy bars barely moved. Willow pointed at the wall. "There's a rope over there." Her three friends grabbed the rope and slowly began to raise the cage.

"Cripes!" wheezed Gemma. "This thing weighs a bleeding ton."

"Hurry, Your Highness," gasped Malvin. "We can't hold it much longer."

Willow dropped to the floor and rolled free of the bars. The cage crashed back down, clanging thunderously. Brand sprung forward to help as she scrambled to her feet.

"How did you find me?" Willow asked. "I thought no one knew where I was."

"No one did." Brand frowned, letting go of her hand. "And perhaps neither should we."

Gemma smacked Brand's arm. "We've already been through this, Sir Brand. The princess needs to be free."

"Aye," agreed Malvin. "We all read the fey history book. Locking Her Highness away solves nothing. In fact, it endangers the entire realm, *including* the princess."

Brand turned troubled eyes to Willow. "Yes, but at least this way she would be here, not on a dangerous quest, all alone."

Malvin and Gemma fell silent. Willow jumped in, changing the subject before things tensed further. "How did you guys find me, anyway?" She started walking toward the door. "I thought no one saw what happened."

Brightening, Malvin joined her at the doorway. "Remember the time you told me of fingerprints? How in Earthworld your sheriff and guards could use them to know who has been in a room and what they had touched?"

Willow nodded. Watching crime shows had been one of her favorite Earth pastimes. She'd told Malvin all about fingerprints, DNA testing, and forensic evidence.

"Well, when we came to your chambers at nine, as we'd agreed, we saw immediately that something was afoot. The first clue being, of course, Headmaster Ewert's one-of-a-kind fey history left lying in the sunlight on your window seat." He gave Willow a headmasterly look of disapproval. Every day, he'd been lecturing her on how to take care of the book: don't expose its pages to sunlight, don't drink or eat while reading, etc. Willow knew better than to deliberately put it in harm's way.

"And the second," added Gemma, "you were missing with not so much as a note to explain your whereabouts."

They walked out the cell door and over the snoring bulk of the dungeon master and another guard that Willow hadn't seen before. On a squat table lay empty dishes and a half-eaten chocolate cake. Willow smirked. Gemma and Malvin must have combined their mage talents and made a "sleeping cake."

"So," continued Malvin, "I applied this 'science,' as you call it, to magic and developed a spell much like your Earth fingerprinting. I infused a powder with the spell and sprinkled it around your chambers. It showed us the queen was the last person to visit you. From there we kept sprinkling it in the hallways, following your trail until it led us here to the dungeon."

"Not a place, mind you," said Gemma, "that I would've guessed on my own."

Brand, who had been trailing them with pursed lips, broke his moody silence. "No. Nor would anyone else have guessed it, I warrant – including the faerie queen." Suddenly he grasped Willow's arm and pulled her around to face him. "Do you not see – the queen has the way of it. Return to the cage. You will be safe there. We will guard you ourselves." He slammed a fist into the wall. "Let the cursed fey fight their own battles," he growled. "Queen Cyrraena can find another strategy. It's not fair to involve you. She should ... she should ..."

Willow blinked, her chest tightening. Brand had tears in his eyes.

He broke away from her, embarrassed. Willow didn't know what to do. What could she say that wouldn't make it worse? Gemma filled in the awkward silence. "You may be right, Sir Brand. The fey *should* fight their own battles. But I still say Her Highness needs to hear the faerie queen out. What say you, Princess? Is it back to the cage? Or forward to the council room?"

All eyes turned to Willow, Brand's dark ones burning with a depth of feeling that filled her with indecision. Finally, she pointed up the winding staircase. "Forward," she said, "to the council room."

CHAPTER 8

On the way, Willow made a detour to her bedchamber to change into a dress. Gemma helped with the ties in the back and brought her gold crown and swan necklace. Willow had decided to go all out with the princess look. Her dress was the elaborate blue and gold court gown that Desma had tried to tempt her with a few days ago. She brushed a hand over its smooth silk, gazing at her reflection, stunned as always when she dressed for court by the regal girl in the mirror.

Gemma set the crown on her head, a narrow gold band studded with sapphires and pearls, made for Willow after she'd returned Diantha's crown. The swan pendant settled just above the scooped neckline of the blue gown. Willow touched the necklace to see if the faerie queen had arrived. The swan sent a warm wave of tingles through her fingers. Queen Cyrraena was definitely here. The necklace always responded when she was nearby.

"She's still here then, is she?" said Gemma, taking a brush to Willow's hair. "We heard she'd arrived this morning, but only the king and queen have been allowed to see her. We feared maybe she'd left already and you'd not get your chance to speak."

Willow sighed. "Yes. Queen Cyrraena is still here." Truthfully, Willow had half-hoped she'd be gone. No doubt only a delay of the inevitable, but a chance to breathe, to really talk things through with her grandparents. She exhaled heavily. "Okay. I'm ready. Let's go."

In the hallway, Brand and Malvin waited, pacing nervously. When Brand saw her all decked out in her princess regalia, he offered her his arm. "Your Highness," he said, bowing his head. This time Willow took his arm with pride, using him and her majestic looks to bolster her confidence. They walked along the corridors to the council room as if they were expected. Courtiers bowed, not seeming the least bit surprised by Willow's presence. Willow relaxed. Obviously her grandmother had told no one of her imprisonment. Getting into the council room, then, wouldn't be difficult.

Outside the council doors, a unit of royal guards blocked the entrance. Willow, with Brand at her side and Malvin and Gemma behind her, straightened her back, held her head high, and sailed up to the doors. Immediately, spear handles barred Willow's way.

"We are sorry, Your Highness, but no one is admitted to the council chamber."

"We are expected. Remove your weapons at once." Willow thought she had done a pretty good imitation of a royal command, but the spear handles remained frozen. Brand jumped into the fray.

"Did you not hear Her Highness's order? Remove your

weapons at once."

The guards continued to stand as still as statues. Willow frowned. There were too many to sleep-spell. She clutched at the swan necklace instead. Heat radiated from it. Queen Cyrraena would know Willow was nearby. *Come on*, she thought urgently, *do something. Make these guards obey me.*

A feeling of warmth spread through Willow. The faerie queen had heard her. The spear handles came apart. One of the guards opened the door for them and stood aside as they passed.

The council chamber had a south-facing wall covered with windows from floor to ceiling, and sunlight flooded the room. Willow squinted at the sudden brightness. Her grandparents, Sir Baldemar, and a few of the other royal councilors sat at one side of the gigantic council table, shocked looks on their faces, while Queen Cyrraena and her contingent of faeries sat on the other end, impassive as always. Willow clutched Brand tighter and let him lead her into the room.

"My netherchild, it is good to see you again. We were just discussing your trip to Clarion." The faerie queen's silky voice reflected none of the turmoil in the humans around her. She was wearing gold today, a simple Grecian dress that gleamed and shimmered in the sunlight, her hair a russet cloak covering her bare arms. "Are you ready, then?" she smiled. Green, tip-tilted eyes pierced Willow. "We have much to discuss."

"*No!* No, we do not." Queen Aleria shot to her feet, glaring at Queen Cyrraena. "Your Majesty," she said tightly, "the deliberations, I believe, have ended. As stated, the princess is to remain here in Mistolear. There *is* nothing further to discuss." She turned her glare to Willow. "Return to your chambers at once. We shall deal with ..."

The words froze in Queen Aleria's mouth. Willow glanced back to see if someone unexpected had entered the room. No one had, but Malvin and Gemma, she noticed, seemed frozen too. She released Brand's arm, which stayed rigid in the air.

"Time is still." The words echoed eerily in the uncanny silence. Willow turned to Queen Cyrraena. The faerie queen and her attendants still moved and breathed, not held immobile like the humans. Cyrraena gestured toward a window that expanded and changed into an open doorway. "Come. We shall walk in the gardens and discuss your trip."

"But ... but ..." Willow passed a hand in front of Brand's eyes. He didn't blink, move, or even seem to be alive. "Are they ... are they okay? They're not ..."

"They are fine. Time is just stilled. When I free it again, they will continue on as if nothing has happened."

Willow followed Queen Cyrraena into the gardens. She stared at Lady Tavia sitting on a bench, her embroidery hoop perched in her paralyzed hands. The gardener stood fixed, admiring his roses, and the cook's kitchen boy lay stationary beneath a shady apple tree. Everything felt surreal, as if Willow had stumbled into Sleeping Beauty's enchanted castle after the sleeping spell.

Sleeping spell? Willow herself could cast a sleeping spell on one or two people. Faerie queens, though, could cast them on a castleful. Heck, Queen Cyrraena could stop time! Willow blinked. *The lesser role of "Once Upon a Time."* She suddenly understood that passage. It meant *Sleeping Beauty* and the rest of the fairy tales she'd grown up with maybe weren't stories at all. Maybe, in fact, were true.

"You are over-quiet, my child. I expected to hear questions fly from your mouth."

"They're not fairy tales, are they?" said Willow. *"Sleeping Beauty ... Snow White ... Cinderella ... Rapunzel ..."*

Queen Cyrraena shook her head. "No, they are true stories. Or at least based on truth."

"Will you make me go if I don't want to?" There. The question was out in the open now. Willow thought she knew how Queen Cyrraena would answer it. But she still held out hope she was wrong.

The faerie queen stopped walking. She faced Willow, puzzlement on her face. "You know that is not my way. I do not *make* you do things. You must decide on a course of action for yourself."

"Yeah, but you stack the deck in your favor. You make it so I don't *really* have a choice. That if I don't do things your way, the cost is too high."

Queen Cyrraena didn't answer. Willow went straight to the point. "What happens if I don't go to Clarion? Will Mistolear be open season for the fey a second time?"

The faerie queen started along the path again. "The cost of that choice, as you say, would allow the fey to come to

Mistolear. However, the cost of going to Clarion may yet allow the same thing."

"So you set me up then."

"Set you up?"

"Yeah. When I accepted a seat on the Council, you knew it meant another Game. But you didn't warn me about that, did you? Made it seem like it was some kind of great honor instead." Willow grabbed Queen Cyrraena's arm. "And my mother – you knew about her all this time. And you didn't tell me."

"Your mother?" Queen Cyrraena appeared confused. "What exactly am I supposed to be informed of?"

"The faerie spell. Don't pretend you don't know about it. She's probably had it on her ever since I agreed to sit on a council seat. How could you not say anything?" Willow's voice cracked.

"Willow, truthfully, I have no idea what you are talking about. The consequences of not going to Clarion would place you in a Game *now*, but you haven't been in one since our agreement. There should be no faerie spell on your mother."

"But ..." Willow thought back to the night when she'd felt the alien magic pattern. She hadn't dreamed it. It had broken her spell and violated her very being. "I felt something in my mom. A pattern that wasn't hers. It ... it attacked me."

"Attacked you?" Concern swept across Cyrraena's usually stoic features. She closed her eyes and became as still as the enchanted humans. Moments later she blinked, betraying a hint of shock. "This does not bode well. I too feel the traces of a discordant pattern, though it tried its best to hide from me."

Willow stared. Her mother lay miles away in Keldoran, but Queen Cyrraena could just close her eyes and check Diantha's magic pattern. It was a bit unsettling.

"Human magic would not try to hide from a faerie."

The cryptic statement pierced through Willow. Had Queen Cyrraena just admitted to the pattern being faerie-made? "So ... so you're saying ..."

"I am saying there may be a Game afoot not sanctioned by the council." For the first time Willow saw true worry on Queen Cyrraena's face. "Willow," she whispered, "you may be right. Perhaps ... perhaps there is no choice. You may *have* to go to Clarion whether you want to or not."

CHAPTER 9

Sure, a small part of Willow had hoped it would be simple. The faerie queen would come. They would talk. Cyrraena would assure her there would be no repercussions. And Willow would be free to decide whether she still wanted a seat on the Clarion Council.

But mostly, Willow had expected the worst.

Which is why, now, pacing among the hedgerows, she felt ambushed by her panicked emotions. Every instinct, every ounce of self-preservation screamed at her to run. To hide. To let Queen Cyrraena fight her own battles. *Why should I have to bear the brunt of everything? Why should it be* me *and not* her *that goes to Clarion?*

The faerie queen watched Willow from a seat beneath a rose-trellised bower, her expression serene and beautiful. Willow wanted to smack her. She controlled the impulse, though. Kept pacing instead. Finally, she couldn't stand it anymore and stormed over to Cyrraena, wagging her finger. "*You,*" she snarled. "You're coming *with* me. This is your doing. *You* should have to help fix it."

Other than a slightly raised eyebrow, no emotion crossed

Queen Cyrraena's tranquil face. "I cannot accompany you to Clarion," she said simply. "My presence here in Mistolear has rules. If I return, I lose my bid for change. I would have to remain in Clarion and be assimilated back into our society." Her green eyes narrowed. "And that, my child, is something I shall never do."

Willow slumped against the trellis. Of course there would be rules governing Queen Cyrraena's presence here. Why hadn't she seen that before? Nethermother or not, Cyrraena was still a faerie. And this was all still just a Game to her.

"You have read the book, have you not?"

Willow nodded.

"Then you know how our society works. We are all bound by the rules. And Jarlath, Nezeral's father, is no exception. If he is behind your mother's illness, then he has found some sort of loophole. For even he cannot break the rules."

"Okay. So what are you getting at?" Cyrraena's habit of dancing around a point frustrated Willow.

"Do you not understand that *your* visit to Clarion has rules?"

Willow blinked. Actually, the thought hadn't crossed her mind.

"These past months I have spent much time mind-locked with the council, preparing new rules that would guarantee your safety. Everyone is in agreement. Even Jarlath. You will go to Clarion, sit with the council for a Mistolearian week, and then return. You will be an observer only, with no requirement to compete in any Games. The only stipulation being, of course, that you go alone."

"So you're saying Nezeral's family can't touch me? As long as I go alone?" It seemed too easy. Willow knew there had to be a catch somewhere. "What about all these rules you've been working on? Do I get to hear them?"

Some hint of emotion flickered in and out of Queen Cyrraena's eyes. Fear? Guilt? Maybe even pity? Willow wasn't sure what it was. She just knew that Cyrraena had immediately clamped down on it.

"No. The rules will not be made clear to you. As an observer, you have no need of them."

Oh great. That was basically faerie-speak for *See you later, kid. You're on your own.* She could break a rule without even knowing it was a rule.

Willow laughed, shaking her head. "Fine. Send me to Clarion. But don't fool yourself, Cyrraena. You're no different than any other fey. I know this is a Game and I'm *your* playing piece." She pushed off from the trellis and began walking back toward the castle. Amazingly enough, Queen Cyrraena had actually frowned. Willow didn't care. She was through letting faeries push her around.

Back inside the council room, Willow positioned herself next to Brand again. Queen Cyrraena materialized back at the table. "Please," she started, "we can ..."

"I don't want to talk about it anymore. Just get it over with."

The faerie queen gazed at Willow, her face inscrutable. "Very well," she agreed finally. Something popped in Willow's ears and Queen Aleria's voice rang again throughout the chamber.

"... you later."

Willow remembered the gist of her grandmother's diatribe, something about deliberations being ended and nothing else to discuss. She squeezed Brand's hand and began to move toward Aleria. "I believe the choice is *mine* to deliberate and not yours nor anyone else's," she said, making Aleria blink at her defiant tone. In front of the table, Willow let go of Brand and spun toward Queen Cyrraena, her defiance turning to sarcasm. "Is that not right, Your Majesty?"

"It is true. Only you have the power to accept or refuse my offer."

"She is a child!" thundered King Ulor, rising to stand beside Aleria. "Under our guardianship, I might add, and as such, cannot accept or refuse anything without our consent." His voice lowered to a growl. "We have rules here as well, Your Majesty. Rules, I believe, that you are sworn to uphold."

"Please, listen," Willow urged, hiding some of the bitterness she felt. "It's not just me who feels the spell on Princess Diantha. Queen Cyrraena feels it too. It's ... it's a faerie spell, Grandfather. They've found some loophole in their rules and are ..."

"Willow, no! Say no more!" But Queen Aleria's plea came too late. The councilors around her had burst into a frightened commotion. Tears of defeat shone in Aleria's eyes. Rules, after all, were rules. And as Willow was bound to obey her grandparents, so her grandparents were bound to obey their royal councilors. Willow sighed. She knew there was no going back now. All she could do was try to comfort them.

"Listen everyone. Please." Willow raised her hands for quiet. The councilors' outburst settled to an agitated murmur. "Queen Cyrraena and I have discussed this. She has negotiated a safe passage for me with the fey council. I'll only be gone for a week and won't have to compete in *any* Games. I'm just an observer. A guest. But I'll still be able to ask about Princess Diantha and what we can do to save her." Willow didn't know if this was true or not. She turned to Queen Cyrraena, who nodded publicly but whispered something different in Willow's head.

Do not query the Council about your mother. Let them speak first. It will be to your advantage if someone admits to the spell.

One councilor, a small anxious man with frightened pop eyes, spoke up over the murmurs. "It's a matter of our kingdom's ... no, our very *world's* security. We have no choice. I vote to send the princess to Clarion at once." A number of councilors added their quick "ayes." One, a braver soul than the others, raised a question to Queen Cyrraena. "Do we have your word then, Your Majesty, that our princess is truly safe? That she will be returned to us, unharmed, in a week's time?"

"You have my word, insofar as the rules are kept, that the Princess Willow will be returned to you, unharmed, in a week's time."

Silence shrouded the room. Everyone suspected Queen Cyrraena's promise was no real promise at all. How could she guarantee that Willow would keep the rules? Especially ones Willow didn't even know. The brave councilor lost his nerve. "Aye," he voted with the others. There were no "nays." Willow's heart drummed in her ears. Her grandparents looked ready to order executions. Sir Baldemar jumped in, taking matters into his own hands.

"Let me go in Her Highness's place," he asserted. "Or at the very least accompany her."

The faerie queen regarded him carefully. "My Lord Baldemar, your offer is both loyal and courageous, yet I am unable to accept it. Only the princess may go to Clarion. There are no exceptions to this." She rose from her chair, her attendants rising behind her. "I shall give you an hour to prepare for her departure. Please use the time wisely." A perfumed breeze swept through the council chamber. Queen Cyrraena and her faeries shone bright for a moment then faded softly.

"Leave us," ordered Queen Aleria. "All of you leave us at once." The councilors, Sir Baldemar, and Willow's friends filed from the room, their eyes downcast and heads bowed. When they were gone, Aleria flew at Willow, not to berate her, but to enfold her into her arms. "Oh my child. My dear, dear child. We are undone."

King Ulor squeezed his wife's shoulder. "Aleria, come now. You shall frighten her." He gently pulled Willow from Aleria's death grip. "Now is the time for praise and approval." His blue eyes gleamed a sad pride. "Our granddaughter quests to save Mistolear. We must send her off with bolstered spirits, not fear and trepidation."

Aleria nodded and wiped her cheeks. Ulor steered them toward chairs and made them sit. "Granddaughter," he began, "you are the faerie queen's netherchild and are gifted with her wisdom." He grasped Willow's hand. "You saved us all once from a faerie spell. I have trust that you shall do it again."

"Yes," said Aleria. "It's true. If I am not allowed to be grandmotherly," she smiled weakly, "and keep you safe here with me, then there is no one – *no one* – in whom I would rather place my faith than you, my dear, to protect us from the fey."

Willow felt her heart break. She hugged her grandparents fiercely. They were both so imposing, so much larger than life. It meant a lot that they actually had confidence in her. She spent her remaining minutes tucked in their arms, reminded that she was their granddaughter and not just Mistolear's princess.

When the hour was nearly gone, King Ulor allowed Brand, Malvin, and Gemma to return to the council room. Willow said her goodbyes, embracing each of them tightly. When she came to Brand, he wouldn't let her go. The emotions she struggled to control threatened to escape. "Brand," she rasped, "it'll be ... it'll be okay. I promise." He let her go, but his eyes never left her.

Queen Cyrraena's image glimmered then appeared sharply before them. "It is time." Her splayed fingers hovered near Willow's shoulders. Energy joined with energy. Every nerve and muscle tingled inside Willow. She panted, her eyes blinking rapidly. The world began to fade. To mist over. Unexpectedly, some force grabbed onto Willow. It squeezed her like a vise, crushing air from her lungs. She screamed, collapsing from the weight. The white mists shifted from gray to black, and she and the unseen force went reeling and plunging through space.

CHAPTER 10

When the cartwheeling, head-spinning motion stopped and Willow realized she wasn't going to puke, she dared to open her eyes, and then instantly clamped them shut against a bright light. She groaned. The cold stone floor pressing into her face was about as comfortable as ... well, a cold stone floor. She tried to raise herself but something heavy was squishing her. *What the* ... Willow craned her neck. Brand was sprawled on top of her, bear-hugging and pinning her to the floor like a wrestler.

"Brand," she groaned. "Get *off*. What ..."

Suddenly, it all came rushing back. Her grandparents. Queen Cyrraena. The trip to Clarion. *No! Oh no, no, no, no, no.* This was not good. This was not good at all. She elbowed Brand when he didn't respond. He grunted and finally released her. Willow climbed to a sitting position. All around the room, impassive, steady eyes watched her.

Willow stared. There were at least sixty faeries, some seated, some standing, some leaning over a stair balustrade, all tall and beautiful, all strangely ageless with skin like fine carved porcelain, the fabrics of their clothing shimmering and pulsing like sunlit water. Willow blinked in surprise at the fluttering ancient tunics worn over modern jeans, velvet Napoleonic jackets, Arabic pantaloons, medieval gowns with floor-touching crimped sleeves, cloaks, furs, even rock star leather. Nothing matched. Every outfit seemed to come from completely random eras and places. An eerie, mixed-up costume party mocking Earth history.

Brand, as wide-eyed and incredulous as Willow, helped her climb to her feet. Round, white, and windowless, the room they stood in looked like a Greek amphitheater, only with a ceiling and a balconied second floor. Willow's gaze circled upwards. More stone-faced faeries peered down from above. She caught her breath. The green ceiling roiled with carved twining vines, an exact replica of the ceiling in the tower where Nezeral had once imprisoned her.

"Ahh – I am reminded of ancient Earth days," rang out a smooth male voice. "Humans on their own were always the poorest players. Already the girl has forfeited." A deep sigh. "It hardly seems fair sport to lay claim to her."

Silver bars suddenly materialized around Willow, and she was caged for the second time today. Brand was caught inside the bars too, clutching them in bewilderment.

"But alas, rules are rules."

Willow finally picked out the speaking faerie. He was one of a number who sat in the chairs behind her. She recognized him immediately, his silver blond hair, green ice-chip eyes, and chiseled face a slightly aged copy of his son's. A soft murmur like a rustling breeze went through the fey. Nezeral's father rose to his feet and addressed the assembly. "As is my right, I, King Jarlath Thornheart, claim the two humans for the House of Jarlath."

Willow gasped. *Oh crap*. This was so not good. She glanced at Brand beside her, his face still slack with shock. She struck his arm. "What are you doing here?" she hissed. He snapped out of his trance and stared at her, his eyes a mixture of fear and desperation.

"I ... I ..." He shook his head, defensive posture slipping back into place. "Already you are betrayed, and you ask me *why* I came?"

A lilting voice stopped Willow's snarly response. One of the seated fey, a female faerie, chided Jarlath. "Really, my lord, is this necessary?" She swept a graceful hand toward the cage. "Do you fear the humans shall ... harm the Council?" Titters of laughter went through the crowd.

Jarlath remained impassive. "Of course, my lady Kestal, I do not fear humans. I only show the court their true nature. That of ... beasts." Willow felt something crawl over her skin. She glanced at Brand. A hybrid of tiger and boy with clawed nails and striped muscular body stood in his place. Fulsome laughter filled her ears. She twitched her own whiskered nose, afraid to look down at what her hands gripping the bars might have become.

"Yes, yes," another faerie spoke up. "Very amusing, my lord Jarlath. But what of your plans? Are you to whisk them away from us? Or will you grant the Council a chance to examine them?"

The illusion or spell or whatever had enveloped Willow dropped from her like a cloak. She strained to hear Jarlath's answer.

"I have no need of haste. Examine them as you wish."

Willow lurched a bit as the bars she leaned on vanished. Jarlath gestured for her and Brand to step forward. "Come. Be questioned." He returned to his seat, watching their approach with cool disinterest.

Catching hold of Brand's sleeve, Willow hissed in his ear. "Don't say *anything*." He glanced at her, his stony gaze promising nothing. *Oh great.* All she needed was Brand mouthing off and making things even worse. She pinched him until he winced, then strode ahead. In front of two lines of seated faeries, whom she assumed must be the Council, she sank into a deep curtsy. Manners, she remembered from her reading, counted for much in Clarion.

"Princess Willow, we greet thee. Rise." Willow got up. She nodded to the faeries and ignored Brand, who refused to bow and stood stubbornly defiant beside her.

"You bring another human. Why is this? Did our lady Cyrraena not make the Council's conditions clear to you?" The male fey who spoke sat in a line of eleven faeries all wearing white. The other row of faeries, where Jarlath sat, all wore black, but there were only ten of them instead of eleven. Willow lowered her gaze deferentially. "Yes, my lord, the conditions were made clear to me."

"Then who is this young man and why is he here?"

"He is Sir Brand Lackwulf, my lord. My sworn knight and protector." She raised her eyes. "And I did not bring him. He forced his way onto the transport spell. There was nothing I could do to stop him."

"This, of course, changes nothing," interrupted Jarlath. "The humans still belong to me."

"Yes. Yes." The faerie in white looked almost impatient. He turned to Brand. "A sworn knight and protector? This seems a poor way to safeguard your princess. To deliberately break the rules governing her safety and draw her into a Game. Were you unaware of the danger?"

"I ... I ..." Willow saw Brand's confusion. Too late, she realized her own mistake. He knew the rule. He'd just never understood why it was so important. In the last hour, she'd explained it more fully to her grandparents, but Brand had only heard her terse goodbye.

"She's in a Game? Because of ... because of ... me?" Understanding passed over him for a moment then quickly turned to defensiveness. "No. It's not true. It was you, not I, who first broke rules. The princess was *already* in a faerie Game. My accompanying her here does not alter this. It does, however, even the score."

The faeries, unnaturally quiet and still, stared blankly at Brand – probably their version of shock. Willow's version, though, consisted of a gaping mouth and the sick feeling of her stomach sinking into her knees. *Don't tell the Council about your mother*, Queen Cyrraena had said. *Don't bring anyone with you.*

Brand was ruining everything. She grabbed his shirtsleeve and yanked him down to whispering level. "*Shut up*, okay! Trust me. And don't say another word."

"Forgive us." Willow curtsied and bobbed her head. "My knight is ... is confused from the transport spell. Of course, he knew I was supposed to come here alone. He just ... he just didn't understand what would happen if I didn't."

Brand looked ready to disagree. She clasped his hand and dug her nails into his palm. He glared at her but kept his silence.

"You do accept then that King Jarlath has a rightful claim? That as his son was defeated by you, he may now attempt to win him back."

Willow blinked at the white-clad faerie. *Win him back?* No. She didn't know that part. She sighed and nodded. "I understand." What else could she say? The faeries had all the playing cards. She was just a poker chip on the table.

"Well then, my lord Jarlath, what is your will in this? Do you challenge the humans or do you give pardon?"

"Challenge, my lord Oberon."

"Very well, then. The humans are yours to Game with." The faerie named Oberon turned a solemn face to Willow and Brand. "It is the will of the Balance that you be placed in Dark. Only Light can set you free again. Do you accept this challenge?"

Willow hesitated. "And if I don't accept it?" she asked. "What happens then?"

"To not accept a challenge justly given is to enslave yourself to the challenger."

"So in other words there is no choice."

Oberon didn't agree or disagree. He just continued to stare solemnly.

"I accept," muttered Willow.

"And I as well." Brand squeezed her hand, trying in his own way to comfort her. She pulled away from him. This was all his fault. Wanting to be the big hero again. "You have me," she cried out to Jarlath. "You don't need Brand. Send him back to Mistolear."

Brand stiffened and gaped at her incredulously. Oberon spoke for Jarlath. "The boy has followed the path of his own Light. He cannot return. You are now bound together in the Game."

Something snapped in Brand then and changed his surprise to anger. He glared at Willow. "Don't worry," he spat at her. "The Game is yours to play. I shall *not* interfere."

"Fine," snarled Willow.

"Fine," agreed Brand.

Neither one of them noticed until their heads started spinning that Jarlath had enveloped them in another spell. A violent force scooped them up, and they hurtled into the air like bowling balls.

CHAPTER 11

Willow and Brand reeled and smashed into each other, everything a blur, wind roaring in their ears. Then – *bam!* – they hit the ground hard and went sprawling across it. Bars sprang up around them and Willow's back slammed into one. Brand hit the bars face on, blood spurting from his nose. They both lay stunned and blinking while Jarlath gazed in at them from the other side of a cage.

"Welcome to the Menagerie," he said. "I have long desired a human specimen for my beast collection. And now I have not one, but two. And a male and female as well." He smiled maliciously. "Perhaps I shall breed you."

"We are not beasts," snuffled Brand, holding his bloody nose. "Release us at once."

Willow gawked, not able to get past the disturbing implications of the word "breed." But a sudden crop of unexpected goose bumps made her look down. All her fine court regalia had vanished and been replaced with a skimpy loincloth and bikini-top ensemble. Not exactly the right outfit to inspire gutsy defiance. She crawled to her knees, huddling against the cage bars.

Jarlath bent closer to peer at Brand, who also wore nothing

but a loincloth. "There are festivities to plan," he drawled. "Tours to conduct." A cryptic smile crossed the faerie king's face. He chuckled, then vanished from sight. Brand hunched forward, cupped hands trying to stem the steady flow of his gushing nose.

"Here, let me help." Willow knelt beside him. Gently she surrounded his face with magic, dulling the pain, then manipulating the cartilage and torn blood vessels back into place and melding them together. The blood stopped spouting, but Brand's face and bare chest were still slick with it. Willow scanned the cage. A water bucket sat beside them. Two corners were piled with straw, one with raggedy blankets. She scooted over to the blanket corner, tearing off a strip from a cloth piece already torn, then dipped it in the water bucket. Brand said nothing as she wiped the blood off, his eyes boring dark holes into the dirt floor. Willow turned to redip the bloody cloth in the water.

"Don't," said Brand. "We may have to drink from that."

Willow instantly froze, her bedraggled reflection looking back at her from the water's clear surface. *Drink from it? Oh jeez. What had Jarlath called them? Animals for his zoo or something.* The red-stained cloth dropped to the ground. Willow sank dejectedly beside Brand, color draining from her face.

Jarlath didn't want a Game. He wanted payback.

"Is what the faerie lord said true? Is it because of me that you are a prisoner?"

Willow looked at Brand. He was sitting too, arms across his knees, wet chest gleaming in the sunlight. Willow tried to swallow. She had never seen Brand shirtless before. He was ripped like a football jock. Quickly, she flitted her eyes away.

"It's ... like ... well ..." Willow took a deep breath. "Yes."

Brand's silence made Willow peek at him. He looked mature, like Sir Baldemar when he had offered to go to Clarion for her. "I don't apologize," he said. "Say what you will, Jarlath means you harm, and with or without my interference, he had a plan to follow. Some scheme that would have tricked you into his clutches. I am your sworn knight, Highness. And a poor protector I would be if I allowed you to enter danger alone."

Willow's sigh filled the cage. She leaned her head back against the bars, staring up at the covered ceiling. She should have seen this coming. Guessed how Brand's mind worked. All along he'd maintained that he wasn't going to let her go to Clarion alone. But over the last few days, the way he had helped with her studying and then agreed to help her escape from the dungeon, he'd lulled her into thinking that he'd accepted the faerie queen's plan. Willow dropped her head and gazed into Brand's expectant eyes. *Darn it*. Maybe she *had* known. The troubling thought took root and began to grow. Had she avoided being alone with him so she wouldn't have to talk about it? Wouldn't have to order him to stay behind? If so, his presence here was partly her fault.

"Look, Brand, I don't know if what you did was right or wrong. But I'm ... I'm glad you're here, okay?"

Brand gave her a crooked smile, then seemed to notice her almost nakedness for the first time. He turned bright red and pinned his eyes to the floor.

Willow glanced outside their cage, trying not to feel embarrassed. A forest of trees surrounded them, entwining around fanciful walkways and ivy-draped arbors that winked with colorful birds. Flowers, bushes, and leafy ferns sprouted in abandon, somehow more potent, more *real* than any Willow had ever seen before.

She turned to the bars and drew herself up. Glistening light caught her eye. Down a grassy knoll and behind a giant tree that draped thick plaits of moss, she could see a green pool and hear the steady splash of its jetting waterfall. Sunshine warmed her bare skin. She drew fresh, perfumed air deep into her lungs. Maybe they were trapped in a cage, she thought, but one set in paradise.

"Willow. What do you make of this?"

Brand usually didn't say her name without a "princess" in front of it. Willow turned to look at him. The cage had a door and he stood there swinging it open.

"It's not locked."

Willow didn't know what to say. She came over and examined the door with him. It didn't even *have* a lock. Just a latch that clicked it shut.

Brand stared at the surreal beauty of the forest. "The faerie said this was a menagerie. I see no animals. No other cages."

Willow followed his gaze. Nor were there any fences or walls. It didn't make sense. "Do you think we should look around? Maybe try and find a way out?"

"Listen," he said. "The birds aren't singing."

Willow listened. Brand was right. She could see birds but not hear them. No insects hummed. No breezes wafted in the tree leaves. Except for the steady splash of the waterfall, the whole forest was silent. Deeply, utterly silent, as if a predator lay in wait for its prey. She shivered. Brand got to his feet, took a step toward the door. She clutched at his arm. "No, don't. Something's wrong. I can feel it."

"I know. I feel it as well." He slipped from her grasp. "Keep watch. I shall only go to that tree by the pond. Perhaps if I climb it, I will see what lies beyond the forest. "

"But ..." Too late. Brand was back in hero mode. He had shut the cage door behind him and was stealthily making his way toward the tree. Willow held tight to the bars, scanning every inch of forest brush for trouble, ready to call him back if something so much as twitched. She didn't see it at first – it had blended in so well with the dark foliage. But once Brand went past the area where he could easily return to the cage, a sleek, black panther revealed itself. It sprang from the bushes, launching onto Brand and knocking him to the ground. Willow screamed. Without thinking, she shoved the door open and bolted to them. Halfway there she realized she had no weapon. No way to rescue Brand. She grabbed rocks, sticks, whatever she could find, and started pelting missiles at the great cat. One struck its rump. Another its ear. The animal snarled at her, then tore off into the woods.

Willow flew to Brand and helped him to his feet. They made it back to the cage and Willow slammed the door, making sure it clicked shut. She turned to Brand. His body had gone slack, his wounds pooling blood on the ground. He swayed and clutched the bars. Quickly, she helped him to one of the straw piles, where he lay panting on his stomach.

Willow's mouth went dry. Four deep gashes spurted blood down Brand's back. He craned his neck to look at her. "Can ... can you heal it?"

Oh God! His wounds were huge, deeper than any she'd healed before. Willow sank to her knees and nearly gagged at the coppery smell of blood. "I'll try," she choked. "I'll try, but don't move, okay. Just don't move." She pushed magic into her hands, letting it grow until it pulsated like a heartbeat. At her touch, Brand moaned but stayed still as a statue. She froze the pain first – more difficult on a large back than a small nose. The effort forced her to rest for a few minutes afterwards. Then she began the healing, the painstaking magical suturing of each torn cell and ragged skin tissue until Brand's back was whole again. It took over an hour. Willow blinked in surprise when the job was finished. She had never before sustained her magic for such a long period of time. She reeled dizzily, pitched forward into the straw beside Brand, and passed out.

Something nudged Willow's shoulder. She moved away from it. It nudged again, and this time a voice accompanied it. "Willow? Willow? Are you well?" She opened one eye and peered up at Brand. "What?" she croaked. "What is it?" Then she noticed his bare chest and remembered what had happened. "Your back ... Is it ... is it okay?" She sat up, ignoring her spinning head and blurry eyesight.

"I think it's fine," said Brand, reaching around to touch his back. He turned to show her. "See? I feel no wound or scar."

Willow squinted. Brand was right. She had healed his back without leaving so much as a scratch. "Try standing," she said. "Stretch up. Make sure everything is connected properly."

"I already have. I am fine." But he did it again anyway, giving her an eye-widening display of flexed muscle.

"Okay," drawled Willow. "I get the point. You can stop showing off now."

He flashed a dimpled grin and dropped back to the straw. His face turned serious again. "I have been watching the forest and there are other predators. A tiger came out from over there." He pointed to one of the walkways where a cluster of fat bushes concealed the path. "And by the water, I think I saw lions."

"'Lions and tigers and bears, oh my.'"

"What?"

Willow shook her head. "It's nothing. Just an old Earth saying." She rested her elbows on her knees, staring glumly around their cage. "So I guess this is home then."

"Yes. I don't want to be some cat's dinner."

A new and terrible thought came to Willow. She gave the cage a careful inspection. "Um ... Brand? Where do we, um ... go to the washroom?"

"Washroom?" He looked at her blankly.

"The privy."

"Oh." Brand's eyes flickered over to the other pile of straw, while Willow's widened in horror.

"No way," she groaned.

"I see no other, um, accommodations. There are two straw piles. One must be for sleeping, the other ..."

"I am *not* going to the washroom there." Willow jumped to her feet and started pacing. The cage and the Tarzan and Jane outfits were one thing, but this was getting out of hand.

"Your Highness." Brand's mouth pursed with amusement. "I believe there are more, um, pressing concerns than a washroom."

Willow glared at him. Yeah, right. Easy for him to say. He didn't have to ... *Oh God!* She didn't even want to think about it. Sunlight beamed onto her face at a hot angle. Probably close to six o'clock, she thought, judging from where the sun rested above the treetops. She glanced at the water bucket, realizing she was thirsty. Hunger gnawed at her next. Willow flopped back down beside Brand. That was it, then. Problem solved. If nothing went in, then nothing came out. She just wouldn't eat or drink anything until they let her out of here.

Brand had no such qualms. He cupped his hands into the water bucket and drank his fill. "Have some," he said, offering her the bucket. Willow just turned her head away. "Oh, come now. You have to drink." He lifted one of the threadbare blankets. "Here, I'll make you a curtain."

Willow snorted. She was about to tell him what he could do

with his curtain when she noticed a rippling movement on one of the walkways. A crowd of faeries had appeared, bright in festive clothing and strolling with lute-playing minstrels. Jarlath led the group, acting as their tour guide. His voice rang vibrantly throughout the wood. "You must see my new specimens. Two humans. Male *and* female. I am thinking of breeding them."

"What a novel idea," trilled a female voice. "Do you recall the Earth younglings? They were quite fetching little creatures. If you decide to raise any, the House of Oram would have a most definite interest."

Others spoke up in agreement. Willow felt queasy. It was bad enough they'd mentioned breeding again, but talking about babies like they were … were *hamsters* was too much. She moved closer to Brand. He wrapped a hand around hers.

The faeries surrounded the cage and stared at them. Shimmering and beautiful, they all looked as if they'd stepped out of a fairy tale book. Willow peered at their puffed and beribboned clothing. No, not fairy tales, she thought – a Shakespearean play. The ladies held feathered masks attached to sticks and the men's masks had horns and long noses. Like a theme party for *Romeo and Juliet*.

"A handsome pair," said one faerie, his horned mask set over brilliant blue eyes. "Strong. Fit. They should produce fine younglings."

"And look at the girl's hair," said another faerie. "The House of Edrea has hair of that color. If she is descended from them, they should be fine Game players as well."

"Yes, Edrea and her ilk were ever known to dally with mortals. The resemblance, though, is really quite striking."

Jarlath's gaze swept over the cage, taking in the blood spattered on Brand and on the ground. He smiled and held up his hands. "Come now, my friends, there is plenty of time to examine the humans. Let us eat now and enjoy the evening." Gauzy tents suddenly appeared, sheltering a glittering array of tables and chairs. Food smells wafted invitingly over to the cage, making Willow's stomach gurgle.

The faeries strolled toward the party tents, but Jarlath lingered behind. "Had a little mishap, did we?" He stared pointedly at the blood. "Sorry. Guess I forgot to mention that little detail about my cats." A haunch of meat, some apples, and a loaf of bread materialized on the cage floor. "Enjoy your dinner ... *Princess.*"

Brand leaped to his feet. "That's right," he called out to Jarlath's retreating back. "She is a princess. One who bested your son. And will, I warrant, best you as well."

Jarlath paused for the barest of seconds before continuing on his way. Brand hurled an apple, which vanished in mid-air. He snorted in disgust and sat down with Willow again. "Swine," he muttered under his breath. "How dare he insult you."

Willow chewed her bottom lip. She had more urgent matters on her mind than a stupid insult. Her knees squeezed involuntarily together. Despite her determination and her earlier precaution, Willow had to pee.

CHAPTER 12

Willow didn't become desperate until late in the night. Most of the fey partygoers had vanished back to wherever they had come from, but a hard-core group of them still twirled away under the stars. Brand had figured out her predicament from her silence and the strained look on her face. To his credit, he'd tried to be sensitive about it. After Willow had knocked down all his suggestions, though, he'd finally lost patience and tossed a blanket over her head. "Do it," he'd ordered. "Or I'll come under there and assist you."

The relief Willow felt at peeing overrode her humiliation. She came out from the blanket smiling sheepishly. Mistolearian guys were a strange bunch. Flash a little midriff or an ankle and they blushed like schoolgirls. But pee in front of them and they weren't even fazed.

"Better?" teased Brand.

"Much."

"Good. Now, eat something." He handed her half the bread he'd saved. "The gods know how long we shall be here. We must keep up our strength."

Willow tore off a small piece of crust and nibbled at it. Next thing she knew, she'd polished off the loaf, some straw-specked meat, two apples, and four palmfuls of water. A burp exploded from her mouth, making Brand grin.

"Er, excuse me," she said, cheeks flaring.

Brand bowed his head. "Of course, *Your Highness.*"

She threw an apple core at him, missed by an inch, so gave him a scowl instead. Slowly, the lights winked out. All the faeries vanished from the grove, along with their party tents and feast tables. For the first time, Willow could hear the hum of insects. The large jungle cats, which had mingled with the faeries like house pets, had disappeared too.

Willow peered through the bars, searching the inky forest for movement. Wind whispered through tree leaves, but the dark underbrush lay still and disturbingly quiet. She made herself comfortable in the straw beside Brand and stared at the bars of the cage, silvered and spectral in the moonlight. A footstep padded in the night. Willow sat back up at the sound. There, standing outside the cage and watching her curiously, was the most amazing-looking girl Willow had ever seen.

Like the bars, the incredible apparition seemed spun out of moonlight and glittering silver, her hair rippling past her waist, gleaming the palest shade of white blond. She stood tall as Willow but thinner, more fragile. A fey angel in a sparkling silver dress come to save them.

Willow shook Brand. He didn't respond. She looked down at him and saw that he slept. Not a real sleep, she was sure, but one the faerie girl had cast on him. Willow's eyes locked back on the faerie, trying to see the hidden danger in her delicately beautiful face.

"You are not what I expected."

The low voice, soft and lyrical, reminded Willow of birdsong or gently plucked harp strings, and made her yearn to hear more. She crept closer, not sure if she was awake or dreaming.

"No," spoke the voice again. "I thought you would be graceless. An ill-favored creature worthy of pity. But Father has again misled me. You appear as fey as I do."

"Who ... who are you?" ventured Willow. The faerie girl *seemed* friendly enough. Maybe she would help them.

"I am Dacia Thornheart, daughter of Jarlath Thornheart, of the House of Jarlath."

Willow gulped. Then again, maybe she wouldn't. "Then you ... you're Nezeral's ... sister?"

"Yes. Nezeral is my elder brother." Dacia peered at Willow, her heart-shaped face pressed against the bars. "You really *do* look fey. Father is trying to hide it with this cage and the rags he dresses you in. But I think no one is fooled." A small, cat-like smile crossed her mouth. "How did you do it, Willow, human princess of Mistolear? How did you defeat my brother?"

Willow stared. For a faerie, the girl seemed almost gleeful. Like she was happy Nezeral was defeated.

"In the end, did he offer you freedom? Did he wish to form a partnership?"

"Yeah. How did you know?"

"I beat him once." Dacia's smile vanished. "He offered to

form a partnership with me as well. A trick that turned my win to a loss. But you, a human, have bested him." The smile came back, radiant as sunlight. "I am pleased to have met you, Willow, princess of Mistolear. It is indeed an honor." Dacia faded and then disappeared altogether as though she had never been. Leaves rustled overhead. A branch snapped in the underbrush. Willow shivered, slipped back to the straw pile, and curled up beside Brand. The image of the beautiful faerie girl swam in her mind. Nezzie's sister – his *true* sister – seemed different from the other fey. Somehow more ... sympathetic.

Willow closed her eyes, remembering Dacia's words. *It is indeed an honor.* Nezzie, or Nezeral, was obviously not Dacia's favorite person. Maybe she could take advantage of that. Find a way to use their possible rivalry to her advantage. Brand twisted in his sleep, his breathing mellow and even. Natural sleep now and not a faerie spell. She pulled the thin blanket over her shoulder. For the first time things didn't feel so bleak. With a possible ally like Jarlath's daughter, maybe she'd find a way out. A way for her and Brand to go home. The thought soothed her mind and she fell easily into sleep.

The bright morning sun and the scratchy straw woke Willow. Eyeing Brand warily, she stole over to the pee-pile of straw and relieved herself under the blanket. She scooped out a couple of handfuls of water to try and neutralize her morning breath. Then, back beside Brand again, she lay in the sleep-straw and pretended to be just waking up.

"All finished?" he drawled, eyes closed.

Willow looked daggers at him. "A true knight, you know, wouldn't *draw* attention to it."

"Truly?" Brand stood up and stretched. "Forgive me, Highness. I must have missed that lesson."

She pitched the blanket at him then turned her back as he went over to the pee-straw himself. *Oh God. Could this be any more embarrassing?* Willow flopped into the sleep-straw, burying her head. She hadn't grown up with boys. No father. No brothers. No boyfriends. Brand's complete lack of bathroom modesty confused her. Especially since he seemed so concerned about other kinds of modesty, namely hers. Something bounced beside her head. She peeked open tightly clenched eyes and saw an orange.

"Our breakfast has arrived."

Willow sat back up, blinking at the food that hadn't been there a minute ago. Bread, cheese, and oranges. She eyed the orange lying on the ground. Water was okay. She'd decided she could handle peeing but just the thought of ... the *other* made her pink with mortification. Food was out of the question.

"I have been thinking of a way to escape from here." Brand averted his eyes from her uncovered body, sucked an orange slice, then chewed it slowly. "What do all animals fear most?"

Guns? Bigger animals? Willow wasn't sure.

"Fire. They *all* fear fire." Brand pointed to some sticks that lay on the ground close by. "Were I to fetch those branches, we could wrap them with the blanket and light them like torches."

Willow stared at the thick branches. How many movies had she seen where the heroes waved fiery torches at their enemies? Quite a few, actually. It could work. They just needed to get the branches into the cage without being attacked, and then find something they could use to start a fire. She looked at Brand speculatively. "Do you have matches?"

"*Matches?*"

"You know, something to start the fire."

"You will start the fire. With your magic."

"My magic?" Willow blinked at Brand. Hadn't he heard about the headmaster's hat? "I'm, uh ... not very good with fire." She looked around at their straw-filled cage, imagining it in flames. "Maybe we should think of something else. Something – Hey," she said, suddenly remembering the faerie girl's visit, "I forgot to tell you. Last night when you were sleeping, we had a visitor."

"A visitor?" Brand munched on some cheese and dared a peek at her. "What sort of a visitor?"

Willow contemplated draping herself with the blanket again. Brand's gaze had drifted to her chest and seemed stuck there.

"Nezeral's *sister*."

That got his attention. Dark eyes flashed back to Willow's face.

"Really? His sister? What did she want?"

"Basically, she congratulated me for beating her brother.

Said it was an *honor* to meet me."

Brand thought about this for a moment. He tore the bread in two and handed her a piece. "Perhaps an enemy of Nezeral's could prove a friend to us. Did she mention Jarlath?"

"Only to say the cage and these ..." Willow looked down at her skimpy loincloth and bikini top, "*outfits* are meant to humiliate us. He wants the other faeries to see us as animals and not as equals."

"Plus he likes to throw parties in the Menagerie and display his latest acquisitions."

Both Willow and Brand spun their heads at the unfamiliar voice. A faerie stood at the side of their cage, watching them with wry amusement. At first glance Willow thought it was Jarlath. Same silver hair. Same chiseled face. But this faerie had laughing eyes and a smiling mouth. Not fey traits at all. He gave Willow a once-over that felt, in fact, very human.

Brand shielded her body with his. "Who are you? What is your purpose here?"

"I am Theon Thornheart," drawled the faerie. "Second son to Jarlath Thornheart, of the House of Jarlath. And as to my purpose – well, let us just say I'm drawn to anyone who has bested Nezeral."

Willow peered around Brand at the faerie boy. *Second son.* So Nezeral had a brother too. A brother wearing hot Romeo tights and a puffy white shirt with leather ties that crisscrossed loosely to the navel. Boots too. Black ones that went right up his muscular thighs. Willow ducked quickly back behind Brand.

Theon Thornheart had seen her looking at him. Had *winked* at her. She flushed from neck to hair roots, suddenly aware of the blood-spattered floor, her stained loincloth, and the sharp smell of urine.

Another voice, sounding somewhat surprised, cut across the clearing. "Theon? What are you doing here?" The faerie girl from last night materialized in the distance, vanished, then burst back into view beside the faerie boy.

Theon didn't even flinch at her sudden appearance. "Hello, Dace," he said casually. "I could ask the same question of you. The Menagerie is hardly your favorite place."

"Nor is it yours." She took hold of Theon's arm and pulled him away from the cage, speaking to him in low, indistinct whispers.

Willow turned to Brand to explain about Dacia, but the words froze in her mouth. Brand was staring at the faerie girl in dumbstruck wonder. Willow followed his gaze. Really, she could understand his reaction. Dacia was *that* gorgeous. But it still made her feel kicked-in-the-gut jealous.

"That's Nezeral's sister. The one that visited me last night."

Brand blinked and looked artlessly at Willow. "Hmm ... what? Did you speak?"

She glared at him. He had enough brains to look sheepish. "Is it Nezeral's sister, then?" he repeated. "The one that visited you."

"Yeah, that's her."

Brand gazed back at the faeries, careful to avoid looking at

Dacia this time. "What do you make of them? They appear to be arguing over us."

Willow glanced at Dacia and Theon. There did indeed seem to be an argument underway. Dacia was jabbing a finger at Theon's chest, her white curls dancing with the movement. The pair broke apart, Dacia serene as though nothing had happened, Theon lit with amusement. Willow studied Nezeral's brother. For a faerie, he displayed awfully human facial expressions. She wondered if it was an act.

"It appears I am needed elsewhere." Theon bowed his head to Willow. "*A pleasure*, Princess," he said. "I'm sure we shall meet again." When he vanished, Willow didn't even blink. She was starting to get used to the way faeries just popped in and out of sight.

"I have petitioned my father for your release." Dacia stepped up to the cage and opened the door. "He won't allow it yet, but he has given permission for you to bathe in the pool and for me to take you on walks. Come. It will be your only opportunity for exercise."

"And the cats?" asked Brand. "Will we be an opportunity for their exercise as well?"

"If you are with me they won't harm you."

"And you will *stay* with us?"

"Yes."

Brand made to leave the cage, as did Willow. Dacia barred the way. "You misunderstand. Only one of you may come with me. The other must remain here."

"Forget it, then," said Willow. "I'm not going anywhere without Brand."

Dacia looked distressed. "Please. You shall *both* be allowed freedom. Just not at the same time."

A hand nudged Willow's shoulder. "You go," said Brand. "I'll stay here and keep watch."

Surprised, Willow glanced at her supposed knight. Brand suddenly trusted faeries now? He didn't look Dacia-dazed anymore. But maybe he still was. Willow narrowed her eyes. Somehow she doubted he'd be so quick to let her go if it was Theon doing the bathing and walking.

"Fine," she said, stepping from the cage. "Let's go."

Dacia walked along the path toward the waterfall pond. Willow stayed by her side, curious to learn more about the faerie girl who claimed to want to help them. "I didn't see you or your brother at the party last night. Is it because of what Theon said before – that you don't like it here?"

A ghost of a smile twitched on Dacia's lips. "Father's *parties*, as you call them, are about as exciting as Council meetings. Theon and I prefer our own friends."

"Oh." Willow touched a fringe of moss that hung from the giant tree Brand had tried to climb. The attack suddenly flared in her mind. *Brand's clawed back. His blood dripping to the cage floor.* She shot panicked glances into the underbrush, not so sure anymore of Dacia's intentions.

The faerie girl sensed her fear. "The cats won't bother us," she said. "I hold them far from here with a spell."

Willow studied Dacia. Was that empathy she saw in the other girl's eyes? Did Dacia fear the cats too? "So why don't *you* like it here?"

Dacia's eyes widened, revealing *silver* irises. She shrugged and began to walk again. "I have no like or dislike for this place. It simply bores me is all."

Something about her indifference contradicted her suddenly purposeful stride. Dacia had a secret. Willow was certain of that. She followed the faerie girl to the pool, not pressing the matter. Faeries probably didn't like it when their human-like qualities were pointed out to them.

At the pool, Dacia surprised Willow by transforming her gown to a top and loincloth similar to Willow's and diving into the clear green water. Willow dove in too, relishing the wet cold against her sweaty skin. The horror of Brand's attack yesterday and her humiliation at being caged like an animal seeped away like the bloodstains from her clothing. She and Dacia swam in the water like old friends, splashing and giggling. For a moment everything felt normal. They ended up on a ledge under the waterfall, hair plastered to their heads, shrieking at the shock of freezing water plunging over them.

Dacia grabbed Willow's hand and pulled her backwards. They tumbled into a dank cave. The water still roared in their ears, but all they could feel was a fine misty spray. Willow saw shells and rocks and two squalid piles of rags tucked in a corner. Dacia stood fixed as stone. "It's all still here," she whispered in disbelief. For a moment she looked ready to cry, then caught herself and turned to Willow, all emotion gone from her face. "Come. Your friend has to bathe as well."

Willow stooped to touch a rag. The moldy fabric broke apart in her hands. "Dacia, what ..." But the faerie girl had already dived through the waterfall, her entry into the pool below a faint slap in the showering thunder. Willow brushed the shreds from her fingers and studied the odd scene. Two piles of rags like ... like beds? And rocks and shells. Pretty. Almost decorative in their arrangement. Willow blinked. Had someone lived here? Had ... *Dacia*?

CHAPTER 13

Over the next week, Dacia, true to her word, came each morning and took Willow and Brand on walks and to the pool. She never mentioned the cave again. As a favor to Willow, she constructed a magic washroom that appeared only when she or Brand called for it, then vanished again into thin air. Other than that, though, Dacia treated them with cordial respect that bordered on aloofness.

Theon came as well, his visits sporadic and never when Dacia was there. He gave them treats like cakes and tarts, and smuggled in for Willow a hair brush and some lip balm. He often offered to take Willow for walks, but unlike Dacia, didn't ask Brand. Willow refused. Theon's long stares and human-like smiles made her uncomfortable.

In the evenings, Jarlath conducted his tours and parties, dancing under the stars with an entourage of costumed guests, the big cats gliding in and out among them like dangerous bodyguards. He never spoke directly to Willow and Brand, only spoke about them as if they couldn't understand his words.

One starry night, though, everything changed. Jarlath made the cage disappear. He dressed Willow and Brand in a white finery that made them look like a bride and groom and invited them to join the feasting.

Willow clutched Brand's hand, her heart racing with fear. Jarlath's grin scared her, as did the sleek tiger that padded along beside him.

The feast tables, arranged in a U shape, sat under crisp white tents whose gauzy curtains billowed in the soft breeze. Flowers garlanded white tablecloths and chair backs, and chains of them crisscrossed the tent ceilings like party streamers. Food and drink covered the tables. There were no torches or fires, but everything seemed flushed with light. *A wedding*, thought Willow. *It looks like a wedding reception.*

Jarlath sat Willow and Brand at the center of the head table and then took a spot next to Willow. "Come," he said. "Eat. Drink. Enjoy yourselves. Tonight is a special night. I share my bounty with everyone." The gold and silver plates on the table filled magically with food. Both Willow and Brand, bored with their simple cage fare, hungered for variety. They dug into the exotically spiced foods with relish. Minstrels appeared around the tents and began performing a haunting song of lost love.

The sad music awoke some warning instinct in Willow. She stared at the beautiful faerie creatures. They glowed with feverish excitement, their jewel-like eyes aglitter with anticipation. Something was going to happen tonight. Something bad. The terrible feeling of dread killed her hunger. Was this the end, then? Were she and Brand having their last meal?

"My princess." Brand leaned in close, his eyes scanning

the tables with the same unease that she felt. "I fear for us this night."

"What?" Willow faced Brand. It was one thing for *her* to be afraid, but to hear it from Brand ...

He stroked her cheek with a callused hand. "In my heart," he whispered. "I have always only sought to protect you. If I have led you into this danger, please forgive me. I shall safeguard you as best I can." He brushed aside a strand of Willow's hair. "Whatever happens, do not separate from me."

"Stop it." Willow jerked her hair from his fingers. "Don't talk like that. We're going to be okay. We ..."

"You're not eating." Jarlath's hand stole around the back of Willow's chair, rubbing her shoulder. "Surely you don't prefer Menagerie food to my feast?"

The light taunt elevated Willow's fear to rage and terror. She snapped around to Jarlath, knocking his hand from her shoulder. "Look," she hissed. "I don't know what you're playing at here, but I didn't harm your son. He's alive and well." Her voice rose hysterically. "I know how this works. There are rules. And you can't hurt us. You ..." Willow's hand flew to her mouth, staunching the flow of panicked words. *What am I doing? I'm only making it worse.*

A white tiger walked up to Jarlath and nudged at his arm. Absently, the faerie king scratched the beast's smooth head, and his turquoise eyes, so like Nezeral's, fixated on Willow. The horror of the moment hit Willow full force. *The cats.* He was going to do something with the cats.

"Oh, my dear foolish princess," he tut-tutted. "I *can* hurt you. You have no idea how much."

Willow's mouth went dry, her heart beating so hard it hurt. For one insane moment, she almost contemplated throwing herself at Jarlath's feet to beg for mercy. But his cold Nezeral-eyes stopped her. Nothing she said or did would change the Game he'd planned. The thought steeled her. She met his stare with a flinty one of her own. "What are you afraid of, Jarlath? Are you afraid Nezeral will grow up like me – like a human? That's it, isn't it? You're scared he'll come back to you more human than faerie."

Jarlath didn't utter a word. Instead, he just ... tightened. Much more chilling, surprisingly, than any angry tirade. Willow felt time shift, as if she'd nodded off for a second. Her eyes blinked. She and Brand were no longer at the table. They stood together in a clearing a few feet away from the feast. Jarlath appeared close by, two enormous white tigers straining against collars he clutched with his fingers. "Run, my humans," he sang out. "Run like the wind."

Not needing a second invitation, Brand grabbed Willow's hand and tore off into the woods, dragging a stumbling Willow behind him. The dress, the beautiful white dress, slowed her down, caught at her feet. She clawed at the fabric, bunching it up as much as she could to free her legs. A cheer broke out. Willow didn't look back. She knew Jarlath had loosed the tigers.

"The water," cried Brand. "We must reach the water!"

The water? Willow peered at the path Brand had chosen.

They were much farther from the pool here than they'd been from the cage. They'd never make it.

Oh God! Oh God! Oh God! Willow summoned every ounce of magic inside her, picturing fire, fire everywhere. Red. Hot. Burning. Something to give them time to get to the pool. And suddenly it was there. A wall of hissing, flickering fire. Only it wasn't behind them, it was in front of them, blocking their path.

"No!" screamed Willow. "*No!*"

Brand reeled to a stop and spun around, searching for escape. The flames shot out all around them. There was nowhere to go. Nowhere to hide. He gave her a desperate look, then threw her to the ground, covering her struggling body with his. The impact came a moment later. Brand shrieked as large jaws shook him like a toy. He held fast to Willow until the second impact finally dislodged him. Willow felt him fly off her like he'd been yanked by a crane. The tigers dragged at him, tore into his flesh, and a horrifying red soaked the white of his clothing.

Willow screamed her throat raw. One of the tigers turned its broad head in her direction, bared glistening teeth, and lunged.

The pain, Willow discovered, was every bit as great as she'd thought it would be.

CHAPTER 14

Willow's eyes flew open. She catapulted to a sitting position, sucking in air in wheezing gasps. She jerked her arms up and stared at them. The tiger had clawed her. Had bit into her collarbone. But she saw nothing. Not a mark, not a speck of blood. *Nothing*. Her hand trailed away from her unmarred neck. She stared uncomprehendingly at her dress. Not white and bloody but whole and blue, the one she was wearing when she'd arrived in Clarion. She whipped her head around, searching the dim room. *Brand!*

"He's fine." Dacia appeared before Willow. She stepped aside and Willow glimpsed Brand's dark hair. He lay stretched out on a stone slab, apparently unharmed. "He's just sleeping," said Dacia. "I will wake him shortly."

"But the ... the ..." Sobs suddenly shook Willow. She still felt Brand's arms around her. Protecting her.

Dacia touched her cheek. "Forgive me. I was forbidden to explain the Menagerie Game to you."

"Game?" Willow pushed Dacia's hand away. "What do you mean *Game*?"

"The Menagerie is a Game. A Game of terror and fear

and ... pain."

"I ... I don't understand. Those tigers were real. They ... they ... *I felt them.*"

Dacia slipped to the edge of Willow's stone bed. A wall lined with shelves swam into view. Dacia pulled something from a high shelf and brought it to Willow.

Cold. The object Dacia placed in Willow's hand was cold as ice, and heavy. Willow stared at it. Shiny cat eyes stared back. Encased in a crystal ball that resembled a snow globe crouched a black panther, teeth bared, one clawed paw ready to strike. Willow tilted the globe's golden base. No sparkly snow. Only a viscous green mist surrounded the cat. "I don't understand." She returned the globe to Dacia. "What is this thing?"

"This is how we play Games." Dacia's finger traced over the markings on the globe's stand. "In the courts of Dark, Games are played in the mind, not body. No death. But fear and pain as *real* as death." Her eyes grew large and luminous. "My brother Nezeral placed me and Theon in the Menagerie Game when we were children. The cats devoured us many times before he released us."

Children? Willow gaped at Dacia, horrified. Saw a tender, fragile child, tow-haired and achingly beautiful, like ... like Nezzie. She blocked out the rest of the grisly scenario. "Then the ... the cave ..." Willow remembered the two little rag piles, the rock and shell decorations. "That *was* you, then, wasn't it?"

Dacia nodded. "There was no cage in our Game. We didn't discover the cave till ... later."

"But why? Why would Nezeral do that to you?" Willow just couldn't wrap her mind around the thought of small children being in the position she'd just been in. It was too sick. Too – Willow studied Dacia a moment. How old was the faerie girl, anyway? She could have been fifteen or thirty in human age, or neither. All faeries had that weird ageless thing about them.

Dacia studied her as well, frowning. "Theon and I are twins."

"Twins?"

"Yes. Twins. Symbols of duality, one the bearer of Light, the other of Dark. But there is no certainty which of us is which." Her silver irises dimmed to gray shadows. "The House of Jarlath serves Dark." She tipped the globe again, watching as green mists shrouded the panther. "We are the Dark faeries of ancient Earth." She glanced back to Willow. "You know of us as the Unseelie Court, don't you?"

The Unseelie Court. Willow's breath caught in her throat. Of course she'd heard of the Unseelie Court. Both the Seelie and the Unseelie Courts were mentioned in the faerie books she'd read on Earth at home with Nana. Courts of Light and Dark. Her hand fluttered back to her undamaged collarbone. The Unseelie Court – *the Dark Court.*

Images of goblins and monsters flitted through Willow's thoughts. The stories of the Unseelie Court were grim and evil. The Unseelie hated humans. She had read there was a faction in their group known as "the host," foul creatures that flew through the air snatching up mortals and torturing them. "Yeah," she said shivering, "I've heard of them before."

"You know then what type of Games we play?"

Willow nodded.

"Then you would understand my family's wish to ensure that the Light, in whichever one of us bears it, is extinguished." She gave a cryptic smile. "Nezeral has always been one to assist in that part of our training."

A worm of disgust wriggled in Willow. If they could let little kids get eaten by tigers, what other horrors were these sick faeries capable of? She swallowed back her distaste. "So – what happens now?" Willow looked around the room, eyes settling on row upon row of crystal globes. Her heart began to hammer, distaste turning to fear. Dacia's words, *This is how we play Games*, echoed inside her head. *All* these countless globes were Games. Possibly even worse, even more horrifying, than the one Willow and Brand had just played!

Dacia shook her head. "I don't know what my father has planned. There is a masked ball tonight, though, that you and Brand are to attend. I am to take you to your chambers and help you prepare." She stepped to the wall of shelves and put away the panther globe, then she went to Brand and passed her hand gently over his face.

Brand flew awake just as Willow had, panting and flailing his arms in panic. Willow sat on the slab bed, trying to soothe him. "It's a Game," she choked. "Just a stupid Game." She rocked him in a tight hug.

"A *Game*?"

When Brand's breathing slowed, Willow explained the

concept of Games in the Unseelie Court. She showed him the panther globe and told him that they were never actually in the cage. It was all in their minds, like a dream.

"None of it was real?" Brand pushed up his sleeve and rubbed a hand gingerly along his unscarred arm.

"Oh no, it was real. *Very* real." Dacia spoke from the doorway, where she stood waiting for Willow and Brand. "Emotions and pain are always real. The mind makes this so. The trick is to learn how to control the mind."

Brand gave Dacia a suspicious look. "And what's it to you, Dacia Thornheart? Why are you helping us?" He led Willow to the doorway and eyed the faerie girl intently. *"You* are Jarlath's daughter. Nezeral's sister. It would seem, despite your professed grudge, that we could only be your enemy. Yet ... yet you persist in making yourself useful. Why is this? Are you, perhaps, playing a Game as well?"

"Perhaps." The faerie girl gave them a cold smile. "But not against you. My father wishes to win Nezeral back. I want him to stay in Mistolear. So, you see, any Game I may be playing will be to your advantage."

Brand returned an equally cold smile. "Yes. Well, you shall forgive me if the words of a faerie don't exactly inspire trust."

"Nor should they." Dacia swept a slender arm into the inky hallway. "Shall we? My father doesn't like to be kept waiting."

The implied threat was enough to silence Brand. He followed Dacia grimly, trying not to flinch when candles along the dark stone hallway burst into flames and sputtered out as they passed. Willow clutched his hand, the cramped passage reminding her too much of dungeons and claustrophobic cages. She shuddered at every corner, her imagination working overtime as she started to remember stories of all the wicked beings that had existed in the Unseelie Court. Bogles, redcaps, banshees – there was a whole horde of nasties to carry out an Unseelie king's business.

Dacia led them through another doorway. Willow gasped when they came to a stop. They stood in a balconied hallway where the vaulted ceiling went up so high Willow had to crane her neck from the railing to see it. Down below, in the great hall, faeries glimmered like specks of jewels. Fountains sprayed crimson water and moonlight made flames of jagged, red-glassed windows. Eerie music climbed to the rafters. Willow stared, mesmerized by the strange, hellish beauty of the scene.

"Gods protect us," whispered Brand. "It's like a dark dream." He jumped when Dacia touched his arm. "Come," she said. "We don't have much time."

She led them to a nearby room, where an elegantly dressed male faerie waited impatiently. "My Lady Dacia, you have given me very little time." His amber eyes gleamed as he looked Willow and Brand over from head to foot. "A handsome pair, these two," he said, circling around them. "Your father made it seem ..."

"Yes, Phelan, I am well aware of my father's descriptions. Come. He won't be happy if we are late."

The male faerie studied Willow. He lifted a strand of hair

and stared at her eyes. "There can only be one outfit for coloring such as this," he announced. Willow felt time shifting again. In a blink, the heavy brocade of her blue dress vanished. In its place fluttered long petals of red silky gauze, light as air, fine as insect wings. She did a half-twirl to see the skirt fly and dance, like spiderwebs dangling in a soft breeze. A mirror appeared before her. She stared at the beautiful faerie gown, its red as dark as rust. A simple bodice wrapped tightly around her upper body, leaving her bare arms and shoulders adorned only by the snaky tendrils of her wildly curled hair. "Oh," she gasped. She didn't know what else to say. It was quite simply the most gorgeous thing she'd ever worn.

The male faerie seemed very satisfied by her reaction. Brand gawked while Dacia looked amused. "Are you sure this is wise, Phelan? A *true* faerie gown? Father may not be pleased."

His arched brows drew together, then drifted apart again. "No," he said, shaking his blond head. "My lord ordered me to follow the natural impulse. This is where it led. I fear no reprisals."

"Very well. And the boy?"

"The boy ..." The words trailed off as Phelan gripped Brand's shoulders. The amber eyes narrowed, then once again things shifted in an eyeblink. Mistolearian tunic and breeches disappeared. Black boots, black leather pants, and a crisp white shirt took their place. Brand's raven hair flowed loose, spilling round his face and softening the hard lines of his jaw.

"Nice," said Dacia. "Very nice."

Willow stared, finding it hard to remember the danger they were in. Brand looked better than nice. He was hot. Like a guy whose photo she'd ogle at in a magazine or hang on her wall.

The designer faerie passed his fingers over Brand's face. A plain white mask appeared, hovering before him.

Willow blinked. A mask had materialized in her hand too. Not plain like Brand's but gold and ornate with slick black feathers that sprouted from the middle.

Dacia grabbed both their arms, her gown suddenly transforming into a silver stardust shimmer. "Come then," she cried, mercury eyes gleaming from behind an ebony mask. "Let us join the revelry."

CHAPTER 15

Willow and Brand clutched hands as Dacia led them through the fantastical crowds. The air, sweet and thick, throbbed with unearthly rhythms. Willow couldn't take her eyes off the costumes. Some of them were like hers, pure faerie, but others mixed time periods in bizarre, unexpected ways. One faerie in an over-large turban, wearing what looked like a medieval jester's outfit, lurched past her, while another in a jean jacket and long-flowing Indian sari made loud tsking sounds. Feathers, furs, and loads of sparkling jewelry accented the getups, and everyone wore masks – some beautiful and ornate like Willow's, some horned and hook-nosed.

Willow touched the detailed edging of her own mask, adjusting it so she could see better. Having half her face hidden made her feel strangely bold and anonymous – just another guest at the party.

"Dace! Over here."

Narrow, red-tinted windows washed red moonlight over a milling group of male faeries. If not for the silver hair and kid-like grin, Willow wouldn't have recognized Theon. He bounded toward them, wearing a black mask, black leather pants and jacket, and criss-crossing silver chains in lieu of a shirt. His friends followed, all in black leather too, like a goth gang but without the piercings.

Her time in the Menagerie had shown Willow that faeries were a lot looser at night than during the day. Seemed, in fact, quite human in their partying. Theon and his friends were no exception. Staggering a little, eyes overbright, they appeared to be drunk.

"By the Trees," whistled Theon. "The clother dressed her like a fey princess!" He sputtered with laughter. "Oh, this will be rich sport. You must allow us, sister dear, to accompany you to Father's throne."

The other leather-clad faeries sobered up quickly at this suggestion. "Ah, listen, Theon, I promised my lady Cynara a dance. I shall meet with you later." One by one Theon's friends made similar excuses and slipped off into the crowds.

"Perhaps they are wise, Theon. Father, I am sure, won't be pleased."

Theon smirked. "Trying to keep all the fun to yourself, Dace?"

Dacia's eyes rolled behind her mask. "Fine. Accompany us if you must. But don't goad Father with your trifling jests." She turned from her brother and began to make her way through the crowd again. Willow followed, this time with both Brand and Theon pressed close to her sides. A whisper-touch of skin brushed her cheek. Theon's head bent low to her ear. "Princess of Mistolear," he said huskily, "I fear you are a flame this night and I a moth."

Willow jerked away from him, sure her face was the only thing flaming. Theon smiled. The black mask he wore emphasized his lips, the top one slightly larger than the bottom, giving him a perpetual pout. Very cute in a boy model kind of way. Willow surprised herself by smiling back.

Brand squeezed her hand, restoring reality. Flirting with faeries, particularly the son of the one who wanted to destroy you, was probably not a good idea.

The pulsing music grew louder, weaving itself snake-like through the room. Willow's toes wanted to point, to leap and twirl and spin her red dress around until it fluttered and waved. Musicians sat on a curved stage that jutted like a tongue from the wall. Beneath them and their long, bulbous instruments danced a frenzied group of faeries. Willow wanted – no, *needed* to join them. Brand seemed anxious to go as well. Theon grabbed both their arms. "Hum," he said. "A song, a march, it matters not. The humming will break the spell."

Willow hummed tunelessly, the vibration in the back of her throat filling her head and lessening the pull of the faerie music. Once past the musicians, the spell seemed to lose its strength. Willow stopped humming and took in deep breaths of sultry air. She realized with a start that Theon, not Brand, was holding her hand. When she tried to pluck it away, he held tight, his eyes glinting amusement at her from behind the mask.

They rounded a thick pillar. Willow blinked. She stopped struggling with Theon and stared up ahead. Mounted on a huge black throne atop a dais, sat Jarlath, resplendent in jewels and shimmering black robes, the two white tigers that had mauled Willow and Brand resting on either side of him. Willow blanched, stomach cramping with terror. Bright blood still speckled the tigers' muzzles. She tried to wrench herself away from Theon again, to escape, but Jarlath's silver-masked face swiveled, the glinting eyeholes piercing her with green mockery.

"Ah," he drawled. "The entertainment has arrived."

Any boldness or anonymity Willow might have felt earlier quickly vanished. Her heart thudded so loudly she thought she could hear it in her ears. The legs that had wanted to dance and spin went suddenly weak, making Willow cling to both Brand and Theon for support. Game or not, she remembered every rip and tear of flesh, every claw and bite. Dacia saw her panic, reached to steady her. "He's only trying to frighten you. Don't be afraid. The tigers won't attack."

Willow fought the scream that had crawled into her throat. Brand pulled her away from Dacia and Theon, his arms tense, his own eyes filled with horror. "Can you be sure, faerie?" he spat at Dacia. "This seems a perfect venue for your kind's grisly entertainments."

Dacia lifted her mask, silver eyes glowing like a cat's in the dark. "If you allow your fear to stand as naked on your face as you do now, then no, *human*, I can't be sure." She replaced the mask, clearly rankled by Brand's insult. "If you don't want my help, then go." She gestured toward Jarlath's throne. "Theon and I won't stop you."

Finding her voice, Willow answered for Brand. "No. He didn't mean it." She felt strength return to her legs. Faeries or not, Dacia and Theon were better allies than none. She pushed away her pride and Brand's arms and stumbled forward, grasping Dacia's sleeve. "Please, don't leave us," she begged. "*Please.*"

Dacia cast a hard glance at Brand. He didn't argue. "Very well." Her silvery hair blazed as she spun back toward Jarlath's throne. The crowd parted and a wide path opened before them. Dacia strode through, head high and confident. Willow tried to copy her, tried to feel safe behind her mask again, but could only cling to Brand, her heart beating like a crazed drum in her ears.

When they reached Jarlath's throne, Dacia hissed at Willow and Brand to kneel. Willow hesitated, but only for a moment. The sight of the bloodstained tigers unnerved her. She dropped to her hands and knees, pressing her feathered forehead to the stone floor and keeping it there. Brand followed suit a few seconds behind her.

"I see my humans are properly subdued," said Jarlath, his voice ringing throughout the room. Willow noticed the music had disappeared. So had the sound of laughter and conversation. Nothing left now but an unnatural hush.

Jarlath filled the silence. "My own daughter and son are another matter, though, aren't they?"

Willow saw Dacia's foot take a backward step. "Father, I ..."

"Don't speak, daughter. *Listen.* You petitioned me to see the humans. I granted your request knowing your curiosity would not be sated until you saw them. I didn't, however, know that at every opportunity you would seek to give them aid. Now *that*, my daughter, is a new revelation."

Dacia said nothing. Fear shivered down Willow's spine as she stared at the faerie girl's dainty, silver-slippered feet. Dacia said she'd had Jarlath's permission to take them on walks and let them bathe in the pool. Had she lied?

"And Theon, *my son*." Jarlath spit the last part out with sarcasm. "You did not even seek my permission to view the humans, for you are drawn to them, are you not, *as a moth to a flame*?"

Willow's heart missed a beat. *Moth to a flame*. Did Jarlath hear and see *everything*? She peeked at Theon. Brand knelt between them. Willow couldn't see the faerie boy's feet. She risked an upward glance. Theon's hands were white-knuckled fists.

"You understand, my court, *this* is what comes of separating the realms. We have children enthralled by humans. *Humans!* Weak, piddling humans hardly worthy of our contempt, let alone our interest." An assenting murmur went through the room.

Willow shifted uncomfortably. Wherever Jarlath was going with this, it couldn't be good.

"Rise, humans. Let me look at you."

Brand helped Willow stand and kept his arm wrapped around her in a protective embrace. Jarlath gazed at them, impassive as stone. Willow felt a flutter of silk against her leg and remembered the red faerie dress. Jarlath was staring at it. She wished she could slip away into the crowd like Theon's friends, anything to escape the contempt emanating from those hard, green eyes.

"Humans acting like faeries. Faeries acting like humans." Jarlath stroked the head of one bloodstained tiger. "Perhaps there is a Game in that. Yes. I believe there is." He pointed at Dacia and Theon. "Since you, my children, have shown yourselves so eager to learn of humans, I shall accelerate your studies." He smiled benignly. "You will enter the next Game with them, *without* your powers."

An excited murmur circled the room. Willow glanced at Dacia and Theon. Both seem unfazed by their father's pronouncements. Jarlath continued. "I will allow one human to possess one human power, but will leave the choice to you, Dacia, as to the human and the power. Now, as to the Game ..." His voice trailed off and his benign smile disappeared. "You shall play the Goblin King's Gauntlet."

This time Dacia and Theon were not unfazed. "Father!" cried Dacia, her voice hardly audible above the fervid din of the crowd. Theon pushed past Brand to glare at Jarlath. "The *Gauntlet*! One power for the Gauntlet? And a human one at that! Surely you jest, Father. You may as well tie ribbons around us and just *give* us to the goblins."

The commotion died down as everyone strained to hear Jarlath's reply. "I could send you in with none." Theon turned pale and stepped back quietly. Dacia held her tongue as well.

"Good." Jarlath stood up and surveyed the room. "It's settled. Come morning, the Game shall commence." He swept his arm over the crowd. "Till then, enjoy the festivities." Music started up and the faeries began to disperse. Jarlath and his tigers vanished from the stage.

"We need to talk," said Dacia. She touched Willow's and Brand's arms. The next thing Willow knew, she, Brand, Dacia, and Theon were outside, standing at the foot of a grand stairway, flanked by lion gargoyles whose open mouths spurted a fiery light. Theon began to pace back and forth between the lions.

"Do you think he really means it, Dace?"

Dacia snorted. "When did Father ever make an idle threat? Of course he means it."

Brand took off his mask, letting it clatter to the stone walkway. "What is this Game your father speaks of? This Gauntlet? Is it some type of race?"

"Oh, it's a race all right," quipped Theon. "A race to survive."

"What does that mean?"

"What do you think it means?" Theon whipped off his own mask, hurling it into the night. Willow and Dacia removed theirs as well and tossed them next to Brand's. Theon smiled bitterly. "You thought the Menagerie Game was bad, didn't you? Well, let's just say the Gauntlet makes it seem a picnic."

Brand gave both Theon and Dacia hard looks. "And your father sends us to this Game that faeries fear to play ... because of you two? Because *you* disobeyed him?"

"Don't dare to blame us, mortal." Theon stepped up to Brand, giving him the same challenging look. Both boys clenched their fists.

Dacia yanked her brother's arm. "Stop it. He's right. We are to blame. Or at least I am. I allowed them to bathe in the pool. I took them for walks. I even provided them with a private toilet." Her eyes fell to Willow. "I know I told you I was allowed these things. But in truth Father only agreed to let me take a look at you."

Theon backed away from Brand. "And I brought them food and gave the girl a brush and lip balm."

"*You did what?*" Dacia glared at Theon. "Well, it's no wonder then that Father seeks to punish us. What a snake you are to go behind my back like that. I told you that first time in the Menagerie to stay away from them. Did you think Father would overlook *both* of us disobeying him?"

"I don't know, Sister. A brush and lip balm are hardly in the same category as a *private toilet*."

Willow thrust herself between the quarreling siblings. "Look, you both helped us. I'm sorry you got into trouble because of it, but that's not the real issue here, is it?" Willow glanced from sister to brother. The bickering, she realized, was only a cover to hide their fear. Anxiety took hold of Willow. What did faeries fear more than being ripped apart by tigers?

"Willow is right." Dacia moved away from Theon and leaned against the lion gargoyle. "The issue is not who to blame but what power to choose."

"But what is this Goblin Game?" said Brand, asking the question whose answer Willow feared.

Dacia looked at Willow before answering. "You say you

146

know of the Unseelie Court. Have you not noticed that our fabled minions are missing?"

Fabled minions? Of course. Willow blinked at her. Where was the Unseelie horde? The goblins, the banshees, the bogles, the demi-fey, all the evil creatures that served the Unseelie Court. She had seen no one here but the faeries.

Dancing flames from the gargoyle's toothy mouth lit Dacia's hair with eerie red highlights. She stared at Willow's feet. "When the Council voted to live on Clarion, it wasn't just humans that we chose to separate ourselves from." An unbroken silence followed Dacia's statement. She looked from Willow to Brand and then to the ground again. "We chose to live only amongst ourselves. All Unseelie creatures who were not royal court fey were sent into the globes. The one holding the goblin king holds the entire Unseelie horde."

"A horde," Theon added, "betrayed by their lords – by *faeries* – and seeking revenge. We shall die a thousand deaths in the Gauntlet, each one an unspeakable horror."

A thousand deaths. Willow thought of just the one death she thought she'd suffered in the Menagerie. Could she go through something like that again? Over and over ...

"Stop it, Theon." Dacia's voice was a whisper. She backed against the gargoyle and sat on its perch.

"I know a human power," Brand said. "One the mage knights use to kill their enemies if their sword arm weakens. Gift me with it. I will use it to protect us in the Gauntlet."

Dacia considered his offer. "And how many can your power

dispatch at once? Can it fell a horde?"

"No. Only one at a time."

"We shall be equipped with regular weapons that can do the same thing. The power we choose must be more far-reaching."

"What about invisibility?" said Willow. Killing did not appeal to her. Never had. But the thought that she could just disappear when threatened, now that was appealing.

Dacia shook her head. "The denizens of the Gauntlet are all magical creatures. Invisibility would be detected."

"What if ..." said Theon, jumping into the conversation. "What if we tell Father we don't want a power? What if we tell him to give us magical weapons instead? Think of it, Dace. Four magical weapons with death spells could plow through a lot of goblins."

Brand nodded in support of Theon's plan. "Aye. As human powers go, magical weapons are by far the most effective means to slay your enemies."

"Weapons can be taken away. What then?"

No one had an answer. Finally Theon scowled at Dacia. "So are you just going to dismiss everyone else's suggestions? Or do you have one of your own?"

Dacia stared at him a moment then took a deep breath. "I do. But I don't think you're going to like it. I claim healing as our power and say it should be given to Willow."

"*Healing?*" sputtered Theon. "Why waste it on that? If we are killed, our wounds will heal themselves. We need a power of protection. One of battle!"

"Theon, we have watched others play the Gauntlet. Do battle powers avail them? No. They all still die horribly. More than once. Think about it. The goblin king knows our wounds do not rejuvenate until *after* death. It's the suffering before that he relishes." Dacia turned to Brand. "I saw how Willow healed your back after the panther attack. Can you imagine your stay in the Menagerie without her powers?"

Brand said nothing. His clenched jaw, though, told Willow that Dacia had made her point.

"Then it's settled." Dacia stood up and placed a hand on Willow's shoulder. "You already possess the power and know how to use it. *You* shall be our healer."

CHAPTER 16

*B*ut it really wasn't settled. They continued to argue through the night. Brand and Theon, not entirely convinced of Dacia's choice of power, kept coming up with opposing ideas. Even Willow, ambivalent about taking responsibility for their one single magic, threw in suggestions – mind control, flight, incredible strength, shape shifting, fire conjuring, illusion. Dacia knocked down every proposal. Finally, the faerie girl had had enough. She said they would sleep on it. The next thing Willow knew, she found herself tucked into a plush bed with a silky nightgown covering her body.

She lay still and gazed at the sky above. The room had no ceiling! Stars twinkled like soft nightlights. She heard the sound of water and sat up, looking around her. The room had a pool in it with a gently gurgling fountain. Open windows sent in faint perfumed breezes that swayed gauzy curtains in a gentle dance.

Almost immediately Willow felt her tension leave. The room was apparently magicked for sleep. *Fine by me*, she thought, yawning. She snuggled under the blankets. *Wake me up when it's over.*

"They all argue against me, Father, but I believe they are beginning to see the wisdom of my choice." Dacia stopped pacing and regarded her father appraisingly. "Even *I* am beginning to see the wisdom of it. Seems strange now that no one has ever used healing as a power in the Gauntlet before. What made you think of it?"

Jarlath stilled. His eyes gleamed in a way that made Dacia uneasy. "There are yet aspects to goblins, my child, that you don't know. Healing will help you against them. But more importantly, if the girl must bind your wounds, she will learn to care for you. Our goal will then be made all the easier. If she befriends you and your brother, it won't seem so wrong to take one of you home."

Mention of Theon made Dacia frown. "You made *me* Game Master, Father. Why did you have to include Theon? I don't need him in this Game. I can win without him."

"I know that, daughter." Jarlath reached out and fingered a lock of Dacia's silken hair. "It was the possibility of choice that made me include him. *Who* will she choose?"

The words lingered in the fragrant night air. Dacia's mouth tightened. Same story as always. Father wanted to test them. Dark or Light? Who would Willow be drawn to? But *both* she and Theon had been brought up in Dark. If one of them had any Light left inside, it would be a twisted, crippled Light. Still, she could see Father's interest in the outcome. Maybe a human could sense things a faerie could not.

"Very well, Father. I shall not disappoint you."

In the morning, Willow noticed that a roof had replaced the sky, and the gurgling fountain had disappeared. Sunlight and fresh air streamed in through the open windows, making her alternately blink and suck in deep breaths. She stretched, climbed out of bed, and discovered she was already dressed: brown boots, brown leggings, loose white shirt, tight leather jerkin, and a sweeping green cloak. Questing clothes, if she'd ever seen them. Brand strode in, similarly attired.

"It appears we've both been readied for battle." He eyed her new outfit and looked around the room. "If we ever see Mistolear again, I, for one, shall sing the praises of these fey rooms. Never have I had such a restful sleep."

Willow nodded. The few hours she'd managed to sleep had left her alert, as if she'd had a pot-load of coffee. She swung her gaze to one of the windows, which opened like a doorway, and saw Dacia and Theon approaching. They stepped inside, their leggings, jerkins, and cloaks similar to Willow and Brand's.

"Come outside," said Dacia. "We shall eat on the verandah." She turned back around, her long hair tied in a single braid that hung below her waist.

On the verandah, Willow and Brand joined Dacia and Theon at a small table for a breakfast of fruit, cheese, and fresh bread.

They ate in silence, Willow studying their extraordinary surroundings in wonder. Jarlath's castle seemed carved from black onyx and gleamed sleek as a raven's wing in the morning sunlight. A handful of other castles jutted from the hilly landscape, each a different bright-colored jewel. Red ruby in the east, white pearl in the west, and blue sapphire and golden amber in the south. The world itself, though, reminded her of Queen Cyrraena's beautiful Timorell. Cloudless, cerulean skies, summer-leaved trees, and water that sparkled an impossible turquoise.

"It's beautiful, isn't it?" Dacia followed Willow's gaze across the rich landscape. "On Earth, it is said, we lived mostly in sithens beneath the ground. Truly, I can't imagine it."

"The goblin king dwells under a mountain," said Theon dryly. "I trust you will be able to imagine it well enough after a visit with him."

Dacia's face stiffened. She picked up a silver goblet and swirled its contents. "Are we all in agreement, then? The power shall be healing, and Willow shall have it?"

No one answered. Brand studied a slice of orange, not meeting Willow's stare. Theon quaffed back his honeyed nectar and slammed the goblet to the table. "Seems you are Game Master, Dacia. We are forced to follow. So – *lead on*!"

"Very well." The faerie girl stood up, looking solemnly proud. "The court awaits us."

Willow felt her stomach slide. The next moment the ballroom with the cavernous ceiling swam before her. Against each wall sat faeries, their poised silence belying their frenzied nighttime personas. Jarlath leaned forward in his black shiny throne, regarding the four of them keenly. No tigers today. Neither Willow nor Brand bowed. There didn't seem a point. Mercy didn't exist in those ice-green eyes.

"So, my daughter, what is to be your choice?"

Dacia stepped forward. "I choose healing for the human princess."

After a moment's hesitation, Jarlath's eyebrows shot up. "*Healing?* You surprise me, daughter, a feat not many accomplish." He turned sharp eyes to his son. "Are you in agreement with this, Theon?"

"Not really. But since you made Dacia Game Master, it seems I have little choice in the matter."

The silence of the room felt heavy. As if the faeries' suppressed excitement had leaped from their wooden bodies and swirled free overhead. Willow's neck and scalp prickled. She wanted to run from the room, hide from all the cold, glittering eyes. She stayed rooted to the floor, though, her heart slamming against her rib cage, her lips twitching anxiously.

"Very well, then. I accept your choice, Dacia. Let the Game *begin.*"

This time Willow felt her stomach lurch, not slide. Her next glance took in thick, pointy-leafed vegetation, a ghostly mist that curled eerie tendrils up stout tree trunks, and a well-trod clay path that twisted through the woods like a snake. Willow gulped and waited for her stomach to settle. She felt weighted down and noticed she and Brand and the faerie twins had rucksacks hanging from their shoulders. They each bore broadswords, but Dacia and Theon carried bows and arrows as well.

"The Gauntlet," whispered Dacia, her eyes enormous. "It seems just a ... a regular path, doesn't it?"

Even Theon had lost his brashness. He shuddered as he stared down the pathway. "Think *he* knows, Dace? Or do you think Father's at least given us the element of surprise?"

"I don't know, Theon. I just ... don't know."

Willow guessed they spoke of the goblin king. She too stared down the path, which disappeared into the dark forest. "Do we just have to walk on the path? That's it? That's the Game?" Somehow she'd pictured something more sinister.

"It isn't just goblins that live in the Gauntlet." Theon kept his voice low, so that Willow had to move closer to hear him. "All manner of fell creature dwell here, and many call the forest their home. The path will lead us to the goblin king, but there will be ... obstacles."

Brand tapped Theon's shoulder. "And why is it," he asked, "that we wish to find this goblin king? Would our interests not be better served to avoid him at all costs?"

"He is the one who decides when it's time to release us."

Both Willow and Brand paled. "But he ... he hates you," stammered Willow. "I don't understand ..."

Theon gave her a pitying look. "I won't lie to you. It won't go well for us. But you and Brand are human, so the goblin king may go easier on you."

"The main thing to remember," added Dacia, "is that

physically we are not really here. In the Menagerie you had no awareness of this, so everything you felt was absolutely real. Being aware changes your perception. It will give you more control over the ... the pain."

"What about physical things like eating and sleeping and, um ... going to the washroom?" Willow remembered the Menagerie in vivid detail. Nothing about it had seemed dreamlike. In fact – she pinched her hand until it stung – nothing about this seemed dreamlike either. Nail indents marked her skin. She shuddered, her mind seeing the tigers again.

"If our physical bodies are in need of those things, then we will be in need here as well."

"So if, say, we didn't eat, could our physical bodies die of starvation?"

Dacia nodded. "Yours could. Not ours. But Father wouldn't allow you to perish that way."

"Let me see if I have this straight then." Willow watched the nail indents fade. "If we do ... *perish*, we wake up whole and healthy again but still here in the Gauntlet. And if we are wounded, our wounds will hurt us just like real ones."

"Yes. And without your healing ability, would take just as long to heal themselves."

A dank breeze creaked branches and stirred the ghostly mist. Moldy decay scented the air. Willow felt prickles start to climb along her spine. Maybe staying in one spot wasn't such a good idea.

Theon unslung his bow and notched an arrow. "Come, I will

take the front and Brand the rear. Speak only if you must and in a whisper."

No one disagreed. Theon began to walk along the narrow path. Dacia followed, then Willow, and then Brand, who'd unsheathed an unusual amber-colored sword and held it, like Theon held the bow, at the ready. There was scrabbling and rustling all around them now. Their heads spun this way and that as they tried to pinpoint sounds that shifted constantly. The wormy smell of rot grew stronger. The tops of evergreen trees crowded together, leaving only a murky light to see by. Willow felt her chest tighten. The farther they traveled down the Gauntlet's path, the deeper they descended into darkness.

"Will? Are you all right?"

Willow started at Brand's touch to her shoulder. She hadn't realized she'd stopped walking, her breathing coming in loud spurts. *Was she all right?* She didn't think so. Fear coursed through her veins. The dark creepy woods made her skin crawl. Made her think of death and dying. "I can't do this," she whispered. "I'm so afraid, Brand. I'm ... *I'm so afraid.*"

"Willow." Brand lifted her chin with his free hand. "You are the bravest girl I know." He waited for her eyes to meet with his. "The faerie queen has faith in you. *I* have faith in you. You can do this. We shall do it together."

Willow took Brand's fingers and squeezed them. His determination seemed to seep into her. She gave him a weak smile. "Thanks." Brand smiled back but his eyes filled with worry. They both turned to the path. Dacia and Theon waited, watching them silently. "We must stay together," said Dacia. She glanced at Willow's still-quivering chin, Brand's clenched jaw. "Yes. Keep your humanness about you. If we are ever separated, make certain everyone you meet *knows* you aren't fey." She gestured for Theon to continue. Willow admired their graceful carriage, their long silver hair that glowed like beacons. She felt fear again but not for herself. Whatever happened to them here, the faeries would get the worst of it.

Brand, who still held her hand, let it go. "Come, Princess. She's right. We must stay together." They began to follow Dacia and Theon, neither mentioning the strange comfort of Dacia's words.

As they walked, the rustling, scrabbling noises intensified. They caught glimpses of movement, some unexplained and others quite evident. A number of crows seemed to find them fascinating sport and flew from branch to branch, cawing down at them disturbingly, as if they were laughing. One deer crossed the path, stopped to stare at Theon's readied bow, then leaped away so fast all Willow saw was a flash of its white tail.

Around noon – well, it felt like noon to Willow's grumbling stomach – the path stopped at a sluggish stream, continuing on the other side. Theon halted far from the water and scouted the area with nervous eyes. Dacia did the same. "Maybe it narrows somewhere," she said, scanning the stream. "Or there's a bridge. Do you think we should look?"

"Of course. Surely you don't wish to go through *that*, do you?"

Willow and Brand shared mystified glances. The stream was all of about ten feet wide and seemed no more than knee-deep. "It appears shallow," offered Brand. "Why do we not just cross here?"

Theon, closer to the water now, continued to search, ignoring his question. Dacia came to stand by Willow and Brand. "Truthfully," she said, "seas and lakes hold more danger than a stream. But even so, without our powers, I'll wager you'll have no wish to meet with a murderous kelpie or a Jenny Greenteeth."

Willow blinked at her. *Kelpie. Jenny Greenteeth.* Vaguely she remembered those names from her faerie books on Earth.

"Found one," hissed Theon. He cleared back from the stream and pointed at some bulrushes. "See there? By the rock."

Willow stared. A brown nose, its nostrils blowing bubbles, surfaced in a stagnant bank of water. A mouth gasped for breath. Then a horse head appeared, long and flat, with dead white eyes that gazed sightlessly. More noses surfaced, so that Willow counted at least four of the creatures – one to attack each of them.

"Kelpies," sniffed Dacia disdainfully. "We're safer here on land." Her eyes strained to see down the stream. "We shall have to leave the path, though. Find another spot to cross."

Brand's sword came out from beneath his cloak. "I fear no blind demons. Why not cross here?"

"Granted, drowning is a relatively painless death," said Theon dryly. "But it will waste time. Which direction, Dacia? East or west?"

"West, I guess. It seems to narrow farther up."

They trudged after Theon through the thick underbrush. Dacia called back softly. "The kelpies, Brand, would have pulled us under the second we set foot in the water. Weapons cannot harm them. Only magic or bribery would have seen us safely across."

Brand said nothing but kept his strange yellow sword at the ready.

Willow pulled her own sword a bit out of its sheath. Also yellow. She tapped Dacia's shoulder. "What's with the swords? How come the metal is all yellow like that?"

"They're made from mithrien, a magic substance that does not harm us like iron does but is just as sharp."

The further along the stream bank they went, the more the vegetation began to thin. Brush and leafy ferns gave way to pebbles and sand and then to boulders and rocks. Theon stopped suddenly and stared up ahead. Two boulders sat inches apart, an easy jump to the other side. But he was looking elsewhere. Just behind the boulder crossing, the water pooled into a lazy pond. On one side knelt what appeared to be a woman. Willow squinted at her. Her bare skinny arms pushed back and forth in a steady rhythm. She seemed to be ... washing clothes.

"*Bean-nighe*," said Dacia, her voice strained.

"What?"

"Bean-nighe. She is a washerwoman, a spirit banshee that portends one or all of our deaths."

Willow blinked. She could see it now. Piles of white clothing spattered red with blood, the pool turning pink from the woman's rinsing.

Theon pushed forward again, easily fording the stream between the two boulders. "Come on," he called back. "She won't harm us."

Dacia followed and then Willow and Brand, each jumping nimbly across the stream. Willow watched the washerwoman. She appeared not to see them, her lank brown hair covering her bowed head. No. Maybe she wouldn't harm them. But Willow felt that someone would and soon. When she looked back from the other side, the washerwoman was gone.

"Draw your weapons," Theon said to Willow and Dacia. "If something is nearby, we must be prepared."

Willow drew the bright mithrien sword, and Dacia, copying Theon, readied her bow and arrow.

"I don't like this." Brand moved closer to Willow. "The princess has no skill with weapons. Here. Hold it more like this." He pushed her fingers down to the sword's hilt. "If we are attacked, stand with your back to mine and thrust like this." He lunged his sword forward and stabbed a tree.

Dacia gasped.

Theon quickly pulled Brand and his sword away from the pierced elm trunk. "Tree spirits," hissed Theon, "are mostly benevolent. But not *here*. Do you want the whole forest against us?"

"I ... I ..." Brand's surprise turned to anger. "Well, how was I to know of ... of *tree spirits*? You haven't warned us of the actual nature of the dangers that dwell here. Only said that danger *does* dwell here!"

Theon ignored him. He touched the split bark. "It isn't deep. Just a scratch. Don't think the trees will turn against us over it. Still, they're a treacherous bunch." He turned to Dacia. "Let's get back to the path as quickly as possible." She nodded and they set off at a fast pace through the woods.

Willow looked at Brand and shrugged. She raised her sword, holding it the way he had shown her. "Thrust like this, right?" she said, lunging forward. "And keep back to back. I'll remember, okay?"

Brand sighed and managed a sullen smile. "Your stance is off, but your grip is good. Come, we'd best follow or be left behind."

The woods on this side of the stream had less of the prickly evergreens and more of the broad, leafy trees. A wind soughed through their branches, sounding an eerie moan. Willow clutched her sword tighter. They passed a copse of stunted, sun-deprived birch trees, whose white bark gleamed in the dim light. The wind grew stronger, bending tree limbs and making leaves murmur in a swishing whisper. Willow felt chills race up her spine. A birch branch reached out like a clawed hand and pressed a twiggy finger against her head. She yelped, racing from the copse with Brand in quick-stepping tow.

Dacia and Theon turned at her cry. The wind died down like a switch had been flicked off. Willow panted, not sure why she'd been so spooked by some trees and a bit of breeze. Dacia and Theon and even Brand stared at her. She looked around. Felt the top of her head. "What? What are you all looking at?"

"*The Mark of White.*" Dacia's voice sounded pitying. "She's been touched by birch. Quick, Theon, take her sword."

Theon dropped his bow, practically attacking Willow to claim her sword. He tore away her bag as well and shouted at Brand to hold her tight.

"What are you doing? *What's wrong?*" said Willow, struggling to escape Brand's grasp.

He tightened his hold and spoke low into her ear. "I know not, Princess. But your head – it ... it glows with a broad white mark."

"Be glad it's only your head and not your heart." Theon stuck her sword in his belt and retrieved his bow, slinging it over his back. "We will have to tie her. Is there rope in our packs, Dace?" He began searching through Willow's bag.

"You've been touched by a birch spirit, one with a white hand," said Dacia. "The mark is only on your head, though. For a short time you will be inflicted with madness. If it had been on your heart, you would be dead a long while, not just the usual hour. You're very lucky."

Willow stayed still. The world around her had suddenly rippled. She could see Dacia's mouth moving but no sounds were coming out. She felt Brand's hold loosen. Without thinking, she sprang into action, elbowing him hard and kicking his shin. Freed, she raced into the forest. The *thing* hadn't fooled her! It'd looked like Dacia at first but then its silver eyes had blazed red. Fangs had protruded from its top lip. She crashed through the underbrush, looking wildly around. They – *the things* – were chasing after her! Three of them, with burning skin and forked tails. No, not things. *Demons!* They were *demons!*

Willow shrieked and kept running. Branches clawed at her face. Rocks appeared from nowhere, tripping her into sneering trees. Crows cawed mockingly. One flew at her eyes. She didn't see the hole in the ground. Or the cunning face. Not until it was too late and she pitched and tumbled downward.

CHAPTER 17

Willow tried to sit. Pain shot up her neck and into her head. She groaned, gingerly feeling a sore temple. *What happened?* She remembered running. Something chasing after her. Then – Willow bolted upright, her mind reeling with the memory of Dacia's red eyes. Dacia, Brand, and Theon had all turned into demons. Had ... had chased her.

A pungent animal smell hit Willow at the same time as the nightmarish memory. She blinked in the darkness. Something was there. Hunched a few feet away, its breathing shallow and phlegmy. She scrabbled back into a wall of moist dirt, clutching at dead leaves. Tree roots jutted into her spine. She seemed to be in a pit or a cave, with a dim light coming in from an above-ground hole. Her eyes began to adjust. The hunched figure grew clearer. It squatted a few feet away, studying her carefully.

Willow's breath caught. She tried to swallow. The small, nimble creature scooted forward into the light. She could vividly see its bulbous head now, its skinny-little-boy upper body, and more horrifically, its hairy, cloven-hoofed goat legs.

"Who ... who ... *What* are you?" she rasped.

The thing's lipless slash of a mouth turned up into a grin.

She stared in horror at its eyes. Instead of eye whites, it had eye *blacks* with small glowing white circles in the middle. Pudgy horns protruded from the tangled hair on its forehead, and to complete the nightmarish picture, pointed, bat-like ears sprouted out from the sides.

"I be Rye Ruskin Wirt, Mistress, a hobgoblin from the Hobs of Rudd." He giggled a high-pitched, gurgly giggle and danced around the pit. "Rye Ruskin Wirt! Rye Ruskin Wirt! No power in names no more. I can sing it to me heart's content. Rye Ruskin Wirt! Rye Ruskin Wirt!" Suddenly, he stopped his whirling and dropped to his knees in front of Willow. "Not that I would mind bein' in yer power, mistress. I served the Unseelie House of Edrea before the Great Exodus, and would serve it again. Yes indeedy do, I would." His pug-like face brightened with desperate hope. "Are ya from her House? Yer hair's like hers. I'll serve ya. I will! I will! Just promise to take me with ya when ol' Gobby sets ya free."

"I ... er, um ..." Willow didn't know what to say. This *hobgoblin* thing thought she was a faerie. Wanted to serve her. Somehow, despite what Dacia had said, correcting him didn't seem like a good idea. "Can you ... um, maybe help me find my, uh, friends?"

"Let Gobby 'ave 'em. Them birches still owe me anudder favor. I'll get 'em to tell ol' Gobby there's only three faeries not four. He'll believe birch trees over lyin' kelpies any day, and ya can stay safe here with me."

"*Another* favor?"

"Aye. I tol' 'em birches to mark ya with the Mark o' White. Went stark ravin' mad ya did. A few of me crow friends helped herd ya over to me hidey-hole, and now here ya are, safe as a mouse from ol' Gobby."

"G-Gobby?" stammered Willow. "Who ... who's Gobby?"

Rye Ruskin Wirt's squinty black eyes widened, the white orbs at their center sparking in surprise. "The goblin king o' course! Who else?" He lifted a scrawny arm and scratched an armpit, his rank animal odor suffusing the air. "He don't know about me little hidey-hole here. We could hide till he's done havin' his fun with yer friends, then his spell'd send ya back and he'd be none the wiser."

Willow's skin crawled. *Having his fun with her friends.* She shook her head. "No. I can't do that. You have to help me find them. And then we'll see about ... about the other."

The hobgoblin grimaced, baring a mouthful of pointy teeth. "No!" he cried out. "No. No. No. The others will hurt Rye. Chase me away." He leaned closer, his hot breath a sharp stink around Willow's face. "Don't ya want to be safe? Don't ..." His words broke off abruptly. He started blinking and sniffing at her. "'Ere now, wot's this?" He grabbed her arm, pushing up her sleeve, his cold wet nose sniffing right against her exposed skin.

Willow tried to pull her arm away. The hobgoblin snarled like a wolf. He yanked her into the light, his strength surprising for a creature only three feet tall. "Ye're not a faerie, are ya?" he growled. "Been foolin' with ol' Rye. Makin' him think ya were. But ye're not!" He sniffed the air all around her. "Ye're as ripe as fruit. No faerie smells like that. What are ya? Who –" Suddenly he stopped his tirade. He stared at her in shock. "I knows that smell," he rasped. "It ... it's *human!*"

The white dot of his eye went red. Willow freed herself from his grasp and shrank against the wall. The hobgoblin grinned evilly. "I likes the taste of humans," he snarled. "Indeedy I do!" He lunged, knocking her to the ground, his jaws snapping and slavering at her throat. Willow screamed. She fought to push him off. He held tight, his teeth gnashing at her neck. She screamed again, surprised that she felt no pain. Had Dacia been right? Had knowing about the Game made her able to control it?

"*Oi now!* Wot's this?" The hobgoblin had pushed her away from him. "Me chompers are workin'," he said, snapping his teeth in a flurry of test clicks, "but yer neck ain't a-tearin'. Ya got some kinda spell on ya or somethin'?"

"*Willow,*" a voice cried out. "Willow, you down there?"

In a flash, the hobgoblin vanished through a black hole in the dirt wall. Willow crawled to her knees. "I'm here!" she cried. "I'm ... I'm right here!" A silvery head appeared above her. "Just a moment. I'll toss you a rope." Willow sighed in relief. It was Theon. She grabbed the rope, and he hauled her out.

"I heard you scream," he said. "Are you all right?"

"I ... I think so." Willow's fingers crept over her throat. Nothing. There wasn't even a tooth mark.

Theon stared back into the dark pit. "I heard another voice. One that was most assuredly not yours." He drew his sword. "Is the creature still down there?"

Willow joined him at the hole's edge. "He ... he said he was a ... a hobgoblin. Thought I was a faerie and wanted to ... to protect me."

"*Protect* you?"

"Yeah. Somehow he thought that we could make a deal. He would protect me from the goblin king if I promised to take him with me when we were released from the Game."

"You screamed though. Did the hob not like your answer?"

Her fingers strayed to her neck again. "When he came close, he, um ... smelled that I was human. He attacked me and I think he was trying to eat me."

Theon examined her dirt-stained clothes. Picked a twig from her hair. "What happened? You have no bites. Did I scare him off?"

"That's the weird thing." Willow showed Theon her neck. "He tried to bite me here. I mean his teeth were chewing away and when he pulled back, he was as surprised as I was that nothing had happened. He asked if I was under some kind of spell or something. What does it mean, Theon? Why couldn't he hurt me?"

Theon looked mystified. "Truthfully, I have no idea. But that's what hobs do, they go for the throat, so I don't doubt your story. A mystery I'm sure Dacia will wish to solve."

"Speaking of Dacia ..." Willow spun her head around to search the wooded area, "where is she? And Brand?"

"I don't know. One minute we were all together searching for you, and the next we weren't." He plunged his sword back into its scabbard and sighed. "One thing we've learned from following this Game is it's never safe to leave the path. Of course, almost everyone has to at some point." He pulled out another sword that had no scabbard but was tucked in his belt. "Here. The Mark has faded. I assume you're sane now. Put your sword in its sheath, take back your rucksack, and we shall search for them. But hold my hand. I won't be separated from you as well."

Obediently, Willow readjusted her sword and rucksack and grasped Theon's hand. She too didn't want to find herself alone in a monster-infested forest. As they walked, Willow thought about something the hobgoblin had said, something she'd heard before. Her hair was the same color as that of the faeries from the House of Edrea. "Theon," she said in a low voice. "What is the House of Edrea?"

He looked at her, his eyes sweeping across her face and hair. "Did the hob think you were Edrea?"

"Well, maybe not *the* Edrea. But definitely from her, um, House. Something to do with my hair color."

Theon studied her features again. "You probably are descended from her." Willow gave him a surprised look. "All humans from Mistolear are descended from faeries. I believe it was up to the seventh bloodlines that were taken there. Blood after that is too diluted for magic."

Willow nodded. She remembered what *The Complete History of Fey Magic Lore* had said. It made sense *now*. How else would humans have a magic gene, if not from the fey? "So you're saying that at some point on Earth, humans and faeries got married?"

"No, we do not marry. We form alliances. But yes, at some point on Earth, faeries and humans commingled and had children together. You Mistolearians are our kindred."

Kindred. That was like being related. Willow glanced at Theon's chiseled profile. They could be distant cousins. Weird.

"Dacia and I were born after the Great Exodus." Theon turned thoughtfully to Willow. "You are the first human I've ever met. I didn't expect you to be like ... like you are."

"Like I am?" Willow raised an eyebrow. "And how exactly is that?"

Theon stopped walking, pinning her with his metallic eyes. "You are like me," he said, "but not. Emotions play across your face as clouds do in a sky. Ever-moving. Ever-changing. Drawing me to search out their meaning." He let go her hand and gently brushed wisps of hair from her cheek. "You make me search inside myself too. Question things I've never questioned before." A smile curved his lips, hinting at amusement. "I haven't decided yet if I desire this curious feeling or detest it, but I do know – it intrigues me."

Willow felt blood rush to her face. She wasn't quite sure what Theon was saying. Was he saying he ... *liked* her?

Theon chuckled, his smile turning to a grin. "Even now your face betrays you. You are drawn to me too, but fight it." He bent his head to hers. "Maybe you shouldn't." Soft lips touched Willow's. Arms slid round her waist. For a second she kissed him back, tasted tangerines and nectar juice, then stiffened with guilt. "Don't." She pushed him away. "Don't do that. I'm ... I'm with Brand."

"Really?" Theon looked over the forest with mocking curiosity. "I thought you were with me."

"You know what I mean. I mean Brand and I are together. A couple."

"A couple. You mean that you are mated?"

Willow's face grew hot. "No! I mean – Look, I can't kiss you, okay. Let's just leave it at that." She plowed past Theon, her blood pulsing in her throat. Truthfully, she had liked the kiss. But how could she have felt that way? She cared about Brand, didn't she?

"Forgive me." Theon strode beside her and took her hand again. "I won't kiss you, unless you wish it. But I don't mind that you are ... with Brand. Faeries can mate with one or many. Eternity lasts a long time. We don't limit our alliances." His fingers squeezed hers. "I will wait, Willow of Mistolear, till you wish to be with me."

Oh great. Just what I need. Willow resisted the urge to free her hand. She was still too afraid of the forest for that. She gave Theon a hard look instead. "I can't *be* with you, okay? Humans are different. We stay together our whole lives."

"Are you and Brand betrothed?"

"No."

"Married?"

"No."

"Then I don't understand. Are humans forced to be with

one person even when they are young? You don't compare different bonds?"

"No. I mean ..." Willow sighed. What did she mean? In a way Theon was right. She'd never had any boyfriend but Brand. And even he had never really asked her to be his girlfriend. It was more like this silent agreement between them. Like it was expected or something. How did she really know that he was "the one" if she'd never even dated anyone else?

"Listen, Theon, I think we've got a lot more important things to be worried about right now. Maybe when this is all over we can talk. But for now, I think we should concentrate on finding Brand and Dacia and getting back on the path."

Theon didn't answer. A half-smile played along his lips.

Fine. Two could play at that game. Willow didn't say anything further either. She concentrated on studying the thick forest around her. If Brand and Dacia were still here, she was determined to find them. Her thoughts, though, kept drifting back to Theon's kiss. She shook her head, let the horror of where she was seep back in. The hobgoblin's nightmarish face flashed in her mind. Would he follow them? Alert the goblin king to their presence? Willow shivered. The memory of those disturbing eyes would no doubt haunt her for weeks to come.

"Are you cold?"

"No." Willow adjusted her cloak. She tried to act natural, as though the kiss had never happened. "I was just thinking about the ... the hobgoblin." Her eyes stayed clear of Theon's mouth. "Do you think he'll tell the goblin king about us?"

"Definitely. As will the kelpies. The birches, though, and the bean-nighe will keep their own counsel. They are spirits and don't serve the goblin king."

"What ... what will he do to us, Theon?"

He took a deep breath and squeezed her hand. "You don't want to know." He kept his gaze straight ahead, not wanting to see her fear, or else trying to hide his own. Willow didn't argue. They walked in silence for a while until Theon stopped and squinted at a gnarled elm tree. "That tree," he said, "we've been by it before. A couple of times." He sighed deeply. "The forest is bespelled. We're going in circles."

Mist, thick as soup, surrounded them. Willow could only make out what was directly in front of her. "Maybe we should rest. Wait for this fog to lift."

Theon nodded. He led her to the elm tree, sat down, and rested against its trunk. Willow sat beside him, the tree trunk wide enough for both of them to lean on. They rummaged through their rucksacks, finding water skins and fresh biscuits, which surprised Theon. His father usually didn't supply food.

"Must be because you're human," he surmised. "Faeries *can* eat but we don't need to."

Willow didn't care about the reason. She was just glad to eat. The water cooled her throat and the biscuits tasted warm. She was joking that his father was a good cook when she noticed that Theon was staring at his feet. Well, not at his feet but at a ring of white-speckled red toadstools that were near his feet.

"I know how to find the path." Theon stretched forward and

picked one of the toadstools. *"'Elf's Cap in a faerie ring to find the path that you are seeking.'"*

"Huh?"

"It's an old faerie spell from Earth. Red toadstools in a ring were magical gateways into the faerie realms. We are not on Earth, granted, and our path is not into the faerie realms, but still – it may work."

Willow eyed the mushroom nervously. It looked creepy and poisonous to her. "What do we have to do with it?"

"Eat it," said Theon, and before she could stop him, he popped the red, rubbery fungus into his mouth.

CHAPTER 18

"*Theon!*" Willow cried. "Are you crazy! What if they're poisonous? You could –" *What? Die?* She suddenly remembered nothing that happened to them here was permanent. But still. She watched Theon's face carefully.

A lazy smile curved his mouth. His already half-closed eyelids slid shut. He tilted his head back against the tree trunk, breathing deep even breaths.

Willow touched his hand. He felt warm. "Theon? Are you ... are you okay?"

His eyes opened partially. He looked at her, then around at the forest. "The mist's gone." His hand started to crawl up her arm.

Willow frowned and shook him off. According to her eyesight the mist wasn't gone. In fact, it was growing thicker.

"Here." Theon held out a mushroom. "Better eat one too." Only his words sounded all slurred together – *BettterEatOneTooo* – like one word instead of four. "The spellll-sssays-something ... ab-about ..." It took great effort but finally Theon got his tongue to manage the words. *"No one follows that hath not eaten."*

Taking the mushroom, Willow grimaced and squeezed its

spongy body. She didn't like the look of Theon's spaced-out eyes or the way his hand was now roving along her leg. She pushed him away again. Whatever these toadstools did, they definitely altered perception. Not something she wanted here in the middle of nowhere with an amorous faerie.

Theon seemed to sense her thoughts. He sat straighter and made an effort to control his wandering hand. "Truly," he rasped, "the mist is gone. You must eat the Elf's Cap to see as I do."

Willow didn't buy it. "Why can't you just lead me? We can hold hands like before."

"No one follows that hath not eaten." Theon's eyes closed and then slowly opened again. "Don't believe me? Put it in your pocket. When we get separated, you'll eat it then." He started to get up.

"Wait." Willow stopped him. "I'll ... I'll eat it now, okay?" She didn't want to, but the prospect of finding herself alone in the creepy forest and maybe running into another hobgoblin, or God knew what, was not something she wanted to risk. She took a deep breath and bit into the Elf's Cap.

At first it tasted normal, dry and flavorless like a regular mushroom, but once she swallowed, its effects were immediate. Blood rushed to her head. She felt warm, slightly dizzy, like she had a fever. A pulse pounded behind her eyelids, making them drift shut. Instantly she began to spiral. Willow grinned. She knew this game. Had played it lots as a kid. Go round and round and round and when you fell down, you still kept spinning inside your head.

"Willow. Open your eyes."

Her neck bobbled as her head whirled. She was really going now. Picking up speed.

Fingers pinched her shoulder. Shook her.

"Huh ... what?" She blinked. The world began to slow down and came back into focus. Theon leaned in close, smiling at her, his fingers brushing her cheek, parting her lips, and then trailing down her throat with shivering jolts of sensation. Willow's heartbeat raced. Theon's lips found hers, kissing them with a fierceness that sent fiery heat blasting through her. She kissed him back, senses reeling. Everything felt charged and nerve endings tingled like electric live wires.

Theon pressed against her, toppling her to the ground. His hands seemed to be everywhere. Touching. Kneading. She felt one slip beneath her shirt, caress her bare back. Something flickered, a kernel of warning that broke through her haze.

"No," she mumbled. "No!" She struggled away from Theon's lips. Something ... something ... She couldn't quite put her finger on it. Shouldn't be doing this. But why? ... Then she saw Brand above them, his eyes dark and accusing. Suddenly Theon was no longer on top of her. She blinked, confused. Brand was an image in her mind, wasn't he? But no, there he was, holding Theon by the throat and strangling him.

"Stop," she croaked. She wobbled to her feet, swaying against the tree trunk for support. Everything seemed brighter somehow. Theon was right. The mist was gone.

"You fey scum!" Brand gave Theon a stomach punch that

sent him crashing to the ground. Willow stumbled over to protect him. Brand grasped her shoulders, about to move her out of the way, then stopped. He stared at her.

At her lips specifically.

Willow tried to cover them. They felt enormous, like clown lips. But Brand grabbed her wrists, pulled them away from her face. He struggled to say something. Anger set his mouth into rigid lines and sent a vein popping along his jaw. Then he just dropped her hands – threw them from his, actually – and turned his back on her.

It felt like when he'd accused her of being wanton, only ten times worse. Willow slumped to the ground, the magical mushroom drug making her head ache. She felt dirty. Wanted more than anything else to shower. To scrub and scrub until she felt clean again.

Dacia wavered in front of her. Helped her stand, then went over to Brand. "It's not what you think." She tugged at his arm. Made him look at the red mushroom in her palm. "They ate Elf's Cap. Probably to see through the spell that's hiding the pathway."

"How does that change what I saw?" Brand's eyes pinned Willow with a cold glare.

"There're side effects," said Dacia. "Anyone who eats Elf's Cap becomes quite, um ... passionate."

Willow's head swiveled to Theon, who'd picked himself up from the ground and was dusting off his pant legs. He grinned at her sheepishly. *The pig!* Willow scowled. He had known all along. Had tricked her into ...

Oh God! Just thinking about it was reviving the magic. She bit her tingling lips and looked around at the forest instead. How much had Brand seen? Would he ever forgive her? Would ... Willow shook her head. Okay, now she wanted to kiss Brand.

"Dacia," she said hoarsely, "when does this spell wear off?"

"Soon. Which is why we must start searching for the path now." She stooped and picked up Willow's rucksack. "Here." She handed it to Willow. "The magic will guide your senses. Just let it."

"But ..." Willow slung the bag over her shoulder, feeling confused, "... don't you and Brand have to, you know, eat it too?"

Dacia gave her brother a quick glance. "No. We can follow. We'll just have to hold hands so we won't lose each other." Dacia grabbed Theon's hand and ordered Brand to take Willow's. Brand hesitated. Looked at Willow as if she were the goblin king himself and then reluctantly obeyed.

They started walking, Dacia and Theon slightly ahead, Willow and Brand following. Willow glared at the back of Theon's head. He had tricked her into eating the mushroom, so he could – what? Kiss her? Take advantage of her? Another thought sidled into Willow's mind. What if he'd known all along Brand was close by? And had orchestrated the whole thing to try and break them up? Willow shook her head. Nah. It didn't make sense that he would go to that much trouble. They were in the Goblin King's Gauntlet, for pete's sake! Not on some romantic walk in the park.

"A hobgoblin captured Willow," Theon announced in a low voice.

Brand's mask of coolness dropped for a second, revealing his concern, then quickly went back up again.

"He thought she was a faerie at first," Theon continued, "but when he discovered she was human, he tried to kill her, or more specifically, eat her."

Brand's hand tightened on Willow's.

"The interesting thing, though, is that while he bit and chewed at her, nothing happened. He never so much as left a mark. What do you make of it, Dacia?"

"I ... I don't know." Dacia looked back at Willow. "Did he say anything about it?"

Willow remembered the hobgoblin's snapping jaws and shuddered. "He was angry. He thought I was under a spell or something."

"Strange," said Dacia. "Very strange. Perhaps Father's added some new element to the Game and neglected to tell us."

Theon snorted. "Don't think there's much chance of that. The hob *couldn't* eat her, Dace. Think Father's going to add an element that benefits a human? No, there's something else going on here." He stared at his sister. "Remember those stories about the Compact between the Seelies and the goblin king? What if they're true?"

"No way, that's ridiculous." Dacia shook her head. "They're just stories, Theon. Stories to scare younglings."

"What are you talking about?" Brand interjected. "What is

this – this Compact?

Theon stopped short and pointed. "The path," he said. "It's just up ahead."

"I see nothing." Brand squinted in the direction Theon had pointed. "This mist is thick as soup."

"No, it's there." Willow could see it, winding forebodingly into the forest. She shivered. Finding their way back to the path didn't feel like a good thing. Only another step closer to the goblin king and whatever fate awaited them.

CHAPTER 19

$\mathcal{B}$ack on the path, Willow's head began to clear. She could see the mist but it wasn't as thick as it had been in the forest. Brand dropped her hand and let her walk ahead of him, as Theon did with Dacia, but somehow Willow sensed Brand's actions had little to do with the narrow path and more to do with not wanting to be near her. She felt her insides crawl with shame. She had a sudden vision of what her kiss with Theon must have looked like to Brand. How it would've looked to her if it'd been Brand and Dacia. She wasn't sure, mushrooms or no mushrooms, she could have forgiven him.

They trod along the pathway for what seemed like hours, no one speaking but everyone jittery and twisting their heads at every little noise. Willow was quite certain they were being followed. Nothing she could catch a glimpse of, but scampering feet and giggling sounds had been giving her chills the whole afternoon.

"It's getting dark." Dacia stopped walking and panned the forest. Willow halted too. She'd been so engrossed with her thoughts, she hadn't noticed how quickly the light was fading. Soon it'd be as black as the hobgoblin's hidey-hole.

"What can we do?" asked Brand. "It's obvious we are being followed." His eyes searched the forest as well. "To set up camp, I wager, would be to invite an ambush."

Theon slipped off his rucksack and glanced at Brand. "Humans need rest," he said. "If we don't stop and face what's out there, you'll be too weary to fight it."

"*Humans* need rest?" Brand scowled. "And I suppose faeries don't."

"Not in the way that you do. We can choose to rest, but we don't need it."

Brand started to argue the point. Dacia cut him off. "No, he's right. I would rather face our foes now by firelight than later in darkness. We shall make camp there, over by that large tree. Brand, you and Willow start a fire. Theon and I will collect firewood."

Willow watched the slender faerie girl pad into the brush, followed obediently by her brother. Quick and confident, that's the way Dacia made decisions. The way Willow wished *she* could make decisions.

Loud clacks grabbed Willow's attention. Brand, crouched to the ground, struck something black against something shiny. Sparks flared. She could see a little billow of smoke curling from a pile of grass.

"Needs kindling," grunted Brand. He nodded to a tree trunk that was peeling gray bark and went back to his task, not so much as giving Willow a glance. Willow collected a handful of thin bark that had fallen to the forest floor and knelt beside

Brand, feeding pieces of it into the small fire he had started. They didn't look at each other or say anything. Finally, Willow broke the uncomfortable silence.

"I'm sorry, Brand. I ... I ..."

Brand glared at her and stalked over to the tree with the peeling bark. He picked up a few more strips, then started collecting small twigs and sticks. Willow watched him, feeling embarrassed, hurt, and angry all at the same time. Tears smarted her eyes.

Dacia emerged from the brush and placed her firewood in a pile beside Willow. She bent close to her ear. "He'll forgive you. Give him time."

"Yeah." Willow nodded. She wiped her tears with her shirt sleeve. "Just wish he'd talk to me is all."

"He will."

Looking at Brand's rigid back, Willow wasn't so sure. On the other hand, Dacia sounded pretty confident. Maybe a little *too* confident. Made Willow wonder what a faerie, who supposedly had no qualms about dating an entire football team at the same time, would know about possessive boyfriends. "Do faeries get jealous?"

"Of course." A hint of a smile lifted Dacia's lips. She seemed to guess where Willow's question had originated from. "What did my brother tell you? That we can mate with one or many?"

"Yeah, something like that. Is it true?"

"It's true. No doubt, though, he neglected to mention all the war Games played if we *do* mate with more than one. I fear faeries and humans are very much of the same ilk when it comes to matters of the heart."

Willow tossed one of the smaller branches into their growing fire. So Theon had known exactly how Brand would react. Had probably planned it. But why? What did he hope to gain by breaking her and Brand up?

The fire crackled and popped. Theon dropped his pile of wood onto Dacia's pile and grinned at Willow. Willow glowered at him, suddenly reminded of the high school boys on Earth. The ones like her old crush, Dean Jarrett. Good-looking. Exciting. Knew exactly what to say and how to say it. Only thing is, they said it to every girl. Maybe Theon was one of those guys, the guys who looked at girls like a contest. Bag a cheerleader – ten points. One with a boyfriend – twenty.

Brand came back with his pile of twigs and bark and began feeding them to the fire. Willow peeked at him, her heart contracting painfully. Brand was not the contest guy. He was the steadfast one. The one who took arrows for you, who followed you into danger. Who used his own body to shield you from tigers. A rush of warmth swept through Willow. And then there it was, plain as the nose on her face – she loved Brand.

Quickly, she lowered her eyes, sure that anyone who saw them would know what she felt. Her heart was pounding now. Her face hot. *She loved Brand*. How could she not have known that?

"Seems Father has added a magical component to our bags," said Dacia, startling Willow. "There's food and water in here. Even napkins." She pulled out a biscuit and took a bite. "Tastes good too. Guess he wants us to keep up our strength."

Theon dug through his bag as well and pulled out another biscuit. "*And* it regenerates. Willow and I ate our biscuits earlier and now here they are again. Fresh and warm."

The words *Willow and I* brought a frown to Brand's face. He stood up and moved a short ways from the fire, settling down on a jutting rock. He drew his sword. "I'll keep first watch."

Willow forced down a biscuit and some water. Her stomach felt too tight to eat. Still, she knew she needed the food, or at least felt like she did. She bit into another biscuit, studying the back of Brand's head. His long dark hair draped loose over the hood of his cloak. She wanted to sit with him. Maybe tie his hair back or brush it from his face. Something she could've easily done before if she hadn't been so dumb and kissed Theon.

A twig plunked on Willow's head and landed in her lap. Surprised, she blinked at it a moment, then looked up. A host of gleaming eyes stared back at her. She didn't have time to scream. Small agile creatures dropped from the tree branches, swarming over the clearing in a matter of seconds. Willow had three of them on her, two clinging to her arms like big squirrels and one piggy-backing around her neck. She shrieked and writhed, bolting up to shake them off.

Brand, sword already out, skewered two of his attackers and leaped to help Willow. He ripped the creatures from her and hurled them into the tree trunk. Willow grabbed her sword, but all of Brand's instructions left her mind as she turned to Dacia and Theon. Except for glimpses of silver hair and green cloak, the two faeries were literally covered in little mud-colored monsters.

Snarling, Brand brushed past her and threw himself into the fray, tearing away creatures and stabbing them with his sword. He seemed to be invincible. Willow saw glints of metal. The monster things were armed, but their daggers and spears had no effect on Brand. He fought them like a machine, impervious to their efforts to attack him. The creatures scattered, most skittering into the dark forest, others squealing in agony as they continued to battle Brand.

Finally, the glade was quiet. Dacia and Theon lay still, their clothing spattered with blood. Willow sprang to Dacia first. She had a stab wound beneath her breast, one in her stomach, and a nasty gash on her forehead. Theon had multiple stab wounds and what looked like bite marks on his cheek and throat. They were both alive but barely. Willow set to work on Theon, whose wounds were deeper and more numerous than Dacia's. Brand helped her to remove Theon's shirt and tunic. He tore cloth strips from a blanket and cleaned up some of the blood.

The blood ...

There was so much blood. The washerwoman and her bloody laundry came vividly back to Willow. She pushed the thought away. Theon and Dacia weren't going to die. Not if she could help it. She didn't bother with freezing the wounds. Theon, already unconscious, wasn't feeling any pain. She went for a staunch spell to stop the bleeding and repair the holes in his body. The magic worked fast, much faster than it did in Mistolear or when she'd been in the Menagerie Game. Almost at the speed of thought.

In no time Theon was completely healed, his eyelids fluttering open. Willow moved to Dacia and repeated the process. When both faeries were healed, Willow looked to Brand, who didn't have so much as a scratch on him. Sighing, she leaned against a tree trunk and ran shaky fingers through her hair. God, she was tired. Like she'd just run a marathon or something. Her eyes caught sight of the little brown bodies scattered around their campsite. She blinked. They weren't what she'd expected. They were like ... like ... *children*.

Willow dragged herself to the nearest ones and studied them closely. They wore nothing except furred loincloths, their bodies human-looking, but tiny and thin, with pudgy little toddler bellies.

Like Nezzie's.

An urge to vomit spasmed through her. She swallowed hard, trying to control it. By the wavering firelight, she could see she'd been wrong about the creatures being brown. They were green as frogs and smooth-skinned like babies. She touched one. Lifted its delicate arm.

"What is it?" Brand knelt beside her, his brows knitted with concern.

"Th-they're like children." Willow's voice wobbled. "Look! Look how tiny they are."

Brand frowned and stood back up. "You saw what they did

to the faeries. They are not children but monsters. Come away from them. I will move their bodies to the bushes."

Willow ignored him. The one little creature she touched had stirred. Its narrow face turned toward her. It had a snout-like nose, chubby cheeks, and a small mouth that grimaced in pain. Almond-shaped eyes opened. All brown with no whites, like a puppy's. She saw the pain and fear. Saw the terrible sword wound in its chest. Instinctively, her hand moved to heal, her magic gathering.

"No! Don't!" Dacia spoke this time, her voice alarmed. She sprang at Willow and knocked her hand away. "You don't understand," she snapped. "The goblins will feel no gratitude for your healing. They are not like you." She drew her sword. "We must kill it. Else it will kill us."

Willow clutched the little goblin in her arms and protected it from Dacia's sword. For some reason the faerie's words bothered her. She wanted to see for herself if goblins were different. She went inside its aura and felt for its soul. It had one. One that seemed surprisingly similar to a human's. But something was different. Something about the way its brain worked. She went deeper. Saw the thing she knew couldn't really be there but that her magic helped her visualize.

A large black thorn lay embedded in its heart.

Willow opened her eyes. "What have you done?" She glared at Dacia. She knew what the black thorn meant. Someone had tampered with biology. Someone had altered this creature's natural pattern so that it wouldn't have a choice. It could only follow one pathway.

A pathway of evil.

Everyone looked at Willow like she was nuts. "What have *I* done?" said Dacia, mystified.

Theon, buttoning up his bloodied shirt, kicked at one of the goblin bodies. "I say kill them all. You're just being sentimental because they're younglings." In agreement, Brand stepped forward to take the goblin from Willow's arms.

"No!" she cried. "Don't touch it." She glared back at Dacia. "There's a thorn blocking this thing's choice patterns. *Someone* put it there. Maybe not you personally. But it's faerie magic, isn't it?" Willow let her gaze fall on all the broken little bodies lying around the glade. "They're all like that, aren't they? They can only choose to do bad."

Lately, Willow had seen traces of certain emotions in Dacia. Traces that made her seem more human. But that suddenly changed. Dacia's fey nature emerged again. The mask came up. The voice went cold. "Goblins serve the Unseelie Court. Evil is what they are. Evil is what they do."

"No. Evil is what they are *made* to be and *made* to do. I saw it, Dacia. I saw the black thorn." Willow turned away from the faeries and Brand. She clutched her tiny burden and reached into its aura again. Quickly, before Dacia's pinching fingers could stop her, she removed the thorn. She healed the goblin's chest wound and sent it into a deep slumber.

Dacia spun her around. "Are you brain-addled?" The stony mask was gone. Anger lit her eyes. "Do you think removing the thorn changes anything? Its nature's been taught from birth. No sweetness and light in a goblin's childhood. First opportunity it'll slit your throat." There was fear just beneath the anger. Looking at Dacia's blood-spattered shirt, Willow felt doubt creep over her.

"Not so fast, Dace." Theon had his tunic back on and was buckling up his sword. "These goblins *are* quite young. Perhaps, surprising as it may seem, someone might like them back." He toed a body at his side. "Think this one's alive. And maybe that one over there. If Willow heals them, we could use them as prisoners. Maybe have a little leverage with the goblin king."

Despite it being Theon's suggestion, Brand warmed to the idea. "Aye. And the ones that ran away might think twice about attacking again if we have their friends as hostages."

"Or," Dacia sighed and slipped her sword back into its scabbard, "they'll come back with twice more to aid them." She turned to Willow. "Do what you will. Kill them. Save them. I see little difference in the outcome."

Willow watched as the faerie girl sat down by the fire and thrust sticks into it. She didn't know if Dacia was right or wrong, she just knew she couldn't kill the goblin children nor let anyone else do it. Gently, she laid her small patient in a grassy knoll and covered him with the torn remains of her blanket. She searched the campsite with her magic, looking for the faint auras of goblins that still lived. Theon was right. Only two others clung to life.

Their wounds gaped in fleshy rips, all the worse on their

small bodies, but Willow grimly set to work on healing them and removing the black thorn embedded in each of their hearts. She sent them into slumber as she had the first goblin and then laid all three of them together on the grassy knoll.

"I'll tie them."

Willow frowned at Theon and the rope he carried. "You don't need to. My sleep spell will keep them out for hours."

"No offense, Princess, but I will not have three loose goblins in our camp, asleep or otherwise." He tied the hands of each goblin, roping the three of them together like a chain gang, then staked the rope ends to the ground with daggers. Willow let him do it. She figured she'd got her way enough tonight and didn't want to push things.

After Brand had removed the dead goblin bodies from their campsite and had collected the discarded weapons, he sat watch again on the jutting rock. Theon took up a spot at the opposite end of the campsite and Dacia stayed by the fire. Willow curled up in her warm cloak and lay near her sleeping charges. She watched them breathing, their vulnerable, puppy-like faces soft in the fire's glow. She hoped she had done the right thing. The image of the goblins swarming Dacia and Theon and the aftermath of blood and death clouded her thoughts. Maybe Dacia was right. Maybe saving the goblins had been just plain dumb. Willow made a pillow with her hands. Yeah. Dumb maybe. But still the only thing keeping her sane and helping her hold on to her humanity. She sighed, closed weary eyes, and wished more than anything that Brand's arm rested on her shoulder.

CHAPTER 20

A crow cawed. Willow's eyes flicked open, taking in a dreamy vision of towering treetops that shut out the dim morning light. Mist curled around the tree trunks and woodsmoke scented the air. She lay still for a peaceful moment until a rush of dark memories spilled in, making her heart thump. She peered around the campsite. Dacia had kept their fire going and still sat by it in a contemplative trance. Brand leaned against a rock, his head cradled on an arm. Theon rested against a tree trunk. Everyone accounted for. Everyone still alive. Willow sighed. They had made it through the night.

Something snorted. Slowly she turned her head. A goblin child stared at her, brown puppy eyes narrowing, baby lips puckered as if he were going to ...

Spit!

Willow pitched to the side, barely avoiding the brownish-green snot gob that landed near her hand. The creature scowled, trying to shake off his wrist ropes but joggling awake his attached companions instead.

"Hey, saphead! Watcha doin'?"

"Yeah! Quit it. Ye're rippin' my arms off!"

Their voices sounded cartoonish, like kids who'd been sucking in helium.

The offending goblin, who still wriggled between them, tried to punch a neighbor with his tied fists, but without enough slack rope, the tugging made the other squeal in pain.

"Ya dirty lump! That *hurt!*"

Then before Willow could stop them, the three goblins commenced a kicking fight, cursing and hurling insults like rowdy little sailors. Theon came over, grabbed hold of the rope, and yanked it hard enough to send all three goblins sprawling flat on their backs. Surprised, they stared wide-eyed at the stone-faced faerie. He held a sword in his other hand and touched its tip to each of their throats. "Not another word," he growled, "or it will be your last." He pointed the sword tip at Willow. "See that gentle princess? You owe her your lives." The goblins lifted their heads to look. Theon immediately yanked the rope tight again and held the sword blade flat over all three of their throats. "But make no mistake, *I* have no qualms in taking them. Now sit there. Shut up. And if one of you so much as pinches the other, I will gag and tie the lot of you into a sack. Is that understood?" The goblins nodded. Theon gave Willow a grin, dropped the rope, and strode over to his rucksack.

The goblins struggled to sit, all the while muttering under their breath and glaring hatefully at Theon's unconcerned back. One, however, turned his hate-glare over to Willow. "Whatcha do to me, faerie? I feels funny. Like me noggin's bigger or somethin'." He started to raise his hand, remembered the ropes, and gave his mop-topped head a quick shake instead. The other two copied him.

"Yeah. Mine feels funny too. All tingly like."

"Mine too."

Willow had been watching the whole performance, from spit gob to head shakes, in horror. What had she done, indeed? Dacia's words came back to haunt her. *Removing the thorn changes nothing.* But then what had she expected? The goblins to wake up all "sweetness and light"?

"A bogie got yer tongue? Whatcha do to my head? And whatcha fix us up fer anyway?" The goblin paled as his mind put it together. "Ya gonna torture us, ain't cha? *Ain't cha?!*" The other two squealed in fright and huddled against the third.

"What? *No!* Of course not." Willow finally gathered her wits. "No one is going to torture anyone."

"Ya gonna trade us then? Pitt there's ol' Gobby's son. And Nox and me is cousins. We should –"

"Aw Lunk, ya great stupid oaf!" One of the goblins jabbed Lunk in the stomach. "Ya gonna tell her where we keeps our gold too?"

"Which one of you is the goblin king's son?" Dacia suddenly loomed over the goblin children, her bow notched with an arrow and pointed at them.

"Dacia, I think –"

"Which one?"

The two goblins at the ends pointed to the one in the middle. "He is," they said in unison.

Dacia lowered her bow. "Maybe I was wrong." She looked at Willow, assessing her with new respect. "A king's son *could* give us a different outcome. You did well to save them." Willow watched Dacia go back to the fire and begin to smother it with dirt. She was pretty certain the faerie girl had just paid her a compliment. Her own doubts started to dwindle. The goblins weren't so bad. A little rough around the edges maybe, but still kind of cute in their own way.

"Hey bird-brain! You with all the straggly robin-breast hair. Don't cha got no food? I ain't eat nothing since yesterday. My stomach's empty as yer fat head."

"Mine too."

"Yeah. Empty as yer fat head."

Willow frowned. Maybe *cute* wasn't exactly the right word for them. Brand came over and tossed the goblins a few biscuits. Instead of scrambling for them, they stared at him in fear. "What?" said Brand. "Why are they looking at me that way? As though they see a ghost?"

"I knifed ya." Pitt, the goblin king's son, squinted nervously at Brand. "I knifed ya real good. And ya didn't feel nuttin' and ya didn't bleed. What are ya then? Ye're no faerie."

Dacia's head cocked at the goblin's words. She beckoned Willow and Brand over to the smothered campfire. Theon ambled over as well. "Is this true, Brand?" she asked, her voice low so the goblins couldn't hear. "Were you unharmed in the attack, just as Willow was unharmed by the hobgoblin?"

"Aye. The princess and I suffered no injuries."

"Oh, come on." Theon snorted in disbelief. "There were dozens of them! You weren't injured *at all*?"

Brand's jaw tightened. His fists clenched and unclenched, itching, no doubt, for another excuse to pound Theon. Willow quickly corroborated the story.

"No, it's true. We were swarmed just like you guys, but nothing seemed to hurt us. I mean, I thought I saw them stab Brand but when I went to heal him, he wasn't ... he wasn't wounded."

"It *must* be the Compact," whispered Theon.

"The Compact?" Dacia looked amused. "As I said before it's just a tale told to scare younglings. You don't seriously believe –"

"What else could it be? Willow and Brand are human. They have both been attacked by goblins and haven't been injured. Either Father has cast a spell to make the Compact look real or it *is* real. There are no other options."

Willow and Brand shared a concerned glance. "What are you talking about?" asked Brand. "What is this *Compact*?"

Dacia sighed. "It's a treaty, supposedly between the Unseelie goblins and the Seelie Court, that protects humans from the Dark. You see, eons ago – when the faerie courts were still on Earth, and before the vote was settled – the two courts warred with each other. In the age just before the Great Earth Exodus, the Seelie Court is said to have tricked the goblin king, who is Lord of the Unseelie demon host, into signing a peace treaty. So then the tale goes that the Unseelie Court, without the goblins or the host to back them up, lost the vote and much of their power."

She paused to exhale a gusty breath. "In the Seelie Court on Clarion, this story is seen as history. But in our Court, it's sneered at as myth or as a tale used to scare younglings." Her eyes darted to Theon. "But Father must know the truth of it. As would the Unseelie lords. They were all *there* after all."

Theon stood silent for a moment, then anger clipped his words. "Yeah, they know. They all know. That's why they always use this Game on us and never on the Seelie Court. The Compact protects them. A Seelie Court faerie would walk through here as the humans do, unharmed."

"But the goblins just accused Brand of *not* being a faerie," Willow pointed out. "Shouldn't they have thought him a Seelie if any of this is true?"

Dacia glanced at the goblins. "They are young. With only Unseelie faeries ever brought to them, I would wager they've never even heard of the Compact. In fact," she chuckled and shook her head, "goblins aren't exactly known for their historical record keeping. I wouldn't be surprised if they've forgotten all about it. This could prove to be quite an interesting Game."

"One other thing." Willow gazed at her hands. "My powers here are about ten times stronger than they were on Mistolear, or even in the Menagerie. I mean you and Theon were almost dead, and I just ... just touched you and ... is that normal? Should I be worried or anything?"

For a moment a wistful shadow touched Dacia's face. She turned to her brother, and Willow saw something like hope pass between them briefly. In an instant, their cool faerie masks came back up and Dacia shook her head. "No. Nothing to worry about. Since we only have the one power, my guess is that yours has been amplified. Perhaps to the strength of a full-fledged mage, not a student."

Willow stared back at her hands, flexing her fingers. Could she ever learn to be this powerful for real? The thought was kind of exciting. She peeked back at the goblins. And if Theon was right about the Compact, then she and Brand couldn't be hurt. Some of the fear seeped out of her. For the first time, she had a sense that things might work out, that she and Brand would make it out of here in one piece. She turned to Brand, expecting to see the same optimism but saw only horror and revulsion.

"You are to come with us." A voice like gravelly thunder echoed around the campsite. Willow whirled to see what Brand had obviously already seen, a nightmarish creature that stood as tall as her, had a man's body but a black sheep head with two horns jutting from its forehead. Its white eyes swept impassively over the group. More of the creatures stepped from the forest, surrounding the campsite.

"Phookas," spat Theon under his breath. He and Brand drew their swords.

The goblin children, still staked to the ground, squealed in fright. One creature snapped a whip in the air, sending it stinging across their helpless legs. Willow made a dive for the goblins and crouched protectively over their bodies. The whip cracked once, twice. She didn't feel anything but saw a new cut begin to ooze on Pitt's exposed foot. She covered it with her hand, then Brand was hugging her, taking the blows from a whip that neither of them could feel.

"Enough," said the gravelly voice. "Let's return. The prince and his followers will be punished more effectively in the dungeons."

The whipping stopped. Brand unfolded Willow from his tight hug. She, in turn, loosened her grip on the whimpering goblins. All three had deep gashes sliced into their legs. Gently she touched the deep wounds, healing them to the wide-eyed astonishment of Pitt and his two friends. With Brand's help, she unstaked the ropes that tied the goblins to the ground, then undid the knots at their wrists. When the goblins were free, they didn't run to the phookas but cowered behind Willow and Brand.

Feeling brave and invincible, Willow faced the phooka carrying the whip. "You will not hurt them again. I forbid it."

"Kill them."

The words were said so matter-of-factly, so indifferently, that Willow thought she'd misheard them. But an instant later, Dacia and Theon lay crumpled on the ground, arrow shafts sticking out from their chests. Willow and Brand blinked. The arrows meant for them had landed in tree trunks. A roar erupted from Brand. He attacked the phookas in a fury as he had the goblin horde, the sheep-headed creatures falling as they tried uselessly to hurt him. In minutes it was over. Some had run away, but the rest lay scattered on the ground as dead as Dacia and Theon.

Willow rushed to the faeries. The arrows had gone clean

through their hearts. They were truly dead this time. There was nothing she could do.

Small green fingers curled around Dacia's arrow shaft and yanked it out. "Takes about an hour," said Pitt, "then they's good as new." Lunk and Nox tugged out Theon's arrow and tossed it in the brush. "Yep, good as new," they echoed.

Willow looked in surprise at the goblin children. "You're still here? You haven't run off with your phooka friends?"

"*Friends?*" Pitt spit on the nearest phooka, his puppy face twisting into a sour grimace. "They ain't my friends. I hates phookas!" Lunk and Nox did a little dance and found more phookas to spit on. "We hates them! Hates them! Hates them!"

Brand came to stand beside her and stared down at Dacia and Theon, his sword still dripping black phooka blood. "Let's move them over there." Willow helped him lift Dacia and Theon to a copse of trees away from the battle carnage, while the goblin children continued their spitting game, hopping from one dead phooka to another, trying to aim their spit at specific facial targets.

"Ten points! I gots an eye!"

"Twenty! I gots a nose!"

"That's *not* twenty! Their noses is half their face!"

"Is so twenty!"

A hitting, kicking, foul-mouthed skirmish exploded and Willow had to stomp over to stop it. She grabbed one goblin arm and then another and yanked two of the squabblers apart. The third was already on the ground. She kept him down with her foot. "Okay, you three. That's enough!"

"*He* started it! Twenty points for a *nose!*" Pitt tried to swing at Nox. "They's *five* points!"

"But I gots it right in his nostril!" Nox tried to swing back but Willow kept her grip firm. Lunk started squirming under her foot. "Nostrils is hard," he agreed with Nox. "Hard as eyes anyways. Should be ten points too."

Pitt was outraged. "He never said no nostrils. He said *nose!*" He wriggled and kicked in an attempt to escape Willow's grasp.

"*Brand!* Are you just going to stand there? Get over here and *help me!*" Willow glared at Brand, who was watching the whole thing with a big grin on his face. He snorted and sauntered over to Willow and the goblins. The goblins stared at the sword, which Brand casually wiped with his cloak, and immediately they stopped struggling. When the sword was clean, he plunked it into his scabbard, scowled at Pitt, Nox, and Lunk, and began to drag away a phooka body.

The goblin boys got the message. The game was over. When Willow let them go they started helping Brand with the phooka bodies, all the while keeping a cautious distance between him and them. They still weren't sure what Brand was, and why he could fight goblins and phookas and not get hurt. Willow heard them murmuring something about spooks and demons. She bent to help them with their heavy burden and saw a white eye flick open. The boys saw it too, unceremoniously dropped the body, and looked for Brand.

"Hey, this one's still kickin'," called out Nox. "Better give 'im another stabbin'.'"

"Yeah, a good one this time."

The phooka's eyes were opened wide now, white orbs of pain and fear. Brand drew his sword, but Willow waved him back. Something compelled her to look past the horrifying sheep head, to see him with magical eyes instead of physical ones. His aura pulled at her. She recognized the feeling, had felt it with the goblin children and with Nezeral when she'd transformed him into a baby. This time she fought it. The goblins had reminded her of puppies, Nezeral of a human, but these ... these *things* with their lipless mouths and nightmare eyes repulsed her.

"What is it, Willow?" Brand's voice sounded concerned, not angry or impatient.

"I don't know," she whispered. "I feel like I ... I *have* to save it. And it scares me."

Brand knelt beside her, staring at the phooka. He didn't make fun of her or say she was dumb. Finally, he spoke. "What if it's Queen Cyrraena's gift? And it compels you to a wisdom that we cannot yet see?"

The wisdom gift. Willow hadn't thought about that. Most of the time she even forgot she had it. "Well, it does feel like I have no choice. Like no matter what something is or what it does, I can't hurt it." She looked at the phooka again and shuddered. "I *have* to help it."

Brand sighed. "My instincts say to kill it. But you are my princess and the faerie queen's champion. I will follow your command."

Brand's faith in her made Willow's heart pang. It brought a jolt of courage as well. She nodded and turned to the phooka, hands outstretched over its gaping stomach wounds. The magic inside her leaped from her fingertips and healed the torn flesh and pierced organs. She reached deeper into the phooka's aura and saw the black thorn, removed it, and then understood something she'd felt before but hadn't mentally connected. The phooka aura was the same as the goblin aura, the same as the faerie's, the same as hers.

They were all the same.

That's why she couldn't kill it. It wasn't their bodies that cried out sameness. It was their souls.

CHAPTER 21

The phooka turned baleful eyes to Willow. His gravelly voice rumbled. "What have you done, faerie?" He sat up, touching his human-looking hand to his muscled belly, then running it through the black matted straggles of his sheep beard. He had a stiff dignity to him that the goblins seemed to lack.

"She's a fixer." Pitt popped up beside Willow's knee, his helium-high voice bright and cheery. "Fixed up me an' Nox an' Lunk. Don't know why. Says she ain't gonna torture us. Guess maybe they's thinkin' on tradin'." He scrunched his little nose up at Willow. "But me fadder don't much like phookas. Says they stink. I'd leave him here iffin I was you."

"And if I were you, Prince Pitt, I would cut out my tongue so it wouldn't babble so much." The phooka stood up and pinned his baleful gaze on Pitt. "*You* don't make much of a trade either. The king has ordered you flayed upon your return."

The little goblin blanched. "Did not!" he jeered, but half-heartedly. Willow gave Pitt a reassuring pat and confronted the phooka, somehow forcing herself to look into his creepy eyes. "I won't let you hurt him," she said. Brand's sword hissed as he unsheathed it, backing up her words. The phooka looked around, saw the pile of his fallen comrades and Brand's amber blade. His sheep face was hard to read, but Willow thought he looked confused. His fingers ran through his muzzle again and then rubbed where the thick horns sprouted.

"I feel strange. As if my skull is larger." He shook his head, thrusting his horns out viciously, so that Willow had to step back to avoid being struck. "What have you done to me, faerie girl?"

"I –"

"I already *told* ya," burst out Pitt. "She's a fixer."

The sheep-man snorted, aiming a savage I'm-about-to-head-butt-you look at the goblin prince. Pitt scurried behind Brand's leg. "Ya was gutted like a fish," he crowed, "and she fixed ya up like new."

"I speak not of sword wounds." He glowered at Willow. "Am I drugged?"

"What? Ya mean the tingly head stuff?" scoffed Pitt. "We had that too. Didn't we fellas?" The other two goblins nodded from their hiding spot behind a rock. "Goes away after a bit."

The unblinking phooka continued to bore holes through Willow. She decided they all needed to hear the truth. "You had a ... a thorn in your heart. All of you did. Not a real one but a magical one that ... that blocked things. I removed them."

"Thorns? That blocked things?" The phooka appeared mystified. "Blocked things like what?"

"I'm, uh, not exactly sure, but I'm guessing, um – good."

"Good?"

"Yeah, you know, things like kindness ... compassion ... um, love." Willow ignored the phooka's skeptical grunt. "No, it's true. The thorn's been blocking half your feelings. Half your thought processes. That's why, I guess, your heads feel bigger. They're running on full now."

The phooka gave another skeptical grunt. He turned his gaze to Brand and the amber sword. "I sense no magic in you, faerie. Yet you stand there unharmed and have slain a battery of phooka soldiers. How is this possible?"

Pitt yanked on Brand's cloak. "Yeah. What goes on with ya? They's never sent us faeries before that couldn't be killed."

"I'm not a faerie. I am human."

"What's a human?"

Brand and the phooka regarded each other, both ignoring Pitt's question. Finally the phooka nodded. "You are protected, then, by the ancient Compact. We cannot harm you. And your healer, she is human as well?"

"Yes."

"What happens next? Are we your prisoners?"

"I don't know." Brand turned to Willow for direction. She shrugged, not knowing what to do with a phooka anymore than Brand did. He decided on his own. "You are free to go. Tell your goblin king that we come and wish to treat with him."

"And the children?"

Brand looked down at Pitt, who suddenly clung to his leg. "You are free to go as well," he said, trying to pry the goblin's fingers from his pant legs.

"No," cried Pitt with a panicky wobble in his voice. He

pushed Brand's hand away. "Me and the fellas'll stay." He gave the phooka a defiant scowl. "Tell Fadder we's takin' 'em to the donjon ourselves."

"Dungeon?" echoed Willow, alarmed.

"No, *don*jon," said Brand. "It's another word for keep or fortress. The goblin proposes to lead us to his stronghold."

The phooka's sheep mouth turned up into something like a mocking smile. He bowed to Brand and Pitt, then disappeared without a word into the thick foliage. Pitt strutted around the campsite, all cocky now like he was suddenly their new leader. "Them faeries'll be wakin' up soon. I thinks we should just sit tight till they do. Maybe go on a search fer somethin' decent to eat." He clouted Lunk and Nox's heads. "C'mon, ya lumps! Let's find us some juicy caterpillars or a nest o' bird eggs or somethin', cuz them biscuits were worse'n eatin' dirt." Lunk and Nox scurried after Pitt, who tromped from the campsite, kicking phooka bodies as he went.

"Winsome little lads, aren't they?" remarked Brand dryly.

Willow chuckled. "Yeah, bunch of real charmers." Her good humor, though, melted away as she stared at the bloodied remains of their attackers. The sick revulsion she felt must have shown on her face. Brand slipped an arm round her shoulder. "Are you well? You look pale." His hand tucked loose curls behind her ear. Lingered in her hair. Brand's way, she knew, of showing he was sorry about how he'd acted over Theon's kiss. The small show of affection almost undid Willow. She choked back tears and hugged Brand tight. She was so glad he was here.

So glad he'd defied the faerie queen to be with her.

"Milady?" Brand sounded confused. "Do you grieve for these ... these monsters?"

"I don't know," sniffed Willow. "I just hate all this blood and killing. *I hate it!*"

Brand nodded. "It's natural for a healing mage to abhor killing, but when it's self-defense ..." His words trailed off in a reproving silence.

"Is it, though? Self-defense?" Willow pulled away from Brand and took his hand. She led him among the dead phooka, through the trees and brush to the glade where they'd placed the goblin bodies the night before. Flies buzzed around the tiny corpses. A terrible smell wafted on dank breezes. Strangely, the desolate scene made Willow think of books she'd read. Fantasy books where humans were always heroes and monsters always slaughtered. No one ever mourned a monster. She swallowed and started breathing through her mouth. "They're still here, Brand. They don't rejuvenate."

He squinted at the goblins, not sure of her point.

"Don't you see?" she cried, grabbing his arm. "They kill us, we live. We kill them, they *die*. How is that self-defense?"

Brand rounded on her, brow knitted. "What would you have me do? Sit back? Let the faeries suffer, while *we* remain uninjured?"

"Yes. *No!* I don't know." Willow sighed. She turned from the sight of the dead goblins and Brand's brutal logic. "It doesn't seem fair, is all. I mean, basically, they're in this Game against their will, they're made to act a certain way, and then they're killed for it. I just don't want you to hurt them anymore."

"Even if they attack us first?"

She nodded. Brand looked at her skeptically. "I am a knight, Your Highness, not a priest." He whipped his sword from its scabbard and pointed it at the goblin corpses. "It's my sacred duty to defend and protect. It's *who* I am! You go too far when you ask me to relinquish this task." The sword scraped back into the scabbard, and he strode from Willow, hiding his hurt with a scowl.

She watched him go. What had happened to his respect for her wisdom gift? His great faith? Her eyes smarted with tears. Guess it only went as far as a wounded pride would let it. Deliberately, she unbuckled the belt of her scabbard. She took it and the sword it contained and laid them both by a small goblin hand. As far as she was concerned, she wouldn't use them anyway.

Back at the camp, Brand crouched by Dacia and Theon's prone bodies. He stared at their wounds, taking no notice of Willow's return. She sat beside him. Touched his hand. "I won't order you not to fight," she said softly. Still no response. Just mulish silence.

An apology edged at the tip of her tongue but didn't come out. She was sorry Brand was upset. She was not sorry for what she had said. Willow's hand drifted from Brand's. Killing something that couldn't kill you sure seemed like murder to her. But maybe with his archaic Mistolearian logic Brand couldn't see that.

"When you ... when you see an aura," Brand said, "what is it like? What do you *see*?" He took Willow's hand back and captured her in his dark stare. "My family only has latent magic. No one wields spells – only swords. Do you see something in these faeries and creatures that I do not?"

"I –" How could she explain it? It wasn't really something she could see with her eyes but something she could feel. "It's like – I don't know, Brand. It's like their auras are outlines of who they are. I don't see the outlines with my eyes, but I can see them in my mind. And – well, their auras look just like ours. So to me, it's like I'm hurting myself or someone like myself if I harm them. It just feels *wrong*."

Brand nodded. "I think I understand." He squeezed her fingers. "I will do as you wish. I will try not to kill in this Game." He folded her into a hug and whispered, "But I am still your knight. Your protection will always be my utmost concern."

"I know." Willow hugged him back, glad he didn't think she was a fool.

Brand broke their embrace and nudged her arm. "Look." A glow began to creep over Dacia and Theon. It shrouded the faeries in eerie light, then flashed a starry, eye-blinking glare that healed their wounds and left their clothing clean and mended. Theon propped himself up on his elbows. "So what did we miss? Nothing too exciting, I hope."

Dacia groaned and climbed to her feet. "Really, Theon, spare us your clever wit." She surveyed the campsite with a sharp gaze.

"The phookas then," she said to Brand, "you defeated them?"

"Aye. As with the goblins, I was immune to their weapons." He rose to his feet and shouldered his rucksack.

Willow rose to her feet too. She'd decided to tell the faeries about her newfound decision not to fight, when Pitt, Lunk, and Nox came racing into the camp.

"*Run!*" shrieked Pitt. "He's loosed the host on us! Fadder's loosed the host!" The goblin children shot past like bullets, leaving Willow, Brand, and the faeries gaping at the quivering gap they'd left in the foliage. Before anyone could move, the campsite echoed with screaming howls and crackling branches. An uncanny wind whipped up out of nowhere. The already dim light faded to darkness, then a macabre, snaking line of flying creatures exploded from the trees, their leathery bat wings whirring and rasping, their fanged mouths slavering and gnashing. Willow's heart froze in her chest. She tried to scream but found her voice frozen as well. Brand, Dacia, and Theon had their swords out. Willow reached for hers. Too late, she remembered her impulsive gesture of remorse. Clawed hands grabbed her cloak, lifted her choking and kicking into the air. More cruel fingers dug into her arms, into her legs, flew her high above the trees into an overcast sky far away from Brand, Dacia, and Theon.

CHAPTER 22

Willow blinked away aura light as horror engulfed her anew. *Black*. The host beings that grasped her had pure *black* auras! She squeezed her eyes, trying to deny what she had felt, trying to hide from the knowledge of what these creatures were, but in the dark of her mind she again saw the swirling black void of their souls. No thorns to pull this time. The host were true demons. Immortal. Immoral. Immune to reason.

Hands slipped from her legs, which suddenly dropped and dangled. Willow gasped, her eyes flying open. Insane giggles erupted all around her. The hands clutching her arms started to let go, then grabbed tight again. They were playing with her. Trying to make her think they would drop her. Willow heard a sob. Realized it was hers and clenched her eyes tight again. She couldn't deal with this. Couldn't deal any longer with monsters and fighting and bloody death. She started to scream. It blocked the sounds of laughter, the nightmarish images of forked tails and cloven feet, of naked bodies, hairless and insect-like in their thinness. She kept screaming uncontrollably. Pointed ears, pointed teeth, wings pulsing with veins, all ran together in her madness.

A sharp dive jolted Willow back to reality, made her open her eyes, changed her screams to one distended wail as she and the host plunged into darkness. Her feet buckled as she hit the ground, her screams and the wind knocked from her. She lay unmoving, trying to catch her breath. Heard other thuds. Dacia, Brand, then Theon sprawled beside her, the three goblin children landing on top of them. The host swooped up to a cavernous ceiling, dove low again, then disappeared down an unlit tunnel in a snaky, howling line.

Pitt, Nox, and Lunk scrambled to their feet and disappeared like shadows into a crowd of onlookers. Willow panted for breath. Her eyes widened. Around them goblins of all shapes and sizes crammed the cave chamber. They loomed from boulders, peered from cracks and alcoves, and even dangled from chains on the ceiling, their eerie torch-lit faces filled with hideous excitement.

Before she and Brand and the faeries could move, red-capped goblins swarmed over them, holding them spread-eagled and helpless. The goblins snatched their bags and weapons then cuffed their wrists in iron shackles. Willow whimpered as goblins poked at her, enjoying her terror. Brand kicked at them with his feet. Theon and Dacia tried to defend themselves as well, but their kicks were slow and weak. Iron from the shackles had already begun to leech their strength away.

"*Enough!*" roared a harsh voice. The red-capped goblins scurried back to their places. Willow threw a fearful glance behind her to where the voice had come from. A stone dais supported a rickety throne. A creature in a spiky black crown leered at her, his jaw protruding so far out that fanged teeth jutted over his upper lip. Willow shuddered, color rushing from her face.

The goblin king was revoltingly ugly with his bulging black eyes, hooked, warty nose, and matted, gray mop of hair. He sniffed at them, curling out his hairy nostrils as though he smelled something foul. "Humans," he grunted. "So 'tis true." He sprang up, his short legs surprisingly agile, and pointed a clawed finger at Willow and Brand. "Tryin' ta fool ol' Gobby, are ya?" His menacing glare fell on Dacia and Theon's pale faces. "And two faeries with no powers. What's the Unseelie Court playin' at now? Is it me birthday?" A gargoylish grin disfigured him even further. "Or is you two payin' a price for a lost bet or some vain lord's dare?"

The faeries didn't answer. The goblin king strutted between them, grabbed their silver hair, and yanked them to their knees. "Been a long time since I 'ad me some faeries 'ere," he rasped. "Ya'd better speak when ye're spoken to."

"We ... we're being punished," said Theon weakly, "for ... for consorting with humans."

The king's shaggy brows drew together. "Punished, is it? Then why's they here?" He jerked the faeries' heads in Willow and Brand's direction. "I can't harm so much as a hair on their heads with the Compact still in force. What's I supposed to do with 'em? Invite 'em to dinner?" A cacophony of laughter burst out among the goblin crowd. "Too bad we couldn't *eat* 'em for dinner!" someone yelled out. "Aye! Nothin' like a good piece of human thigh meat!"

"Well?" The king tightened his grip on Dacia and Theon's hair, then shook them like rag dolls.

"Stop!" Dacia cried out. "We don't know! We don't know!"

"She's right!" Willow found her voice. "Stop it! They didn't even believe in the Compact." She started to stand but was forced to her knees by a red-capped goblin who held her there with his pinching fingers. "It's not their fault," she tried again. "Their father did this. *He* put us here."

"Father, is it?" The goblin king snorted and pulled Dacia's face close to his. "And who be yer father, faerie girlie? And don't lie neither."

"Jarlath," Dacia whispered. "Jarlath Thornheart."

The goblin king let go of Dacia and Theon's hair and stood stock-still, ignoring the clambering noise around him. *Who did she say? Who's 'er father? Jarlath. Jarlath Thornheart.* The hissing sounds of the faerie king's name traveled through the room like wildfire, leaping from goblin to goblin until the name crescendoed into an eerie bedlam. Ol' Gobby roared for quiet but didn't get any until he sent his red-capped guards into the audience to smash a few mouths shut.

"So he's one of the ten, eh?" The king still leered at the faeries but had lost some of his bravado.

"Th-the ten?" stammered Theon.

"Aye, the ten traitorous Unseelie kings that duped us all – their own loyal servants – into this ruddy hell of a Game spell.

One of *those* ten cur rotters!"

"But you *do* tend to get duped a lot, don't you, King Gobb?"

"What's that?" The goblin king turned his attention back to Dacia, his left eye twitching psychotically.

"I said you get duped a lot."

Willow blinked at Dacia. What was the faerie girl *doing*? Goading the goblin king!

"Wasn't it *you*, after all, the Seelies duped into signing the Compact in the first place, thus rendering your so-called *loyal* services to us useless? No wonder you were sent here. I'm just surprised you're still king." An ominous silence struck the crowd. Dacia had her cold faerie-face on, but Willow could see the strain of holding it there in the tightness around her lips. "Maybe the goblins need a new leader!" she cried. "One to take you back to the Unseelie Court!" This time the uproar became a ruckus. Goblins surged over the stone platform, shouts of *Unseelie Court! Unseelie Court!* and *Down with ol' Gobby!* spitting from their fangs. The goblin king wasn't fazed. He nodded and hundreds of red-capped guards hurled themselves into the crowd, thumping and pounding with clubs until things were quiet again.

"This is some new Game, isn't it?" he said. "A test maybe." He looked perplexed, frowning at Dacia's unexpected boldness. He fingered a strand of her hair and sniffed at it thoughtfully. "Faerie kings is always findin' ways to test ol' Gobby. But they's never sent me a princess before. No humans neither." Silver hair drifted like gossamer threads from his fingerclaws. A new realization dawned in his bulging eyes. He spun round to Willow and Brand. "The realms are supposed to be separate!" he roared. "This must be a trick!" Immediately a sword was in his hand. He raised it and came at Willow with murder in his eyes. She squeaked out a scream but before the sword could reach her, Brand pushed aside her guard and flung himself over her.

The crowd cheered as King Gobb uselessly slashed the sword over and over again through Brand's back. He gave up after about the twelfth stroke and ordered Brand torn off Willow instead. He grabbed a hank of her hair and sniffed it like he'd sniffed Dacia's. Wonder replaced his crazed anger. He hauled Willow to her feet and thrust her forward like a prize trophy. "Wait, me fiends and monsters! Look! Humans and faeries *together*! Maybe the realms be combined again. Maybe they needs us again! Needs ol' Gobby's goblin horde!"

Thunderous jubilation roared to the ceiling tops. King Gobb hair-dragged Willow back and forth across the stage, his cry one of triumph. Finally, he thrust her to a guard. "Quick," he ordered. "Find 'em a cell. Gut anyone who tries to stop ya." Willow, Brand, Dacia, and Theon were hustled behind the platform. Guards moved a boulder and pushed them into a cramped tunnel, where they had to duck to keep from hitting their heads. A few twists and turns and the tunnel opened into a large corridor lined with closed wooden doors. The guards unshackled them and shoved them roughly into an unlit room.

At first Willow saw only darkness but after a moment made out a large crack under the cell door that let in light. Her eyes soon adjusted to the dimness. Stone outlines of a cave room came into view, along with Brand's inky silhouette as it felt around the walls. He must be looking for an escape route, she thought. Dacia and Theon leaned against a stone wall. Willow squinted at them. She'd never seen faeries in the dark before. They glowed. But in a strange way, like photo negatives.

"Well, sister." Theon turned to Dacia, his eyes and lips gleaming silver against the new velvety darkness of his skin. "I see now why you are the better Game player." He shook his head, chuckling. "Making them think we're here to liberate them. Stroke of brilliance. Pure brilliance. Why, you practically deposed the goblin king! You know, if we keep playing like this, we may end up with only the one death. Some sort of Gauntlet record, I'm sure."

Willow felt nauseated. She heaved herself to her knees and retched noisily in the corner. Brand came to her side, gently held back her hair while she puked until there was nothing left inside to puke up. She collapsed into Brand's lap, weak and trembling, her mind consumed with horrible images of white-dotted eye-blacks, dead goblin children, and whirring, pulsing demon wings. "I can't do this anymore," she whispered. "I just can't." Maybe it was only a game to the faeries, a knightly quest to Brand, but to her it was all too *real*. She wished there was a bed around, so she could hide under it.

The faerie twins knelt beside her. "Are you sick?" Theon's fingers brushed a tear-stained cheek. Willow shook her head. Dacia's silver eyes bore into hers. "No," Dacia said softly. "She isn't ill, Theon. She's sick of heart."

Brand's arms tightened around Willow. "Leave her be," he ordered. "She will be well in a moment."

Would she, though? Willow wasn't so sure. She watched the faeries lean back on the stone walls, still weary from the effects of the iron shackles. Her mind again spun with images. Dacia, ghostly in the moonlight on that first night Willow had seen her through the cage bars. Her face always a mask. Theon with his human smiles. His sarcasm. The urgent touch of his lips. *What did they want from her? Why were they even here?*

Brand stroked her hair, whispered in her ear. "We were not plucked up till the tail end of the demon chain. I thought ... I thought when they first took you, you were lost to me. It was as black a moment as the one that entombed me in a chess piece." He pressed her head to his chest. "Forgive me for doubting you with Theon. For ... for treating you as a lackwit when you forbade the killing of goblins." A smile twitched his lips. "Don't mistake me, though. I am *still* unsure about this queer ban on goblin killing. But I am trying to understand it."

Willow surprised herself by returning his smile. Leave it to Brand to admit to being a jerk just when she needed to be shocked out of a nervous breakdown. She snuggled into his shoulder, glad to be reminded of the normal stuff, like fights and boyfriends and making up. He rested his chin on the top of her head. A gesture that felt so natural. That made her feel safe. A new yearning filled her. She thought of Mistolear and her family. She missed her mom and dad and little Nezzie, and wondered if

Diantha knew yet that she was gone. Hoped not. Hoped her mom was safely oblivious in Keldoran and not any sicker. Hoped Gemma and Malvin would forgive her and Brand for leaving them behind. Even hoped her grandmother would have some good arguments for her when she got back home.

Home. Willow blinked. It had just occurred to her that home was Mistolear. Not Earth. She was homesick for Mistolear! Her head popped up from Brand's chest. She felt strangely euphoric. Like things might be okay after all. "You know, I think I'd kiss you," she said, "if my breath wasn't all barfy."

"Barfy?"

"Pukey. Vomitous."

"Oh." Brand smiled, lifted her chin. "I care not." He moved to kiss her, but Willow jerked her head away. "Just a sec," she said. No way she was kissing him with gross puke breath. She magicked the sour saliva in her mouth and made it taste like chocolate mint, then snuggled into him. His lips pressed against hers. Softly at first and then harder. Lips that wanted something. That weren't chaste or honorable. Willow answered them. This was the Brand she yearned for. The real one. Not the knight one.

"You know that I ... I love you, don't you?" he whispered brokenly. "Since that day I first saw you alone in your chambers and gave you my fealty pledge." Willow nodded. "I know." She tried to say it back to him but the words stuck in her throat. "I ... I ..."

"Are you two quite finished?" drawled Theon. "Seems to me we should be discussing strategies, not trying to copulate."

His words were like cold water. Brand stiffened, practically tossing Willow from his arms. "Not that it's your business, but I was comforting the princess."

"*Comforting?* Is that what they call it now?"

Willow burned with embarrassment. She'd forgotten about Theon and Dacia.

"Do you sully my lady's good name, faerie?"

"No. I think you were doing a good enough job of sullying it yourself."

In a fury, Brand rose to his feet. Dacia stepped in front of him. "He's just teasing you, Brand. Ignore him."

"Yes. No hard feelings, eh?" Theon grinned at Brand, his white teeth bright against his glowing face. Willow stared. Despite the jokes, Theon seemed angry. As though he was – jealous?

Sullenly, Brand sat back down and clasped her hand again. He looked up at Dacia. "So what do we do now? Await the goblin king's pleasure?"

Dacia ignored his sarcasm. "His pleasure," she said, settling herself back on the floor, "may not be what it once was. King Gobb hopes the realms are combined again and that maybe we are here to liberate him. Although, I'm sure once he has time to think about it, he'll realize that even if this were true and the realms *were* once more combined, he and his goblins would mean little to the Unseelie Court with the Compact still in force. But if we convince him that it can be broken –" She swallowed. "Maybe then he won't torture us. Me and Theon, I mean."

Willow barely heard Dacia. Theon had her glued in his

sights, his flaming eyes boring a hole into her. He *was* angry. She just didn't understand why. Could he possibly have been serious about wanting a relationship with her? Or an *alliance*? She dropped her gaze to where Brand's hand held hers securely. Forget Theon. The guy had drugged her for pete's sake! He had no right to act all hurt and angry now, like she'd *betrayed* him or something.

"Don't you think so, Willow?"

"What?" Willow looked back up. She'd been lost in thought, not listening to Dacia.

The faerie girl repeated her question. "The black thorns. Don't you think their removal could convince the goblin king that the Compact had been lifted?"

"I ... well –"

Their cell door suddenly swung open, bright torchlight making them all shield their eyes. Pitt strutted in, followed by Lunk and Nox. "Me fadder sent me to fetch ya." He pointed at Willow. "Human girlie with the fox hair."

"Princess Willow," provided Brand dryly.

"Aye. Her. She's ta come with us." Pitt's puppy nose wrinkled in disgust. "*Gor!* What's the stink? Someone blow grub in here?"

Blow grub. That was a new one. Willow rose gingerly to her feet, Brand rising with her. The faeries started to stand as well but Pitt stopped them. "Nah. The rest of yas may as well stay on yer rumps. Da only wants the human girlie." He strode over to Willow, grinning up at her. "Told 'im all about how ya fixed me and the fellas and even Raal the phooka. Only clouted me ear once, he did, and said maybe I'm only *half* as stupid as he thought." Pitt's chest swelled with pride. "Sent me and the fellas to guard ya. C'mon. He's all set out in his talkin' chambers." He took Willow's hand and started to tug but Brand moved to follow.

Pitt gave him a puzzled look. "You can't come. I told ya, Fadder only wants her."

"I am Sir Brand Lackwulf, *knight* to Her Highness. Where she goes, I go."

"Aw, c'mon. Don't make me get them." Pitt glanced over his shoulder. Two hulking lumps taller than the doorway stood outside it. "They's pretty mean. And, well ..." Pitt leaned in close to Brand, "stupid too. Don't want yas ta get hurt. 'Sides, Fadder's only gonna talk to her. She'll be back afore ya kin even miss her."

"It's okay, Brand." Willow gave his hand a squeeze. "I think I should go with them." Thoughts of the bestial goblin king were making her heart race alarmingly, but she really didn't want anyone to tangle with whatever waited outside their cell.

Dacia attempted to mouth instructions. It looked like *remember the compass*. Willow squinted at her. "Huh?" Pitt hustled her past the faerie girl, though, before Dacia could try again. *Remember the compass? Remember the* ... not compass – Compact. Dacia must have been saying *remember the Compact*.

CHAPTER 23

*O*nce outside their cell, the door slammed shut. Willow caught a glimpse of meaty, oversized hands, and the blobby outline of an enormous head that stretched up into the shadows of the ceiling. Pitt hurried her along. "Them trolls look hungry. Don't want 'em gettin' any ideas."

"What?" Willow stopped walking, causing Lunk and Nox to bump into her. If Pitt thought she'd leave Brand and the faeries with a couple of hungry trolls, he had another thing coming.

Pitt and his buddies started to giggle. Lunk grabbed one hand, Pitt the other, and Nox started pushing her from behind. "I's just jokin' with ya," snorted Pitt. "Trolls is always hungry. But they likes their grub *cooked*, not raw."

Was that supposed to make her feel better? Reluctantly, Willow let the goblin children lead her down the passageway. Somehow she didn't think they meant to harm anyone. The goblin king on the other hand – she wasn't too sure about him.

The cave tunnel turned sharply and became high-ceilinged and wide. Instead of torches, wrought iron lamps hung from chains attached to the ceiling, casting light that shivered eerily over the gargoyle faces carved into the walls. A gate loomed at the end of the tunnel like a square of iron lace. Fire burned on braziers, winking red-eyed light through the gate holes. Willow trembled. How many fantasy books had a tunnel scene like this? Almost made her feel like she'd been here before. But books didn't *smell* like rotting fungus. You didn't *hear* spooky crackling or weird echoes. You didn't *feel* damp air skitter over your skin.

"You okay?" Pitt looked up at her, his eyes blinking curiously. "Ye're twitchin' like a rat's nose and yer hand's all sweaty. Ye're not gonna blow grub, are ya?"

Willow gave a half-hysterical laugh. Pitt's way with words lessened her tension. "No. I think I blew enough of it back in the cell. But, you know, thanks for asking."

Pitt nodded, took her hand back. "Ye're scared then, ain't cha?"

Willow stared at his green fingers. Was Pitt *concerned* for her? She felt a tiny hope-seed begin to grow. Maybe Dacia'd been wrong. Maybe a thornless heart could learn to feel. It just needed time. "Yeah, I'm scared. Your dad's a bit ... um ..."

"Blood-freezin'," supplied Lunk.

"A goon bully," added Nox.

"Well, I was going to say intimidating." Willow grinned. "But, yeah, I guess he's those things too."

Pitt stopped walking. "Ya needs to whizzle or anythin'? I always does that afore I sees him."

"Whizzle?"

"Yeah. You know, whizzle, piddle, pee."

The word "pee" she recognized. "Uh, no that's okay. Think

I'll make it till later."

"Well, I'm goin' ta."

"Me too."

"Me too."

The goblin boys turned to the wall and peed three decorative streams onto the stone. The smell of urine mixed with the smell of rotting fungus. *Nice*, Willow thought, rolling her eyes. But still, it had been kind of thoughtful of Pitt to ask. The boys began fighting over whose pee had made the biggest mark. She rolled her eyes again and started walking down the passageway without them.

"Hey, wait for us!" cried Pitt. He and Lunk and Nox scurried to catch up. At the end of the corridor, red-capped goblin guards swung open the gate from the other side. The boys, each clinging to an edge of her cloak, ushered Willow in. She stopped to look around. It was like being inside a snow globe, the room was so round and smooth.

"Come in. Come in. Don't be 'fraid of ol' Gobby."

Willow peered at King Gobb. He sat on a fur-covered throne, waving her and the boys forward, the fiery braziers lighting him devilishly. She began to sweat. Pitt, Lunk, and Nox pushed her toward the goblin king.

"So, me boy here tells me ye're a fixer. Fixed him an' his chums and even ol' Raal up." A phooka stepped out from behind a brazier and nodded at Willow.

"Yeah, Fadder, look." Pitt stuck out his round green tummy. "Had me a gut wound, right here. Now I don'ts even have a scar." Lunk and Nox rolled up their shirts and sleeves to display their smooth skin too. The king didn't even glance at them. "So me question," he said, pinning Willow with black, gleaming eyes, "is *why*? Why would ya fix 'em and not leave 'em to die with the others?"

Good question. Willow wished she knew the answer to it herself. "I ... I grew up on Earth," she stammered. "I've ... I've never killed anyone before. I –"

"Earth, is it?" The goblin king pressed back into his furry throne. "I remembers the Earthworld. Human. Faerie. Goblin folk. We all lived together then. Till the faeries ruined it, that is, with their tricks and warrin'." He spit next to Willow's boot and squinted at her. "Been o'er a thousand years since those days, girlie. Tell me the truth, now. Be the realms combined again?"

"I ... well ..." Willow made a face. The king's bulldog teeth had left gross bumpy wrinkles on his top lip. She noticed his clawed grip tightening on the armrests. "No. N-not yet," she said quickly. Wait. Oh shoot! Hadn't Dacia *wanted* him to believe they were combined? *Crap!*

King Gobb's fangs pressed deep into his lip ruts. Guess he wasn't too happy with her answer either. He shifted the subject back to healing. "And what's this I hears about black thorns stickin' like pins in our hearts? Ya tryin' to fool us into some tricky spell?"

In answer Willow unfocused her gaze, saw the foggy halo of King Gobb's aura. Her rosy hope that the goblins could reform had made her brave. If she could remove the king's thorn maybe she could remove them from all the goblins.

"'Ere now! Stop it. Ya ain't touchin' me with that zombie look on yer face."

Willow blinked. Pitt pushed against her leg. The phooka grabbed her arm.

"Don't be takin' liberties with me," growled the king. "Maybe I can't pain ya proper cuz o' the Compact. But there's other ways ta hurt. Ways that don't cut the skin." His face lunged close to Willow's. "Ya gettin' my drift, girlie?"

His breath was a hot miasma of moldy stench. Willow felt her knees go weak. The demon host. The guards. It had just hit her. *How* had they captured her and Brand? How had they been able to put them in a prison cell? "W-what do you mean?" she stammered. "I – I don't understand."

"As long as there's no murder in me heart and I'm not tryin' ta bodily harm ya, I can pretty much do with ya what I will. The Compact won't interfere."

"But ... but ..." That didn't sound very good. Willow tried to take a step backwards but found Lunk and Nox blocking her from behind. Pitt stared up at her, an idea forming in his eyes.

"Hey, Fadder! When we plays with the faeries, ya can use 'er as yer fixer. That way ya won't hafta wait the whole hour for them to wake up again."

Lunk and Nox agreed.

"Yep, she's real quick."

"*Real* quick."

Willow's head bobbed from goblin to goblin, horror

replacing shock. Oh no. No, no, no. This was not good. She had to think of something and fast. No way was she being used as an aid for torture. "I have been sent here to –" *Darn!* Her words came out in a squeak. What she needed to do was mimic Dacia. Sound cool and confident. She cleared her throat. "You wish to escape this Game? To be free of the Compact?" Her princess voice echoed throughout the chamber. "Then let me remove the thorn. Let me free you from your bondage." After the way the goblin boys had just acted, she wasn't sure anymore that removing the thorn really changed anything. But maybe it would buy Dacia and Theon some time before ... before ... Her mind slammed closed at the vile possibilities.

"Here, take me knife." King Gobb handed a sharp blade to Raal. "Stab her."

For a moment the phooka hesitated. Willow tried to escape but the goblin boys held her fast. In a lightning strike the knife slashed through her stomach. Willow cried out. Peered down. But nothing had happened.

"Looks like *he's* not free from the Compact." King Gobb thrummed a finger along his armrest. "Bite her boys."

Small feral teeth glinted in the firelight. Pitt went first, opening wide and trying to take a chunk out of her leg. Lunk and Nox followed suit. But just like before, nothing happened. It *looked* like they were chowing down on her calves. But it was like an illusion. Like she was a ghost and their teeth were going right through her.

The king scowled. "Nope. They's not free of it neither. Any

other lies ya wish to tell me?"

Willow shook Lunk – who was still chewing away – off her leg. "I ... um –" Suddenly an idea flashed in her mind. "The Compact will not be lifted," she cried, "till every thorn is pulled. Till every goblin is made free from their bondage." Maybe a bit evangelistic, but hey, if it worked, it worked.

"And why would ya be doin' that for us, now? What's in it for *you*? For all I know them thorns is keepin' us safe from some flippin' faerie spell or other."

Willow shook her head. She had to make him understand. "No, don't you see. The thorns *are* the faerie spell. They put them in you ages ago to make you their servants, to *bind* you to them so you didn't have any choices."

King Gobb snorted. He nodded to Raal. "What about it? Ya feels like ya got any choices?"

Raal's eye-whites reflected the flames, his dour sheep face still as a statue. "I do not know about choices, Your Majesty, but I do feel different."

"How so?"

The phooka's nose quivered. "She spared my life today. I came home thinking nothing of it. But when my mate and son greeted me, I felt ... *pleased*." An ear twitched spasmodically. Raal gave his horned head a furious shake.

"Pleased?" King Gobb looked puzzled. "Whatcha mean by that? Pleased like when ya guts someone with them great horns o' yers?"

"Yes, Sire. A very similar feeling."

The king squinted at Pitt. "What about you?" he growled. "Ya feel *pleased* when ya saw yer ol' fadder?"

Pitt frowned, his little brow furrowed in thought. "Nah," he said finally. "I just got squeamish."

King Gobb roared with laughter. "You boys take her outta here. Me an' Raal is gonna talk some more 'bout his new *feelin's*."

The way he said feelings, like they were something weak and namby-pamby, made Willow think Raal was in trouble. She glared at the goblin king, trying to resist Pitt and Lunk's vigorous tugging, but then Nox joined in and the three of them forced her toward the doorway. Iron gates opened and slammed behind her as the goblin children hustled her out.

"Whatcha fightin' us for?" Pitt gave her an exasperated look. "Do ya *wants* to watch a phooka scourgin'?"

"Scourging? You mean ... you mean he's going to *beat* him?"

"Yeah, he strings 'em up by their horns. Sometimes even dangles 'em over a fire."

A sharp crack, followed by a horrible puling cry, resounded through the corridor. Willow felt ill again. Raal's scream was just like a sheep's high-pitched bleat.

Pitt and the boys hurried her along the twisting corridors. The grim sounds from King Gobb's room faded, then disappeared altogether. Willow noticed the tunnels becoming narrower and the ceiling lower, until she had to stoop to go through. "Um, Pitt," she said, making the goblin boys stop. "Where are you taking me? I don't remember this passageway."

Lunk and Nox suddenly seemed to notice their new whereabouts as well. Their surprised eyes widened. "Thought we was takin' 'er back to the cell," said Nox uneasily. "What's we doin' here in the hidey-holes?"

Hidey-holes. Where had Willow heard that expression before?

"Well, well. We meets again," said a familiar gurgly voice.

Willow blinked. Out of the shadows stepped Rye Ruskin Wirt, the human-eating hobgoblin from the Hobs of Rudd.

CHAPTER 24

Rye Ruskin Wirt tossed a small jingly bag to the ground. "Ye're a good lad, Pitt. I added some extra sparklies for yer trouble. Bit of a bonus ya might say."

"Deal's off, Rye." Pitt kicked the bag back to the hobgoblin. "Fadder knows she's here. Sent the demon host after us, he did. I brung her for Sab."

"Sab?" Rye's pug face squinched into a frown. He pocketed his bag of sparklies and looked up at Willow. "Why should she get 'er? She's got no sparklies. They's *all* mine!"

"Nobody's *gettin'* her. I already tol' ya, Fadder knows she's here. I brung her ta fix Sab's foot."

The hobgoblin's eyes narrowed to a disbelieving squint. "What fer? She's the best crawler I gots." He blocked the tunnel with his skinny arms. "I don't know what ye're on about, Prince Pitt. But I ain't lettin' ya inta me hidey-holes if ye're gonna be messin' around with me crawlers."

Pitt shoved Rye, who was no taller than the goblin boy, to the floor. "That's right. It's *Prince* Pitt, and don't *you* be forgettin' it. If I wants to go in yer hidey-holes, I'll go in yer hidey-holes. Now bring me to Sab. Or I'll tell Fadder 'bout yer little games."

The hobgoblin scrambled to his goat hooves, nodding and bowing, eyes wide with fear. "Yes, me prince. Sorry. Sorry. I'll take ya to 'er right away. Right away." He click-clacked down the tunnel, still mumbling *right away, right away.*

"Pitt, what's going on?" hissed Willow.

"I'll tells ya when we gets there. We gots to keep up, though, okay?"

Willow would've stopped, made the goblin prince explain things to her, but Rye Ruskin Wirt was going fast and the tunnel they were in had suddenly opened up to a maze of holes and fissures. Losing the hobgoblin now was obviously not a good idea.

Things slowed when they had to crawl through a low passageway. Crawling for the goblins, though, of course, meant belly-slithering for Willow. She wormed forward on her elbows. Dusty air. No light. The walls began to constrict like a stomach trying to digest her. Willow panicked. *"Pitt.* Pitt! I can't ... I can't breathe!"

"If ye're talkin', ye're breathin'. Just keep yer head. We's almost there."

Pitt's logic made sense. Willow found she could gulp in breath, and noticed Pitt's butt outlined in front of her face. Somewhere up ahead light was seeping into the tunnel. Willow relaxed. She could see a distinct gap now. Not too far. Only a few more elbow shuffles.

They slid from the gap opening into a low-ceilinged cavern.

One dim brazier fire flickered light over a rag-tag huddle of tiny creatures. Willow stared. Someone stood up. A small goblin child like Pitt. He pumped a fist into the air. "Look!" he cried. "Rye's brung us a faerie! Can we plays with her, Rye? Can we plays with her?" His other arm pumped a nubby stump. More little creatures stood. All children. All with something damaged or missing. An eye. A foot. A hand.

Rye plowed into the roiling group. "Settle down. Settle down." He knocked a few back to their bottoms. "She ain't ours. Belongs to the prince, she does. Now shut up, the lot o' ya!"

The goblin children grew sullen and quite. They stared at Pitt with scowls and bitter glares.

Shivers crept up Willow's spine. "What is this, Pitt? Where have you brought me?"

The goblin prince pointed at someone in the middle of the crowd. "That's Sab. She gots a crushed foot." His brown puppy eyes turned to Willow. "Can ya fix 'er? Can ya makes it so she don't got ta be a crawler no more?"

Were those tears in Pitt's eyes? Willow bent down on her knees and grasped Pitt by his skinny arms. "You *do* feel it, don't you? That stuff with your dad, it was just an act, wasn't it?"

Pitt struggled away from her. "Let go o' me! I don't know what ye're talkin' 'bout. I just want ya ta fix Sab's foot."

Willow hugged the affronted goblin prince before releasing him. Her hunch had to be right. Pitt was trying to do his first good deed. He scurried into the crowd, returning with a small goblin girl, who hop-walked with a crutch, dragging a leg behind her.

"This here's Willow, Sab. She's a fixer. I brung her to fix yer foot."

The little goblin girl looked up at Willow with wide, button eyes. Butterscotch hair stuck out in tangles around a pixie-doll head. Her nose twitched. Except for her little fang teeth and pointed snout, she looked like a *Dark Crystal* gelfling Muppet. Willow smiled at her. "Hi."

Sab ignored the greeting, stuck out her lame foot instead. From mid-calf to ankle there was a terrible twist that turned her foot out at a weird angle. The foot itself looked oddly flat like it'd been crushed. Willow touched the twisted bone knob. "What happened?" she asked softly.

"Pitt made me play in the rock piles." Sab's voice was an *Alvin-and-the-Chipmunks*-notch higher than a goblin boy's. She lifted her chin. "And I weren't scared neither. Even when they falled on me."

Willow glanced at Pitt. He wouldn't meet her eyes. "It was my fault," he whispered. "I broked her."

Magic gathered in Willow's fingers. She drew it there with a calm sense of rightness. It was right that Pitt felt guilty. That he had brought her here. When the magic filled her hands and plugged her fingers, Willow grasped Sab's ankle. The goblin girl flinched but didn't pull away. Willow closed her eyes, saw the crook-mended ankle bone and the shattered foot fragments. She resculpted them in her mind. Smoothed the ankle straight. Puzzle-pieced all the splinters and chips back together again.

Then she sent magic up the leg, through the midriff, and plucked the black thorn from Sab's beating heart.

A collective gasp went through the room. Willow opened her eyes. Goblin children pressed all around her, mesmerized and awed by Sab's perfect new limb. "Fix me!" someone cried. "Fix me! Fix me!" They began to tug on Willow's cloak, jump on her back, wrap their tiny arms round her legs, her neck. "*Help!*" Willow managed to squeeze out before she collapsed under the weight. This time she really couldn't breathe. She could hear Pitt, Lunk, and Nox yelling at the others, "Get off! Get off!" Then Rye Ruskin Wirt must have started to help, because little bodies began to peel off her at a tremendous rate. Finally she could breathe again. The goblin children still pressed close but left enough space for her to sit up. Rye started pushing them farther back.

"Git away, ya pack o' dogs!" he barked. "She bloody well ain't fixin' no one else. Now back to work! Break's over!" The crawlers didn't much like Rye's orders and swarmed over him, knocking him down.

"Hey!" hollered Pitt, swinging his fist around. "I brung her for Sab. *Not* you lot! Now get lost. We's leavin'."

"No. No." Little hands reached out to Willow. "Don't leave. Fix us too!"

"Pitt." Willow stopped him from shoving the boy with the nubby arm stump. "We can't just leave them here." Her face set resolutely. "I'm staying."

Pitt looked as if he were about to argue, then shifted his gaze to the injured goblin children. Willow thought she saw something pass through his eyes. Surprise first and then – understanding? "All right," he growled. "Ya can fix 'em too. But we's got to be quick afore Fadder knows ye're missin'." He grabbed the boy with the nubby arm stump and hauled him in front of Willow. "Fix up Nim, then. I'll line the rest up for ya."

"Stop!" roared the hobgoblin. "Who'll crawl in me hidey-holes? Who'll find me sparklies?"

"Shove it, Rye." A gang of goblin children held down the struggling hobgoblin and stuffed a rag into his mouth.

Willow touched the nubby arm stump, grew bone, blood, and flesh and stretched it into a hand. She made a blind eye see again and a bent back straight, pulling each and every black thorn as she went. She mended more broken bones than she could count, erased scars that would chill Frankenstein, and healed thirty-six pairs of scabby, scuffed up knees. Apparently crawling through Rye Ruskin Wirt's hidey-holes searching for sparklies was a way of life for an injured goblin child. The last creature in line was Rye himself. He had calmed down somewhat and now showed her a painful cut between his hoof and leg. She healed and de-thorned him as well.

"Been botherin' me for a long time, that has." Rye hopped from hoof to hoof. "Kept splittin' open. Good as new now, though. Good as new." He tossed Willow something from his bag of sparklies. "For yer services," he said. "For yer services."

The large green gem covered Willow's palm. She stared at it, suddenly remembering Rye's earlier words. *A bit of a bonus you might say.* What had he meant by that?

She pulled Pitt away from his healed buddies and showed him the gem. *"The deal's off.* What did that mean, Pitt? Were you going to sell me to Rye Ruskin Wirt?"

Pitt sighed and rolled his eyes. "No. O' course not. Well not since ya fixed me up anyway. Ya see, Rye were the one that tol' me 'bout ya bein' here. 'Member when we first tried to ambush ya in the woods? Well, if we hadda won and captured ya, I was supposed to bring ya to Rye without me fadder knowin' 'bout it. Course Raal blabbed everythin' so the deal was off."

"And, um ..." Willow glanced at the jaunty hobgoblin. "Exactly what kind of games does he like to play?" She remembered Pitt's threat of telling his father about Rye's games.

"Games?" Pitt squinted and followed her gaze to Rye Ruskin Wirt. A grin broke out on his face. "Oh, I sees. Ya was thinkin' I was takin' ya to a new torturer." He shook his head, snorting laughter. "Rye likes to play ... likes to play ... *pretend.*"

"Pretend?"

"Yeah. He likes to pretend he's at the faerie court. Only he makes us be the faeries and order him around. It's kinda fun. He's got this room and everythin' wheres we can dress up. Guess he wanted ya to be the faerie queen or somethin'."

Willow's mouth tweaked up at the corners. Rye came bouncing over to them with the white pinpoint of his eye gleaming. "Do ya have to leave now? Do we have time for a game? Time for a game?" The other goblin children took up the cry. "Yeah! We gots a real faerie now. She can be the queen!"

"No. No. No." Pitt gestured for quiet. "We can't stay. I's supposed to be takin' her back to her cell. Fadder finds out she's not there ..." He didn't need to finish his sentence. Their wide eyes told Willow the goblin children feared Pitt's father as much as he did.

"Well, c'mon then," said Rye. "I'll lead yas to the main tunnels."

"We's goin' too, Rye." Some of the newly healed goblin boys crowded around Rye Ruskin Wirt. "Ya can't keep us now we's all fixed. We wants to go too."

The hobgoblin started to protest, but thought better of it when he saw some of the children pick up rocks. "Well, will yas come back," he said, "if I ... if I ..." His face screwed up as if in pain. "If maybe I, um, divvy up me sparklies with ya? We could maybe play more games too." The children cheered at this new arrangement and quickly agreed. Rye then took Willow, the goblin boys, and all his crawlers back to the large passageway through which Pitt, Lunk, and Nox had brought Willow. All the crawler children ran off in different directions, and Rye headed again for his hidey-holes. "If ya gets a chance," he called over a shoulder, "come back for a game of faerie court. Ya'd make a great Queen Edrea."

Pitt didn't answer. He grabbed Willow's hand and started hurrying along the corridor. "We's got to get ya back," he panted. "Da finds out ya fixed them crawlers, he'll string us up like phookas."

Oh great. The bleating phooka scream. Just the thing she

wanted to remember. Willow felt relieved as soon as she saw the trolls still hulking outside her cell. She wanted to see Brand. Tell him about Rye and the goblin children. Tell him how Pitt and Raal had changed. Lunk lifted the bar and Nox opened the door. It was still dark inside.

"Brand? Brand?"

Pitt brought in a wall torch. He kicked Lunk's leg. "Ruddy hell!" The room was empty.

CHAPTER 25

"They ain't in here," whispered Nox, voice shaky, eyes twin circles of panic. "I'm goin' back to the hidey-holes. Yer fadder finds out she wasn't with the others, we's all troll feed for sure." Lunk's terror mirrored Nox's. "I'm goin' with ya."

"Hey, wait a minute!" ordered Pitt. Too late. Nox and Lunk bolted like scared rabbits from the cell. Pitt handed the torch to Willow. "We'll be back," he called out. "Soon as I can find 'em."

Willow started to protest, but a big hairy troll hand reached through the cell opening and slammed the door.

All alone in the dank cave, she set the torch in a wall bracket and sank wearily to the floor. *What next?* Where was Brand? And poor Dacia and Theon? What would the goblin king do to them? Her head dropped to her knees. She was tired. So tired even breathing seemed like an effort. Her eyes fell shut. The darkness behind her lids suddenly dipped and whirled, and she plunged into it, as if stepping off a cliff.

Willow gasped, her eyes popping open. The cave cell was gone. In its place twined the familiar leaves and vines of the faeries' council room ceiling. She sprang up. The Fey Council sat before her, the ten Unseelie Court kings and queens in their robes of black and the eleven Seelies in white. Like chess, thought Willow – black on one side, white on the other. Willow herself was in her royal blue gown again.

A Seelie queen spoke first. "*You* set the rules, Jarlath. I see no reason to change them now, just because your daughter and this girl have found a way to beat you."

Beat him? Willow jerked around to stare at the beautiful Seelie queen. If she and Dacia were winning the Gauntlet Game it was news to her.

"They disrupt the Balance," said a stern-faced Unseelie king. "You have your pixies, your brownies, your sprites. We have our goblins. It has always been so."

Someone snorted on the Seelie side. "Disrupt the Balance? When has that ever been a concern of yours, except when it doesn't favor you?" One of the Seelie kings leaned forward in his chair. "I say she be returned to the Game and allowed to continue."

A clamor rose from the black side. "Nay. Nay," someone shouted out. An Unseelie queen stood up. "You are a fool Oberon Foxglove! Jarlath seeks only a way to save his son from the humans. If the girl wins, the way will be lost."

"Yes," added an Unseelie king. "Let the Balance tip toward us, Oberon. If she continues to pull thorns, you must release the goblins from the Compact. I guarantee if it means the goblins can do to her what they do to us, she will pull no more thorns."

Now the clamor rose on the white side. "It's a ploy! The Compact gives the Seelies power. You don't want to save a youngling. You want to rule over *us*!"

"Release only the goblins from the Compact, then," said the Unseelie king, "not the demon host. You will still have the Balance of Power on your side. And she," he pointed an accusing finger at Willow, "will not weaken our position further by pulling more thorns."

The puzzling exchange fascinated Willow. Did the faerie courts really think she could win the Gauntlet Game? Could even shift the Balance of Power?

The Seelie king named Oberon stood up, his face as tranquil as a summer morning. "I vote *no* to releasing the goblins from the Compact." All the other Seelie kings and queens stood up as well. "No. No. No," went down their shining line until all eleven of them had spoken. The Unseelie kings and queens stood next, each uttering a curt, pointless *yes*. Eleven nos to ten yeses. The Unseelies could never win.

But a surprising thing happened next. All eyes turned to Willow. "What is your vote, human?" said King Oberon. "Do you vote yes to releasing the goblins from the Compact, or do you vote no?"

Vote? Willow blinked at the faeries, comprehension suddenly dawning. Of course, vote. She was a member of their Council now. Something she'd totally forgotten. Her eyes locked with Jarlath's. He hadn't argued one way or the other, and he smirked like a cat with cream on his whiskers. Willow squinted at him. Oh yeah, he was up to something. But what? Did he still think he could somehow win Nezeral back?

A new realization hit her full force. *Another yes would tie the vote*. Is that what Jarlath thought? That she would vote to free the goblins?

"What if I tie the vote?" she asked. "What'll that do?"

King Oberon gave her a cryptic smile. "A tie keeps everything in place. The Game and Compact will remain as they are."

Willow glanced back at Jarlath. Her vote changed nothing. So why did he still look so smug? Like he knew something the Seelie king didn't.

She took a deep breath. "I vote no," she said, keeping an eye on Jarlath's reaction. He smiled and tipped his head in her direction as though she'd done him a favor. Willow's stomach whirled. *Shoot*. Wrong choice. Next thing she knew she was back in the cave cell, Jarlath's laughter echoing in her ears.

"Willow! Where did *you* come from?"

She opened her eyes. Theon sat beside her, surprise full on his face. Brand shot from across the room to crouch at her feet and Dacia spun around from where she stood at the door.

"Are you well?" Brand squeezed her knee. "The goblin king didn't ... didn't ..."

"No. No. I'm fine."

Dacia knelt too. "You were outside the Game. What's going on?"

"Outside the Game? What do you mean?" asked Brand. "How could she be outside the Game?"

"No one just appears or disappears unless they have the

power, which *we* do not. What did Father say to you?"

Willow stared at Dacia's determined face, suddenly unsure what to say. The Council had reminded her of the true fey nature. Everything a Game. Nothing as it seemed. "He just ... he just wanted to gloat," she lied. "To make me scared."

"He did you no harm, then?" Brand looked her over, checking for himself.

"I'm fine." She swung out her arms and legs to prove it. "He didn't hurt me, okay?"

Brand still didn't appear convinced. "And what about the goblin king? Did you see him as well?"

"I did."

"And?"

"He wanted ... he wanted to know if the realms were combined."

Dacia stiffened. "What did you tell him?"

"That they weren't." The faerie girl's shoulders slumped. For a second, Willow saw her as a child huddled in the cave in the Menagerie. She cast Dacia some hope. "The goblin king asked about the black thorns too. I told him if they were all gone the Compact would be broken."

"Did he believe you?"

"I don't know." Willow sighed. She leaned against the stone wall but bounced right back up again. She hadn't asked anything about them. "No one was here when Pitt brought me back. Did you guys see the goblin king too?"

Her three companions looked confused. "We've been here

the whole time," said Theon. "You and that torch are the only things that just appeared out of nowhere."

"No doubt Father's doing." Dacia stood up. "Willow, you did well. There's a chance now that if the goblin king believed you about the thorns, he may be more hesitant to – he shall be careful in how he treats us." Her silver eyes lit up. "Plus, I really don't believe Father pulled you from the Game to gloat. More likely he fears that we've found a way to win the Game. Was it the thorns he tried to frighten you about?"

Willow only nodded. Dacia seemed sincere but so had Theon when he'd given her the mushrooms. Brand was right not to trust them. She was going to have to figure things out on her own.

A key clicking in the lock made them all turn toward the doorway. A phooka stood there, staring at them. Brand leaped to his feet, ready to fight bare-fisted if he had to.

Theon rose as well. "What do you want, *phooka*?" He said it like a swear word, contempt dripping from his voice. Willow frowned. Phookas had killed him and Dacia once already. She didn't think it wise to provoke them.

"I come to see the human healer."

Willow recognized the gravelly voice. "Raal?" She climbed to her feet. *What could he want?*

Raal nodded. Willow caught a motion behind him. Something small peered out from around his thighs. Raal's hand went down and pushed the creature forward. "My son, Tark. And my mate," he reached back and pulled someone else from the shadowed hallway, "Maela."

Willow squinted at Raal's family. They looked exactly like him but shorter with no jutting horns, and Maela wore a dress. They came inside the cell and Raal closed the door. Willow noticed his stiff movements. Remembered what had happened to him. She felt uneasy, hearing his screams again in her head.

"I wish you to remove their thorns."

Brand and Theon both relaxed. Dacia even smiled. Willow's stomach sank. She remembered Jarlath's laughter. His calm acceptance of the vote. Somehow pulling the thorns benefited him. But what could she do now? She couldn't refuse to pull them. Not after she'd made up that whole thorn story for Dacia. Maybe she could just pretend to remove them. She stepped toward Raal.

The little phooka boy scrambled back behind his father. "Don't like her. Don't want my thorn removed." An eye-white peeped out fearfully. "Don't let her hurt me, Da." Raal's mate seemed scared too, cowering next to her son. Raal pushed them both forward. "Do not be afraid. You will feel no pain." Maela scowled at him. "No pain *now* maybe. But if the king hears of this, we will be scourged as you were." The boy gave a thin cry and clung to his father's leg.

"Um, Raal, are you sure you want me to do this?" Willow stayed put, ignoring Dacia's frown. Maybe she wouldn't have to pretend. If everyone heard what happened to Raal, no one else would want their thorns pulled either.

Raal knelt down to talk to his son. Willow could see the

terrible criss-crossing gashes that striped his back. "These thorns are ... are wrong, my son. They keep our minds in tiny spaces and enslave us to the goblin king. I would have you free of it." He looked up at his mate. "And you as well." Maela's eyes glowed in fear. Willow could almost see the thought bubble outside her head. *Who is this phooka?* Then fear switched to anger and her eyes turned to Willow. The thought bubble changed too. *And what have you done to him?*

Raal stood back up but the sight of his whip marks still burned in Willow's brain. Her magic instinctively began to gather. She would heal him at least. "Raal, your back. Let me –"

"No." The phooka shook his head, his great horns swinging in firm resolve. "The king would know that I have been here. I want them safe." He rested a hand on his son's black lamb head. "I want them free."

The magic shone white in her fingers now. Willow knew she couldn't just pretend to pull the thorns. Raal was real. Not just some monster, but a *person* risking death to save his family. She couldn't deceive him. Her hand touched the phooka boy's arm. He cringed from her. Raal held him steady. Willow's magic poured through the child, making a lightning-quick beeline for his thorn. The speed surprised Willow. Almost made her pull back. The thorn shattered in an explosion of black fragments.

"See? I told you it would not hurt." Raal gave his son's head a pat. "Now you, Maela." The phooka woman didn't move. Fear still shone in her eyes. Willow reached for her, this time trying to keep a tight rein on her magic. It surged away from her, again blasting the thorn like a bomb.

"Thank you." Raal gave her a dignified bow, then he and his family left the prison cell, locking the door behind them.

Willow stared at the spot where the phookas had stood, Jarlath's laughter echoing once more inside her head. Somehow it wasn't a choice anymore. Something was forcing her to remove the thorns. But there was another factor involved. Something even more important. She had seen it in Raal's eyes. In Pitt's eyes too.

Love.

CHAPTER 26

$\mathcal{D}$acia grabbed Willow's arm and spun her around. "What *really* happened with my father? You just pulled thorns with enough power to light a city. How? What did he do to you?"

"What? What are you talking about?"

"Willow, I've seen you pull thorns. You don't usually pulse with magic." Dacia turned Willow's hand palm up. "Look. Even now you're still glowing."

"Huh?" Willow stared at her hand and wrist. Dacia was right. She glowed white like she had in Nezeral's chess Game.

Theon peered at her hands too. "Game glow," he muttered. "Means you don't have control over something."

"What do you mean?" interrupted Brand. "We glowed in Nezeral's chess Game but still had control."

"What piece did you play?"

"Knight."

Dacia considered his answer. "Could you travel without your horse?"

"No."

"Then there was something out of your control." Dacia let go of Willow's hand. "What happened, Willow? What has Father changed in the Game?"

Willow's heart sank. *He* had changed nothing. It had been her. "It wasn't your father." She decided to tell them the truth. "He didn't pull me out of the Game. It was ... it was the Council. I had to vote."

"Vote?" Dacia looked incredulous. "On what?"

"On whether or not the Seelies should release the goblins from the Compact."

Theon's eyes widened. "So it really does exist, then?" He seemed stunned. "I thought perhaps Father had some nefarious scheme for making the Compact real in this particular Game ... but ..." He shook his head. "They lied to us, Dace. *All* this time they've lied to us. They made us believe the Seelies had Balance of Power on their side because they won the vote to leave Earthworld. But it was the Compact that shifted the Balance, not the vote. So why lie about it? Why not just tell us the truth?"

"Truth?" Dacia snorted. "Truth makes Unseelies look weak. You should know that by now, little brother. Father and the Unseelie kings have been lying to us younger faeries because the truth probably shows that *they* were the ones the Seelies tricked into the Compact, not the goblins. Then they sealed the goblins in this Game so they wouldn't be reminded of their failure."

"Well, whether this Compact's real or not," interrupted Willow, "everyone's worried that it will disrupt the Balance."

"Disrupt the Balance?" echoed Dacia. "How?"

Willow sagged against the stone wall, shaking her head. "I don't know. Removing the thorns with the Compact still in place somehow makes the goblins free – free from the goblin king *and* the Unseelies. Which, I guess, must weaken the Dark side of the Balance even further. The Unseelies wanted the Seelies to release the goblins but not the demon host from the Compact, which the Unseelies said would keep me from pulling more thorns and would push that Balance thing a little toward the Dark side, but not enough to change the Balance of Power. The Seelies didn't believe them and thought it was a trick. They all voted no to releasing the goblins from the Compact."

"How did you vote?"

"I voted no too."

"But then that would change nothing," pointed out Theon. "Father could not alter the Rules, nor could the Seelies. The Game should have remained the same." He stepped by Dacia and clutched Willow's hand, peeling back her tunic sleeve. The glow went up her arm. "Who did this, then? Who controls you?"

"I don't ... I don't know."

Brand suddenly pushed between Willow and the faeries. "Enough. Leave her be." He sat Willow down on his cloak and sank beside her. "You need rest," he said gently. "You are as pale as Malvin when the Imp is loose."

A giggle escaped from Willow. She leaned her head on Brand's shoulder, grateful for his intervention. Truth was, she felt tired enough to sleep for a week. Her lids closed halfway. She noticed the glow in her hands fading. Had it really come from somewhere else? Or had she done it? Made the magic surge like a tidal wave?

"The Game glow is gone now," grumbled Theon. "That shouldn't happen either. Something's not right."

The door to their prison cell opened. A strange, officious-looking goblin bustled inside, shuffling papers and mumbling under his breath. "Extra bogiechops. Check. Told hags. Check. Four more for dinner. Ah – here we are." He looked up from his papers, his small face overwhelmed by a foot-sized nose and huge waggling ears. "I be the chief steward." He snapped his heels together and gave a little bow. "Ye're all to follow me to his Majesty's feast hall for dinner."

"As guests?" said Theon dryly. "Or one of the main courses?" The goblin riffled through his papers again. "Says guests here. But ya never know with ol' Gobby." He grinned, affording everyone a wide view of his nostrils.

Brand gave Willow a hand up. Simultaneously they noticed her shimmering fingers. He said nothing, but quickly pulled her cloak-edges together, hiding her glow from the others.

In the hallway, a red-capped goblin guard awaited them. "Ah, good," said the steward, "ye've sent the trolls off. There's just no trustin' 'em once they starts droolin'." The guard grunted and chuckled. The steward set off at a brisk pace down the corridor, followed by the faeries, Willow, Brand, and the guard.

Willow began to sweat. Magic pumped like hot blood under her skin. Weird magic that required no conscious effort. As if her body was *blushing* it. She stopped in her tracks. *That's* what it felt like. Like the magic was just happening to her and she had no control. Same as a blush.

The goblin guard pushed her. Magic shot from Willow into the guard's hand and up to his heart, exploding the black thorn. "'Ere now!" he growled. "I got a shock from 'er!"

Two and two suddenly made four. A blush needed a trigger – usually embarrassment. Alone in the cell with only Brand, Dacia, and Theon, Willow had stopped glowing. As soon as the steward entered, she'd started up again. Something was triggering her magic. Something the goblins had that she, Brand, and the faeries didn't. *Thorns.*

Brand slipped a hand behind her back. "Are you well?"

She nodded. Her fingers still glowed. One more thorn. She needed to test her theory. She bolted from Brand and grabbed the steward's arm, magic instantly bursting his thorn.

"Hey!" he cried. "Whatcha doin'?"

Willow looked at her hands. The glow didn't linger as long this time, fading away to skin.

"Well, what is it? Ya got a question or not? Ye're holdin' us up."

"I – no, it's nothing. Forget it."

The steward gave her a disdainful sniff and started down the corridor again. Theon brushed close to Willow. "Careful," he whispered. "Goblin king sees that, you might be pulling out more than just thorns."

Oh God. The goblin king. How was she going to hide her glow from him? "Theon, I can't control it. Soon as I'm around thorns my magic takes over. What am I going to do?"

Dacia answered. "Convince King Gobb the thorns keep the

Compact going, and you'll have nothing to worry about."

"Until the thorns are gone," hissed Brand, "and nothing happens."

The guard shoved a spear handle into Brand's back. "Quit yer yakkin'."

No one spoke again. With each step, Willow felt more and more uneasy. Before the vote, her magic had been her own. Now it wasn't. Someone controlled her. Someone, no doubt, who stood to gain from removing the thorns. But who?

Meaty odors and a swelling din filled the corridor. Drums pounded tuneless rhythms. A vast cavern sprawled open before them, fires dancing in barbecue pits, goblin hordes feasting like wolves on whole carcasses. Willow started to twitch. A sea of thorns called out to her, making magic bubble and boil in her veins. Brand and the faeries saw what was happening. Dacia pulled up Willow's cloak hood to hide the strobing glow, and the boys tried to shield her with their bodies.

More red-capped guards joined their entourage, brutally cutting a path through the crowds. They led them straight to the goblin king, who sat on his throne atop a stone dais, white, fleshless bones strewn at his feet. Ten cages swayed from chains around his head. Willow could see tiny pleading hands dangling through some of the bars. Four of the cages appeared empty. Guess the steward was wrong about their dinner invitation.

"I hear ye've being doin' some thorn pullin'," said the king in a dangerously calm voice. He lifted a haunch of meat the size of Willow's thigh and poked it at a cage bottom, sending the iron coop swinging in crazy arcs. Squeals ensued. Little snouts stuck out through the bars. Willow saw Pitt, Lunk, and Nox stuffed in one cage, Rye Ruskin Wirt and his crawlers in the others.

"Help us, Willow!" cried Pitt. "He's gonna roast us!"

The king ignored his son's plea. He squinted at Willow, trying to see under her hood. "Whatcha hidin', girlie? Somethin' under there I should know 'bout?" A guard ripped off Willow's cloak. Light beamed out of her so bright the goblin king and the guards shielded their eyes.

Brand tried to protect her, but other guards pulled him back. They forced Willow up onto the dais, her magic shooting off sparks that removed their thorns in a prickly burst. One guard shoved her face into the stone, striking her temple. She gasped and didn't fight him when he kept her on her knees and yanked back her head. Something warm streamed down a cheek. *Tears? Blood?*

It took a moment for the king to see Willow properly. When he did, he touched the wet trickle on her skin. The thorn inside him exploded like a belching volcano. He blinked at her, surprised. His finger curled into a claw and scratched a deep gouge into Willow's face. She cried out from the searing pain.

"Ya spoke truth afore," he whispered harshly. "The Compact *is* crumblin'. Ya gotta remove them thorns. *Now.* All of 'em!"

Willow stared at him in horror. Blood dripped from his fingers. *Her blood!*

The goblin king's voice became a mighty thunder, reverberating throughout the cavern. "My goblins," he roared, "today we be free of the Compact! *Free!*" He grabbed Willow and lifted her straight over his head. "See this girl? This girl that glows like a sun?" His subjects stopped their feasting to watch their king strut around with Willow's struggling body. "She's loaded with magic. I want every last one of ya to touch her. Ya understand? *Every last one of ya!*" The goblins started to howl. They pressed themselves against the dais, arms reaching with frenzied excitement. Willow twisted and thrashed. She felt the king jerk her forward, then a whoosh of air as he pitched her into the seething crowd.

Hands grasped at her everywhere. Willow fought to escape but was surfed along the frenzied goblin ocean like live bait. Razor-sharp nails gouged searingly into her arms and legs and raked vicious scratches across her face. She shrieked in agony as chunks of hair ripped from her head. A fist slammed into her nose, and a sickening crunch told her it was broken. Blood erupted everywhere, choking Willow and gagging her screams.

She tried to use her magic. Numb the terrible pain. But nothing was hers anymore. Not her magic. Not her body. Not even her mind. Whatever possessed her swelled inside like an evil, surging tide, drowning every cell of her being.

Willow's back hit hard stone. Goblin bodies swarmed over her, grabbing, grasping, suffocating her. She heard cloth tearing. Felt her jerkin rip away, her bare flesh being bitten. But it was the magic that held her fast. The magic that violated her. It used her body like a channel, forcing itself through her again and again and again. Willow recognized it now. The same magic that held her mother. She squeezed her eyes tight and curled up into a tiny place in her mind, away, far far away from the goblin king's feast hall.

CHAPTER 27

*T*he magic began to clear out in a purging gush. Physical pain filled the void it left. Pain that Willow couldn't hide from. When she opened her eyes, she was alone at the edge of a dim-lit cave, bruised, battered, and abandoned like a broken toy. Goblin cries echoed in the distant hallways. Drums still throbbed. She swallowed, tasted the tang of her own blood. Whimpers pushed up her throat and turned to sobs.

She dragged herself to a sitting position, the movement enflaming her oozing wounds. Her clothing lay in tattered shreds around the stone altar the goblins had placed her on. *Cold. It was so cold.* Willow shuddered. Chills wracked her body. She curled into a ball and rocked steadily back and forth, back and forth, reason and intellect slipping away, instincts settling on survivor mode.

She felt a touch on her shoulder that sent raw adrenalin raging through her. Snarling, scratching, she flew at her attacker until he caught her in a bear hug and made her stop. Through a muddled haze, Willow saw Theon shimmering like a dream.

"It's okay," he whispered. "It's okay."

Willow crumpled against him. He wrapped her in his cloak

and held her tight. A gentle hand brushed at her hair. "My poor princess. What have they done to you?"

The whimpers started in her throat again. "I can't ... I can't ..."

"Sshhh. It's okay. Don't speak." Theon cradled her face, wiped off blood and tears, then scooped her into his arms. She nestled into him, relief spreading like wings. He felt like a tree. Strong and sturdy. She clung to his familiar tunic. *Theon would save her. He would get her out of here.* He carried her out of the darkness, away from the cave room and the bloodstained altar. Theon's powerful voice rang out in the corridor.

"It's finished, Father! The Game is over! Let her leave."

Light burned Willow's eyes. She gulped fresh air, her irises rolling back into the easy dark of unconsciousness.

When she woke up, Brand was beside her, face worried yet remote, Theon and Dacia hovering behind him. Her eyes locked on Theon, and it all came back: the goblin king throwing her into the mob, monsters clawing and biting, and Theon holding her, wiping away blood. *Saving her.*

"You ... you got us out, d-didn't you?" she stammered. "Out of the Game."

"No. It wasn't me. It was you." Theon pushed past Brand to help her sit up. "There's no Game now. No Compact either. You destroyed them both."

Pitt popped into view. "It's true. Me and the boys ain't gotta roast no more." His hand patted hers. Willow stared at his small green fingers, trying to hide her revulsion. She was glad he was free, but they were wrong. She hadn't done it.

Brand moved closer, his chair legs scraping the floor. "Forgive me, Your Highness. I ... I ..." But Willow had focused back on Theon, her heart swelling with gratitude. His words had forced Jarlath to release them. *He* had been the one to save them. Brand leaned toward her, blocking Theon from her gaze. He clutched her hand, making her meet his earnest eyes. "Your Highness, please ... please forgive me. I failed you. I should have been at your side."

He was using his knight voice, the formal one that Willow hated. It made her sad. Weren't they past all that? "Why?" she asked. "What could you have done?"

Brand frowned. He stood up and glared at Theon. "Perhaps I should have hid in a cage as he did. Then, at least, I would have been there for you at the end, instead of useless and dead." He turned and strode from the room, his back stiff with anger.

"Aye," added Pitt. "He didn't even have no weapon, but he fought like a demon. Had more nooks in 'im than Rye's hidey-holes. Guards killed 'im dead, though. And her too." He pointed at Dacia. "Was the faerie prince that loosed us. He let me and the boys and Rye and all the crawlers outta the cages."

Confusion spun in Willow. *Brand fought for her? He – he died?* But ... but Theon had saved her. They were wrong. He'd saved them all. Hadn't he? Willow's eyes brimmed with tears. She didn't know. She didn't know anything anymore. Emptiness yawned inside her. Nothing was right. She felt chopped up. Like the Game had broken her, severed her into tiny pieces that couldn't fit back together again

Dacia reached out and cupped Willow's cheek. "He'll be back. Once he forgives himself."

Tears spilled down Willow's face. She let Dacia hug her. Let her think she cried for Brand. But it was the emptiness that filled her that made her sob like a lost child.

No one noticed when Jarlath appeared in the room. Then Willow saw him over Dacia's shoulder, watching them impassively. Next thing she knew it was Jarlath and not Dacia that sat beside her. They were alone in a garden, sitting on a cushioned bench.

"You are a remarkable young woman."

Willow stared. She thought she should feel anger or at least contempt for someone who had caused her this much pain. But she felt nothing. Absolutely nothing.

"I placed you in the Goblin King's Gauntlet," continued Jarlath, "to cow you to my will. I did not expect you to win the Game."

She laughed wearily. "I didn't win anything. And I think you know it." She studied the faerie king's face, searching for a chink in his smooth facade. But he was unreadable. Someone you didn't want to play poker with. Finally, she sighed. "What do you want from me, Jarlath? Why am I really here?"

A long silence ensued. Jarlath looked at her with new eyes. Appreciative eyes. "Very well, then," he said evenly. "What I really want is for you to agree to take either Dacia or Theon back to Mistolear with you."

Emotion flickered in Willow. *Back to Mistolear.* She could go home?

"I want one of them to stay with you until Nezeral is grown again."

Nezeral. Willow's mouth tightened. "And if I refuse?"

"Your mother will die."

This time emotion crashed through her, ramming panicked memories into her mind. She remembered that alien power slicing through her body again, slicing through her mother's. "What is it?" she hissed. "What kind of magic can *do* what that magic did? Can force itself into people like ... like...?" *Like what? An army? A predator?* "Is it yours?"

"Yes – and no. It's the Balance."

"The Balance?" Willow didn't understand. The Balance was the power that controlled faeries. What did it have to do with her and her mother?

"What did Cyrraena tell you about the Balance?" asked Jarlath. "That it's like a weighing scale? That it strives to be even?" He laughed. "The Balance is *me*, Willow. It's Cyrraena. It's all faeries. And it doesn't struggle to be even. It's not a scale. It's a pendulum. A pendulum that forever swings back and forth, back and forth, *balancing* between Light and Dark."

Willow saw the swinging motion in her mind. Light and Dark. Light and Dark. What was Jarlath trying to tell her? That it was Dark's turn on the Balance now?

"I knew when it interfered with your mother it was planning to shift." He assessed her with a mocking eye. "Cyrraena knew it too. She bundled you off here, quick as a wink, didn't she? Thought you'd keep the power balanced. But you tipped the Balance instead."

Rage began to build in Willow. Cyrraena knew. *She knew!*

"It's strange how the Balance works, though. It *seems* as if it's serving one side, when in reality it's really gathering enough momentum to swing back to the other. So when the Council neglected to stop you from pulling my thorns –"

"*Your* thorns?"

"Of course. Jarlath *Thornheart*. Goblin thorns were my invention. If anyone else had tried to pull them, the Council would never have allowed it. But with you, a human, they were fooled. They gave the Balance its opportunity to shift. It took you over, pulled the thorns, and stretched the pendulum so far into Light, the Balance could only swing back into Dark. And that swing back released the goblins and the demon host from the Compact, thus ensuring Dark once again reigns in the Balance of Power."

Willow cradled her spinning head. Why was he telling her all this? What did he want from her? She blinked, remembering he'd already told her what he wanted. Take either Dacia or Theon back to Mistolear. Her mother would die if she didn't.

She frowned at Jarlath. Was he trying to trick her? "I don't get it, then," she said. "If Dark has the power now, and the Balance has what it wants, why would it still be interfering with my mother?"

"Clever girl." Jarlath arched an eyebrow. "You're right. The Balance has indeed left your mother. But it's *me* now you need worry about. Balance of Power brings certain liberties with it. Liberties that, I assure you, you and your mother won't like."

"And what if I don't believe you?"

A trace of humor softened Jarlath's face. He closed his eyes. Willow saw magic emanate from him in a long wavy tendril that danced and swayed hypnotically. Gentle as a spider web, it tickled her cheek, her neck, the tops of her hands, anywhere her skin was exposed. She moaned, terror freezing her to the seat. Nezeral had done the same before trying to strangle her. But somehow she knew Jarlath meant to do worse. Far worse.

The magic doubled her over, knifing straight to her core. "No!" she cried out. "Please –" But it was too late. Snakes crawled over her, cold and heavy, hissing obscenely. She felt a tremendous force pushing her into a dark hole, crushing the writhing snakes against her face. She struggled to speak. Gasped for breath. But couldn't find air. Couldn't move. With a final effort the words came screaming out of her. "*Nooooo!* Stop! I'll do what you want!"

Instantly the writhing pressure vanished. She sat on the bench like she'd never left it. Like nothing had happened. Then she realized nothing had. The magic had made her see those things in her head. She gaped wide-eyed and panting at Jarlath. Could he do that to her mother? Turn her into a madwoman?

"Not very pleasant, is it? Would take – oh, perhaps only a

few days for a mortal to go insane. Death would follow, of course, but not right away."

Willow was trapped. A lie? The truth? *She didn't know*. She didn't know! The snakes hissed in her mind, pulsed against her. She pushed them away, pushed everything away. The emptiness claimed her again. She didn't care about the faeries and their stupid Games. She knew only one thing – she wanted to leave here and never come back.

"I'll do it," she said. "I'll take one of them home with me."

When the time came for Willow and Brand to leave Clarion, the faeries made a great show of it. Both courts showed up in the Greek-like amphitheater, a shining host of gods and goddesses. The Seelies, though, had the lesser amount of Council seats this time, and stood behind their Council members with subdued splendor, their pixies and sprites quiet like chastened children. The Unseelies, in comparison, seemed all dark glitter and movement, goblins darting here and there, excited as uncaged monkeys.

Willow stood beside Brand, eyeing the empty Council seat that stood between the two sides. Her seat. The one she hoped, after this, never to see again. Brand's arm slipped reassuringly around her shoulders. His way of apologizing again. Willow didn't know how to warn him. She gave him an urgent look. *I'm sorry*, her eyes pleaded. *Please don't hate me*. She stepped from his reach and went straight to the Council chair. Once Brand knew of the decision she had to make, he would try and stop her. It was better that she stayed away from him.

Jarlath stood up from his chair, his black councilor robes billowing around him. "The princess Willow has proven herself a worthy Game player." He bowed in Willow's direction. "It is her wish that she and the human, Sir Brand Lackwulf, be allowed to return to Mistolear. I grant this wish ..." He paused and directed his gaze along the row of Seelie Council lords. "And ask that she grants one for me."

The whole room became still. Even the goblins stopped to listen. Willow focused on a blue speck in the floor tiles, letting it fill the empty shell of her mind. Jarlath spoke his wish. "My son, Nezeral, needs fey guidance. I ask the princess her permission to allow either my daughter Dacia or my son Theon to accompany her back to Mistolear, to stay in that realm until Nezeral is grown again and can return to Clarion."

Excitement went through the crowd. Willow heard Brand's outraged shout. She stared at Dacia and Theon, both blank as slate. No surprise. No expectation. Willow couldn't tell if they knew of their father's plans or not. She stood up. The crowd went silent again. She said nothing, just continued staring at the faerie twins. Her brain had refused to think before. Now she forced it to consider her options. Forced it to remember that one faerie represented Dark and the other Light.

Dacia, shining and beautiful, smiled at her sweetly. Willow remembered how she'd first thought her an angel. She admired the faerie girl. Her confidence. Her intelligence. But there was something about her. A coldness that Willow didn't trust. A coldness that could maybe mask a different nature. She turned to Theon.

Brash, arrogant Theon. He felt real. Almost human. He stared at her now with sad, ocean-deep eyes. Willow swallowed. She again felt Theon's strong arms cradling her against him. Heard his voice ringing in the corridor, ordering his father to release them from the Game. He had been so gentle with her. So kind. Willow knew he cared about humans. He wouldn't hurt them like Nezeral had wanted to. *It must be him.* She took a deep breath.

"I choose ... I choose *Theon.*"

Once the words were uttered, Willow felt snapped out of a trance. She saw the fury blaze in Dacia's eyes, the triumph in Theon's, and when she looked around the room, she saw Brand. Her breath caught. He was pale as ash, his dark eyes pinning her with such contempt that she recoiled. Everything they'd been through together came flooding back. She remembered how he'd thrown his body over hers to protect her from the tigers. What Pitt had said about him fighting the goblins weaponless, trying to save her. And her love – that came back with a sickening jolt that weakened her knees. *She loved Brand.* That's what was real in all this. That's what she needed to cling to.

Willow took a step toward Brand but faltered. The kiss she and Theon had shared flashed in her mind with a stunning realization. Brand thought she'd chosen Theon because of that.

He thought she *liked* him.

Theon came to join her. He took her hand and brushed it with his lips. "You chose well, Princess."

Willow blanched. *Oh, what had she done? What had she done?* She pushed Theon away, turned to Brand. He just stood there as if in deep shock. Pitt pulled at his arm. "C'mon, ya great lump! They're sendin' ya home. Ya gots to get over with Willow." Brand didn't move. A war waged behind his eyes. Finally he let Pitt lead him to Willow's side, but he looked through her like she wasn't there. Jarlath nodded. A spell wrapped around them, and they returned, finally, to Mistolear.

CHAPTER 28

Willow awoke with a start, the bite of goblin fangs searing her flesh. Instinctively, she clutched at her arm, felt around her neck and chest. No blood. No gaping wounds. Just a nightmare. Only a nightmare. She slumped back onto her pillows, heart racing like an Indy engine. Jeez! She hated these dreams. *Hated them!*

Her breath came out in labored huffs. A whole week back in Mistolear, and still she couldn't shake the horror of what had happened to her in the faerie world. In daylight, it crouched just below the surface of her thoughts, flashing unexpected images. But at night, it all became real again.

Sweat trickled down Willow's neck. She longed to kick the bedcovers away. The fear was always strongest, though, when she first woke up, when it was still dark. The blankets became her armor then – nothing could harm her as long as she remained under them. She had to fight the fear in stages.

Stage one: find her happy thought.

The happiest thought Willow could think of was seeing her mom again. The moment Diantha had embraced her, Willow knew the parasitic magic had left her mother. The princess glowed with health and vitality and didn't have Nezzie attached to her like a third arm anymore.

Willow smiled. Her mom had been making up for lost time with both Willow and Alaric, going riding with them, going for walks together, picnicking in the woods. Willow closed her eyes. Let the good feelings of being someone's daughter, a part of someone's family, fill her up. Everything she'd been through, she told herself, was worth it if her mom was okay, and ... and if Jarlath kept his word.

The doubts started to niggle. Yeah, *so far*, Jarlath had kept his word. No alien faerie magic disturbed Mistolear. But there was still Theon running around – a full-grown faerie with no power limitations. She doubted very much that *babysitting* was his true purpose.

The sweat soaked into Willow's shift. Still, she wasn't ready to push the blankets back. *What was Theon's true purpose?* This single question propelled her fear. Made her tremble. Why was he really here? Would he hurt Nezzie? Embroil them all in faerie Games again? She grabbed the blankets, pulling them higher. The guilt rushed in. She cursed Cyrraena under her breath. The faerie queen should be the one to feel guilty, not her. But Cyrraena had not shown her face in Carrus since she'd transported Willow to Clarion. Willow cringed. And it was Willow herself who'd brought Theon here. If anything happened, that part would still be her fault.

Every night she went over the conversation with Jarlath. What had been wrong with her? Game shock? A spell or something? She'd given in with hardly a fight. Now, of course, her mind teemed with all kinds of things she could've said or done. She could've made a deal. Why hadn't she bargained? Said Theon could come, but not unless he had his powers removed like he'd had in the Goblin Game? Or at least reduced, so they were human-sized? Or she could have offered to give Nezzie back to Jarlath and just been done with it.

She sighed. Nix that last option. Faerie or not, Nezzie was her little brother. She remembered how he'd locked his small arms around her legs and clung to them. *Will, stay here. Don't go 'way again.* She'd breathed in his sweet baby fragrance until tears ran down her cheeks and he'd squirmed to escape. *Don't cwy, Will. Don't cwy. I be good boy.* No. Giving Nezzie back was not an option.

Light filtered into her room, illuminating the heavy furniture. *Morning.* Mornings were safe. She finally pushed the blankets off and sat up, her damp shift sticking to her like Saran Wrap. The cool air gave her goose bumps. Summer was almost over, the suddenly chill mornings and evenings flirting with fall. She rose to her feet, creeping to the balcony and peeking past its velvet curtain. Theon was out there again. Down by the mist-covered pond, just sitting on a rock. What was he doing? Meditating?

Willow studied his straight back, his wave of silver hair. So far, he'd proven the perfect castle guest. Polite. Charming. Enthusiastically interested in everything and everyone around him. Courtiers fawned over him. Lovestruck ladies-in-waiting stalked him. He'd even won her grandparents over, and they'd originally wanted to clap him in irons.

The fear twisted in Willow's stomach again. One person wasn't too thrilled with Theon. Was terrified of him, in fact. *Nezzie*. Theon couldn't even go near him without the little guy screaming bloody murder. Willow hadn't figured out why yet, but she worried Nezzie knew something she didn't.

A movement in the bushes caught Willow's attention. She squinted at a small figure that prowled stealthily toward Theon. The sun hadn't risen yet, so shadows fogged the courtyard. Still, she made out a shaggy head, a toddler-size body, and knew Pitt was out there, spying on Theon.

Willow chuckled. While Nezzie had immediately disliked Theon, he'd been enthralled with Pitt, thinking the goblin prince his new plaything. The two were now inseparable, Pitt having elected himself Nezzie's guardian.

She held her breath. Theon had just turned.

Pitt froze. Theon appeared to listen, nodded, and went back to staring at the pond. Pitt stayed put behind a bush, close enough now to keep an eye on Theon. When he wasn't guarding Nezzie, that's what Pitt did – watch Theon like a hawk.

Warmth spread through Willow. The little goblin had surprised her. Not being a faerie, he could travel the realms without restriction, and had chosen on his own to accompany her to Mistolear. It made her feel good – maybe the whole thorn-pulling debacle hadn't been a total disaster. Of course, it worried her too. If one goblin could come, so could others. And what about the demon host? She shuddered, not wanting to even think about what they could do.

The sun began to rise over the far eastern forest. Willow's thoughts reluctantly turned to Brand. Another day to face his coldness. Another day of indifferent looks and clipped replies. Her heart began to ache. She wanted so much just to talk to him, to let him hear her side of things. But he wouldn't be alone with her. Wouldn't listen to anything she had to say.

Willow dropped the curtain and went back to her bed. She wondered what would have happened if she'd picked Dacia – would Brand still treat her like this? But maybe he just despised her for giving in to Jarlath. For being so weak she'd had to bring a faerie – any faerie – back from Clarion. She clutched her pillow, curling it into a ball. "I'm sorry," she whispered. *So sorry*. God, she'd made such a mess of everything. *Why, why, why had she just given in like that?* If only she'd told Brand what Jarlath had offered. Brand would've helped her to be strong. He would've helped her to come up with a better plan. She gave a weary sigh. Wished she could just stay asleep and not worry anymore. But the dreams ...

She sat up, sleep suddenly losing its appeal. Her robe lay at the foot of her bed. She got up, pulled it on, and left the room. When she was little, she remembered having bad dreams and sneaking into Nana's bed to snuggle with her until she felt better. Not that she could do that with her parents. Willow smirked at the thought. But there was someone else she could snuggle with.

The guard outside the nursery nodded sleepily and opened the door for Willow. She crept past the dozing nurses and slipped into the adjoining room where Nezzie slept. His crib was backed against the wall. Willow stared down at him and smiled. He'd found his thumb while she'd been away and was sucking it in blissful slumber. She reached in and scooped him out of the crib. His jewel eyes winked open, saw it was her, and shut again. He nestled into her shoulder. She carried him over to the spare empty bed, the one her mother used to sleep in. Diantha had gone back to sleeping with Alaric, and it was Pitt's bed now, but he was still out spying on Theon. Willow squeezed herself and Nezzie onto the narrow mattress and tucked the covers around them. Pitt's slightly gamy scent made her wrinkle her nose. She pressed her face into Nezzie's hair, breathing him in like the scent of a flower.

"I won't let Theon hurt you," she whispered. "Or anyone else. I promise." She kissed the top of his head and cuddled him to her chest. The tension she had felt began to drain. Having someone to protect made her feel in control again. Gave her something else, besides her own fear, to focus on. She let her breathing deepen.

Pitt's head suddenly appeared over the edge of the bed. "You 'ere again?" he grumbled. "I needs a bigger cot." He pushed in beside Nezzie and Willow and yanked over some of the blankets. Willow stared down at him, bemused. She'd avoided him at first because he reminded her too much of the Gauntlet Game, but he was beginning to grow on her again. He piqued her curiosity.

"Pitt? Um, how come you want to protect Nezzie? You know he's a faerie, right?"

"I knows."

Willow waited for him to elaborate. The goblin turned over so she couldn't see his face.

"I used to have lots and lots o' brudders and sisters," he murmured. "Me fadder, though, don't like it when we gets too old. He's afeared we'll take his throne. He murders us all afore we can grow up. I'm the youngest. So I still have me a few more years."

Willow blinked in shock. Holy jeez! She touched his shoulder and felt it quivering. "Pitt, I'm –" But Pitt interrupted her. "I likes Nezzie," he said, "cuz he's little like me. Kinda like one of me brudders. I couldn't help them, but maybe ... maybe I can help him."

"Oh, Pitt." Willow enfolded the tiny goblin in her arms, squishing Nezzie between them. "I'm *so* sorry about your brothers and sisters. I can't believe your father ... he ... he ... You know you're safe here, okay? No one's going to hurt you. And you can stay as long as you want. You don't *ever* have to go back."

Pitt nodded. Willow heard sniffs and saw him wipe his eyes. She gazed at him in wonder. He really had changed since she'd pulled his thorn. A moment from yesterday flashed in her mind – Pitt comforting Nezzie who was crying from a fall in the garden. The goblin prince had had to learn about bathing and wearing clothes and how to eat with forks and knives, but it was what he was learning about caring that made Willow's heart soar. And if Pitt could learn to care, so could Nezzie.

It hit her then like a ton of bricks. *She had done the right thing.* Maybe not every little part had worked out perfectly, but the really important parts – saving her mom and pulling the thorns – had worked out right. She just needed to believe it herself and then maybe Brand would believe it. She snuggled into Nezzie and Pitt and closed her eyes. It was going to be okay, she told herself. *It was going to be okay ...*

In all her life, Dacia Thornheart had never felt this way, rage quivering in every nerve ending, threatening to blast out of her in a devastating hurricane of power. She breathed raggedly, forcing herself to stay calm. Theon's voice still echoed in her head. *We have to work together, Dace. I need you. Why do you keep blocking me?* She saw his mist-covered pond, felt him searching for her.

Never! All her defenses slammed into place. Let him call to her every hour on the hour if he liked. She would *never* help Theon win Father's Game.

Just thinking of her father made Dacia's rage stir again. How dare he use her like a pawn! He'd promised the Game was *hers* to play and then had pitted Theon against her. And all the *lies* he had told. Lies about humans. Lies about the Compact. Her fists clenched. She should have guessed he was up to something when he'd told her to pick healing as their power. *Healing!* She shook her head. What a fool she had been. She had actually thought he'd picked healing to help her and Theon with their injuries, to help them bond with the humans. Not to tip the Balance! And now everyone would think it was Theon who'd won the Game. *Theon* who'd given Dark back its power.

"Down!" she cried to her gargoyle. "*Down!*" The great beast obeyed, folding its wings and pitching them into a free-fall dive. Dacia screamed her anger into the wind as she and the plummeting gargoyle spiraled to the ground. When it seemed they would crash, the gargoyle's leathery wings suddenly swept into an upstroke that landed them safely. Panting, Dacia slipped from its back. Gargoyle joyriding was her only escape these days. The only thing that cleared her head. She gave the gargoyle's lion ears a quick scratch, froze him into place, and strode off to the cypress grove.

The brisk air mixed with the fresh tang of cypress resin helped to restore her equilibrium. She breathed the heady fragrance, willing her nerves to steady. The grove was her most private, spell-hidden place. It sat high on a distant hillside overlooking the gem-like palaces of all the Unseelie lords. Sunlight barely crested the horizon, making her father's palace, the House of Jarlath, wink back at her like a gargoyle eye. Dacia frowned at the glinting castle. Someday she would have her own house – the House of Dacia. She was not out of this Game yet. Far from it!

Dacia settled herself in a comfortable spot between the cypress trees. Faeries' true bodies were impervious to cold and heat, but Dacia let the cool winds whip her hair and form goose bumps on her skin. She enjoyed feeling so aware of her body. The surge of her elemental being. She closed her eyes, looking instead with the mind's eye. With the new Balance of Power, she could go places she had never gone before. See Mistolear as if she walked there freely. And if she wished it, she could make herself known to Theon – or any other faerie.

Her mouth curved into a smile. She refused to be anything but ghostly film to Theon. But to Nezeral – to *him* she was real. She'd given Theon a monster's head and had whispered to little Nezzie to beware of his brother's sharp teeth. She laughed. Let Theon try to influence him now. He couldn't even get near the child without him going berserk.

Dacia appeared in Willow's room, hoping to catch the stupid girl writhing in one of her nightmares. She was disappointed, though. Willow wasn't there. Dacia followed the girl's essence and found her in bed with Nezeral's baby-form and the dirty goblin child.

Disgust curled Dacia's nose. That's right. Surround yourself with ignorant brats, you stupid, *stupid* girl! For the millionth time, Dacia posed the question she couldn't get out of her head. *How could Willow have chosen Theon over her?* Theon with his crocodile smiles and his incredibly pathetic attempts at a romantic alliance. Was the girl truly so gullible? Dacia sighed. It was her own fault. She'd misjudged the effect of the goblin attack. Who knew they'd bite and claw like that? The king had just said to *touch*. Stupid goblins. Dacia chewed her lip, glaring at Pitt. If only she'd hidden away as Theon had, then she could've rescued Willow herself and the human would've picked her.

All too late for that now, though. Dacia faded from the nursery and reappeared in Brand's room. She would play the Game another way. Let Theon use Willow if he wanted. She would use Brand.

The human boy slept all tangled in his sheets, his long dark hair veiling his face. Dacia's finger trailed along a jagged strand. She wondered at its texture and itched to brush it back, but in Mistolear her touch was as insubstantial as butterfly breath. She could not make Brand see or feel her. She could not move his hair. Her finger trailed across the boy's forehead and stopped just between his eyes, sketching a fey rune of peace. But there was one thing she could do. Oh yes. One thing that would make all the difference. She could come to him in his dreams.

Coming in Spring 2012

The Divided Realms
Book 3

Following the nightmare of the Goblin's Gauntlet, Willow faces life with a broken spirit and a broken heart. She is easy prey for the seductive faerie prince, Theon Thornheart, who tempts her with a powerful, addictive elixir that warps her magic. Meanwhile, dark forces in Clarion set the stage for a new Game that will place humans, faeries, and goblins in a magical battle of wits. Does Willow have the strength to resist Theon's temptation and the ability to restore the Balance of the realms?